# H. P. OLIVER

OMNIBUS

## FIFTEEN TALES
## FROM THEN AND NOW

HPO Productions
8698 Elk Grove Boulevard, Suite 1-271
Elk Grove, California 95624


Cover art and book design by Steve Eitzen


Printed in the United States of America


ISBN: 978-0-9994150-6-1

MYSTERIES IN HISTORY

## DEDICATION

Dedicated to the thing all fiction writers prize most, regardless of genre or style. Dedicated to the story.

## AUTHOR WEBSITE

You are cordially invited to visit the author's website at http://www.hpoliver.com for many free features related to this and other H. P. Oliver books. These include a unique VISUALIZATION section with illustrated quotes from OMNIBUS that will increase your reading enjoyment by allowing you to "see" parts of the story. (use link below.)

http://www.HPOliver.com/BOOKS/OMNIBUS/VISUALIZATIONS/index.html

# ACKNOWLEDGMENTS

The author gratefully acknowledges the following research sources used in the writing of stories in this book: CULT OF GLORY, Doug J. Swanson; Niles Essanay Silent Film Museum; WINGING IT, H. P. Oliver; Catalina Island Conservancy; HARLEM OF THE WEST, Elizabeth Pepin; TheHotelBurlington.com; Palm Springs Air Museum; City of Brookings. Also, appreciation to Gary Weisenberger for keeping the author honest.

# PLEASE NOTE

This novel occasionally refers to individuals and groups in terms considered disrespectful and inappropriate today. These terms, however, were in common usage during the historical periods in which some of these stories are set and are included here solely for the purpose of accurately depicting the attitudes and customs of the day.

# Contents

# A Tale of the Texas Rangers

## Thursday, February 28, 1878—Allen, Texas

There is lots of reasons cowpokes remember a town. Some of 'em is good, and some ain't so good.

Reasons that make a feller think kindly of a town is friendly folks, saloons that don't water their liquor, and a decent cathouse . . . stuff like that. Some of the bad things about towns that make cowpokes take the long way around might be a sheriff whose nose gets all out of joint when cowboys let off a little steam or womenfolk who look down their noses at a feller who earns his livin' in a saddle. Worst of all is a one-horse town that's just plain dead from the tail both up-ways and down.

Sad to say, that last reason fits Allen, Texas like a pair of Kansas boots. I say that's sad cuz it appeared I was gonna be in Allen for a time. Ya see, I'm a Texas Ranger and our company has spent the last few weeks chasin' a gang that stuck up a train near Allen.

Yup, I said they stuck up a train. Now, that's been done other places, but ain't nobody ever done it in Texas before. Them fellers made history that day, but not no good kinda history.

The robber gang was a pretty slick outfit and we didn't have no luck trackin' 'em down right off, so the boss of our outfit, Lieutenant Peak, figured we'd do better if we split up. He planted me and a couple other boys in the Allen area a-thinkin' them robbers might show up here again.

So that's why I'm coolin' my heels in Allen, Texas and keepin' my eyes open for Mister Sam Bass and his boys. Bass was identified as the leader of the train robbers. Bass had three other fellers with him, Frank Jackson, Tom Spotswood, and a local hand who goes by the handle Seaborn Barnes. Yeah, Seaborn. All told, the Bass gang rode away with about one-thousand-three-hundred dollars.

Now, if that weren't enough to keep us busy, we had a bunch

1

of Pinkerton boys out there a-messin' up Bass's trail. Six months before the Allen train robbery, a Union Pacific train from the San Francisco mint was stuck up in a place just across the Nebraska border called Big Springs. This one was a big deal cuz them robbers made off with sixty-thousand-dollars.

Not taking kindly to losin' that kind of freight, the railroad brought in the Pinkertons to get it back. So when the Allen train was robbed, the Pinkerton boys figured it was the same bunch that done the Nebraska stick-up.

WANTED

SAM BASS

And His Gang

REWARD

$1,000.00 Dead or Alive

Anyways, I've been hangin' out here in Allen with my Ranger badge pinned inside my jacket and lookin' for Sam Bass. I even have a picture of Bass and his sidekicks from a wanted poster, but that don't make 'em any easier to find. I didn't much feel like I was earnin' my thirty dollars per month.

I gotta admit, though, duty in Allen wasn't too awful. That's cuz I made the acquaintance of a sweet little gal name of Emma Parker and we started keepin' company in our spare time. Emma, or Em as I call her, is a workin' woman.

Naw, not that kind of workin' woman, you jackass. She's a schoolmarm at the Allen Academy—a private school for the youngins of rich folks in northeast Texas. Schoolmarm or not, Em is just pretty as a picture, but why a beautiful and educated woman like her would cotton to a no account feller like me was a mystery.

Emma woulda made a good Ranger, though. She has a way of thinkin' that makes sense out of things that downright puzzle me. Like why local folks, 'specially the farmers, seem to have the idea Sam Bass was a right feller. Here he is robbin' trains and stagecoaches, and nobody aside from me is anxious to see him locked up in the calaboose.

But Emma, she knowed exactly why that was. She said it this way, "Walter, farmers and ranchers despise the railroad because they are at its mercy for shipping their produce and stock to town."

Getting' the picture, I said, "That's because there's only one railroad in these parts, right?"

"That is exactly right. The Union Pacific is the only railroad serving this part of the country so they can charge whatever they want to haul produce and stock to market. When Mister Bass robs a train, folks see that as striking back at the railroad."

EMMA PARKER

Emma smiled at me and said, "There might even be more to it than that. Elderly train passengers see Sam Bass as a friend because he is always polite to them and does not take their money. One woman on a train he robbed said Mister Bass told her, 'That's all right, mother. You keep your purse. I can see you surely worked hard for your money.'"

I saw what Emma was a gettin' at. "Ain't that somethin'? I even heared he sometimes gives poor folks a helpin' hand by tossin' 'em a few coins for food. I guess he's sorta like that feller who stole from rich folks and gave their money to the poor. You know who I mean?"

She smiled a smile at me that would charm a sidewinder. "That was Robin Hood of Sherwood Forest."

"Yeah, that's the feller. Say, where is that Sherwood Forest? I never heared of no place called that in these parts."

"That is because Sherwood Forest is clear across the Atlantic Ocean in England."

"Dang, you're smart! Oh, pardon my language, Em."

Em just gave me another one of them sweet smiles and hooked her arm through mine as I walked her home to the Austin House hotel on Allen Street where it crosses McDermott. Walkin' her home earned me another smile and a shake of her hand. I was always careful not to squeeze her tiny hand too hard.

## Friday, March 8, 1878—Allen, Texas

Then, about a week later, I got word that Sam and his boys stepped things up some. I'd just et my breakfast at the Allen House and was takin' a walk through town to see what I could see when the kid who runs messages for the telegraph office came runnin' up Deshon Street a-hollerin' my name and wavin' a piece of paper.

"Mister McCadden . . . Mister McCadden . . . telegram for

you!"

"Okay, son. Ya found me."

The boy handed me the paper and I tossed him a nickel. He thanked me and I read the telegram. It was from Lieutenant Peak and it went like this:

**BASS GANG HELD UP RR N OF MCKINNEY THURS NT•**
**KEEP EYE OUT•**

Now, that was a right interestin' piece of news. McKinney, Texas is only about ten miles up the track from Allen. That means Sam Bass and his boys was right close and if I got to it, I might just find 'em. I trotted on up to the livery and told the feller who runs the place to saddle my horse, which he did pronto. After that, I made me some tracks up the McKinney road.

If Allen, Texas is a one-horse town, then McKinney is almost a two-horse town. Let's call it a one-horse and one-mule town. The railroad track runs north to south on the east side of town, but there wasn't nary a train in sight at the station.

By asking a few questions I got about all of what there was to know about the train robbery. The train didn't have much worth stealin' on it, so the gang didn't get much to show for the trouble of robbin' it. The most helpful part I learned was the Bass gang made their escape along the tracks to the south.

That didn't make a whole lot of sense to me because it meant they rode right through McKinney to wherever they was headed. Seems Sam was so cocksure of himself he wasn't even worried about anyone seein' which way he went. As a rule, robbers who get to thinkin' they can't be caught is the next ones to get caught.

I set out along the tracks back toward Allen. A short way from the depot, the tracks entered a forest so thick and dark it felt like I was ridin' in a cave. That slowed me down some. If Sam and his boys were holed up somewheres along the track, they'd hear me comin' and I'd be right on top of 'em before I knew they was there.

At the rate I was makin' my way back to Allen, it was pure dark by the time I got there. I left my horse with the fellow at the livery stable and set out toward the Allen Cafe for some grub. My path took me by the Austin House hotel where Emma lives.

I happened to glance up to her window, which I just naturally did most every time I passed the hotel. This time, though, I saw something mighty peculiar. I saw a man in her room. He was standing with his back to the window, so I couldn't see who he was.

Now, a man bein' in Emma's room might be none of my blamed business. I don't have no brand on her or nothin', but knowin' how puritan Em is, I thought it might be a good idea to look in on her and make sure there wasn't nothin' bad goin' on up there.

Em's room is at the end of the second floor hall and I heared voices when I got to the door. Emma must have been talkin' to the man I seen in the window. "Sam, you must be more careful. Coming to see me here could . . . ."

I didn't hear all of what she said, but what I heared was enough. The whole durn sichiation was suddenly clear as day. Em was in cahoots with Sam Bass and she was hangin' around with me to find out what us Rangers was up to so she could tell him.

Feelin' like an addle-headed tinhorn for lettin' a little gal like Em fool me, I drawed my Colt Frontier and banged the door so hard rattled on its hinges. "Ranger! Open up in thar!"

I surprised 'em. Everything got real quiet on the other side of the door, and then I heared a window open. Backing up a step or two, I kicked that old door hard as I could. The doorframe splintered all to hell and the door swung open with a bang.

Two things caught my eye right off. A man's leg was a goin' out the window and Em was sittin' on the bed half out of her dress. Seein' her like that musta distracted me just long enough so Bass was already clear of the window when I fired off my big Colt.

I runned to the window and looked for Bass. He was just dropping off the roof of the first-floor porch. I couldn't hit him from there and I knowed he'd be long gone by the time I could get down to the street.

Turnin' to Em, I said, "Well, you sure enough played me for a fool, didn't ya, Missy?"

She just sat there lookin' away and not sayin' nothin'. I said, "All right, Emma get yourself decent. We're goin' to pay a visit over to the Sheriff's office."

By this time there was several fellers standin' out in the hall. One of 'em took a step forward and said, "Hey, who you think you are treatin' this sweet little gal that a-way?

I held my jacket open to show him my Ranger Badge and said, "I think I'm a Texas Ranger and you'd do well to keep your distance. This here 'sweet little gal' is a-goin' to the hoosegow."

Well, sir, Emma Parker, iff'n that was even her real name, spent the next few days in custody of the Collin County Sheriff until a Ranger showed up to collect her back to headquarters in Austin. My report went there with her, but I took no pride in what them papers said. It was downright embarrassin' to get took in by a pretty little gal like that, and I knowed I was in for a razzin' next time I showed my face in Austin.

Iff'n you is wonderin' what come of Sam Bass, he and his boys headed down south to a place called Round Rock, but this time we knowed where he was. That's cuz Jim Murphy, one of Bass's gang worked a deal with the State of Texas to rat on Bass in exchange for what they call clemency. That means the state promised not to arrest Murphy with the gang iff'n he helped catch Bass.

So Bass and his boys come into Round Rock to scout the bank they was aimin' to rob and they was spotted. Well, ever-body started in to shootin' and Bass was hit in the gut. He got on his horse, but his gang left him behind just outside of town cuz he couldn't stay in the saddle. The Rangers caught him, but two days later, he ups and kicks the bucket. Turns out Sam's life ended on his twenty-seventh birthday.

Them sixty-thousand gold coins Bass took off the first train he robbed—the one up in Nebraska—ain't never been found, so there's all kinda rumors 'bout where he mighta hid them coins. Most folks think he hid the coins in a cave up near Allen, but everyone knows where that cave is and ain't nobody ever walked out of it with the coins, at least they didn't say nothin' about it iff'n they did.

That's pretty much the story of Sam Bass as I know it. Last I heared about Emma Parker was a judge in Austin cut her loose cuz, with Sam dead, puttin' such a pretty little gal through a trial didn't make much sense. Besides, holdin' a trial for Sam Bass's gal friend wouldn't set too good with folks in these parts, especially them what think Sam was a hero like that Robbin' Hood feller.

Sometimes I get to wonderin' if maybe Sam told Emma where them gold coins from his first train stick-up was hid. With that much money, Em could put a lot of distance twixt her and Texas. Bein' a Ranger and all, I guess I shouldn't be sayin' this, but I kinda hope that's what happened to that pretty little gal.

## THE END

# Edna and the Louse

February 8, 1915
Essanay Film Manufacturing Company—Niles, California

My profession is assembling order out of chaos. In other words, I am a motion picture production manager. It is my job to make sure a film's director, actors, cameramen, helpers, props, camera, and the sun all end up on the film stage when it's time to shoot a scene. Oh, and film. We must not forget to load film in the camera!

I perform this lengthy litany of tasks for the Essanay Film Manufacturing Company. I know, the name is goofy. It was someone's brilliant idea to make the company's name up out of the owners' initials: S and A, which stand for Spoor and Anderson, George and Gilbert respectively. They are the guys I work for.

Actually, I work more for Gilbert Anderson than for his partner. While Anderson is in charge of things out here in California, George Spoor runs the other half of the company back in Chicago. By the way, Gilbert Anderson is much better known by the name of the cowpoke hero he portrays in Essanay western picture plays, "Broncho Billy." The kids love him.

Forgive me if I talk and work at the same time. We have a scene to make in a little while and it's for a Chaplin picture, so I am sure to catch pure hell if I don't get the preparations exactly right. The Great Chaplin is a considerable pain in the posterior.

When Chaplin joined us last December, we were all pretty excited about George Spoor stealing him away from Keystone Studios down in Los Angeles. After dealing with The Great Chaplin's annoying personality for a couple of months, though, I'm not convinced we stole him. I think a much more likely scenario is Mack Sennett was deliriously happy to get the guy out of his hair. The Great Chaplin is impossible to please.

Worse yet, Chaplin negotiated a bunch of special clauses in his contract with Essanay, like he writes and directs all of his own pictures, and Chaplin gets to work at his own pace, which is just plain nuts. Chaplin produced his first Essanay motion picture, HIS NEW JOB, in Chicago and decided he didn't care for the Windy City, so he came out here to Niles and we've been cranking out two or even three of his two-reelers a month since.

The Great Chaplain also gets to pick and choose his costars. In his first Essanay picture play, he worked with fellow comedy actor, Ben Turpin, but you could tell right off, Chaplin doesn't like sharing the stage, especially with an established comedian like Turpin.

While shooting his second project, A NIGHT OUT, Chaplin stopped the entire operation to audition for a new leading lady. He claimed none of the studio's contract actresses were right for the part, including little Gloria Swanson, who had a bit part in HIS NEW JOB and did a swell job.

CHAPLIN & PURVIANCE

I have to admit, though, The Great Chaplin made an excellent choice out of the auditions for a new leading lady. She is a secretary from up in San Francisco by the name of Edna Purviance. This young woman is cute as a bug's ear and actually has a little stage acting experience. I strongly suspect, however, The Great Chaplin picked her for qualities one would not be likely to find in an acting resume.

Please don't read anything into what I just said about Miss Purviance. She's a sweet girl and entirely on the level. It's Chaplin who is out of whack.

## February 19, 1915
## Essanay Film Manufacturing Company—Niles, California

As you probably know, Essanay released A NIGHT OUT at the beginning of the week, and it seems to be doing all right so far. Now we're working on THE CHAMPION. In this epic tale The Great Chaplin plays a boxer. With any luck at all, Ernie Van Pelt, who plays Chaplin's boxing opponent will accidentally knock the Great One on his tail.

Edna Purviance has a part in THE CHAMPION, too. She played her role in A NIGHT OUT to perfection, proving again that Chaplin picked a winner. Ben Turpin is also in the new project, but The Great Chaplin has him playing a ringside vendor at the boxing matches, a relatively minor role with last billing in the players' credits. That should not come as any surprise when you remember Chaplin is writing and directing all of his own films here.

EDNA PURVIANCE

It's rather amusing to watch the relationship between The Great Chaplin and his new leading lady. Miss Purviance is staying in one of the player cottages here on the lot, and I've heard Chaplin has flowers delivered to her cottage every day. I hope she isn't allergic to the local flora.

The Great Chaplin's love life, of course, is his own business, but some of us feel bad for Miss Purviance. Just the other day I saw Gil Anderson shaking his head while watching her take Chaplin's arm to be escorted back to her cottage after shooting a scene. Anderson muttered, "That SOB will do her dirt sure as shootin'."

That was the general consensus of opinion where Edna and The Louse were concerned, and there wasn't much any of us could do about it. We figured Chaplin would show his true colors sooner or later, but by then it might be too late. I vowed to myself, though, if Chaplin broke Miss Purviance's heart, I would personally knock him into the middle of next week, which would be a surefire way to lose my job. Despite Gilbert Anderson sharing my opinion of The Great Chaplin, there was little doubt who the loser would be if push came to shove at Essanay.

Anyway, we had THE CHAMPION in the can and released on March 11. Then we immediately went to work on a one-reeler called IN THE PARK. The cast of players for the new project included Miss Purviance, Ernie Van Pelt, and a raucous redhead named Leona Anderson. We had a week to produce IN THE PARK, and during that week The Great Chaplin proved to everyone on the lot that he was a louse of the first order.

9

## March 12, 1915
## Essanay Film Manufacturing Company—Niles, California

Edna Purviance and I were in my office, where I was going over the scenario for IN THE PARK with her. Chaplin had scribbled pencil notations all over her copy and I was trying to help her make sense of them. She couldn't ask The Louse to decipher them because he was supposedly in the house he rented recovering from a cold. I say "supposedly" because it turned out that wasn't quite the case.

The window in my office overlooks the street on the other side of some railroad tracks next to the studio. A train went by, which made conversation impossible, so there was a lull in our discussion while we waited for the racket to pass. I was studying the scenario, but Edna was looking out the window. When the train was gone, I offered a suggestion as to what one line of Chaplin's scribbles might mean, but Edna didn't reply.

1915 PIERCE ARROW

I looked up from the scenario and saw that Edna's attention was still glued to something outside the window, and whatever was out there, clearly did not make her happy. Out of curiosity, I turned to look, too. What I saw was a shiny Pierce-Arrow roadster. I recognized it as one I saw The Great Chaplin driving around town. At the moment, though, he wasn't driving. He was too busy kissing the redhead beside him in the Pierce-Arrow's passenger seat. The redhead, of course, was Leona Anderson.

I turned back to look at Edna and saw her expression transform from shock to heartbreak. Clearly, Chaplin kissing another woman was not something Edna expected to see. Even though I was not nearly as surprised as she by Chaplin's behavior and could have predicted something of this sort, I could not help but feel sorry for Edna.

In an feeble effort to take her mind off the love scene being played out in front of the studio, I suggested to Edna we take a break from our efforts to decipher Chaplin's notes on the scenario and ask the man himself what they meant later. She quickly agreed, and after a pause, asked if I would escort her to her player bungalow at the back of the studio lot.

Under the circumstances, I had little choice but to do as she asked. At Edna's bungalow, she unlocked the door and turned to thank me for walking with her. Instead, she burst into tears. Seconds later Edna was sobbing hysterically in my arms. I quickly escorted her into the bungalow and onto a loveseat in her living room.

It certainly was not that I didn't enjoy holding the beautiful Edna in my arms, I just didn't want The Louse to show up at the still open bungalow door and catch me doing so. Regardless of his abominable behavior, a word from Chaplin could terminate my employment at Essanay in a heartbeat.

## April 9, 1915
### Essanay Film Manufacturing Company—Niles, California

Despite there being an obvious cooling of Chaplin's relationship with Edna, I managed to keep production on IN THE PARK moving so that we released on the eighteenth of March as scheduled. The next project was a terrible scenario called A JITNEY ELOPEMENT in which Chaplin plays a fake count intent on marrying Edna. The rest of the troop consisted of folks we began calling The Chaplin Regulars, a group of actors The Louse knew made him look good and included in every film he did.

There was no role for Leona Anderson in the new project. Whether that was simply due to the lack of a second female lead in the story, or because The Louse was trying to patch things up with Edna I could not say. I did know he was still seeing Leona, but now it was strictly on the sly.

Edna must have figured that was the case because she made it known to me in a coy and ladylike, fashion she would not mind spending some of her off-time in my company. We did so cautiously, however, because as long as The Louse was still interested in Edna, my job was at risk. For the same reason Edna and I were careful to mind our Ps and Qs during working hours, lest Chaplin get suspicious.

I always enjoyed time spent with Edna. In a word, she was "fun." She turned simple walks in the nearby hills into adventures, sometimes even naughty adventures. Once or twice, we went to see motion pictures at the Edison Theater on Niles Street, and even held hands in the dark while we sat through four or five reels of drama or comedy or whatever the featured presentation happened to be. We called these occasions our bus-mans' holidays.

Most of us at Essanay knew in fairly short order that The Louse's sixth Essanay project was destined for motion picture history. Called simply THE TRAMP, it was the first picture in which Chaplin played what would become his signature character. I knew he'd been developing the role the entire time he was in Niles, and Chaplin now decided it was time to trot the character out and see if his rapidly growing multitude of fans across the country liked the little tramp.

Once again, I have to hand it to The Louse. He played the character as a sympathetic little fellow who wants to be a rogue, but the fates seem to be against him. It was love at first sight for legions of movie goers.

In his role as the leading character in THE TRAMP, Chaplin wooed Edna in scene after scene. In his role as the film's director, however, The Louse criticized everything she did. Edna simply could not please him, no matter how hard she tried, and I knew she was trying as hard as she could. Sadly, I thought I knew what The Louse was up to. It turned out I had him pegged.

### April 16, 1915
### Essanay Film Manufacturing Company—Niles, California

CHAPLIN'S LITTLE TRAMP

Essanay released THE TRAMP on the eleventh of April, and within a week we all knew Chaplin's future was signed sealed and delivered. Motion picture fans throughout the country immediately fell in love with The Louse's tramp character.

The final scene shows the sad little tramp walking dejectedly away from the camera along a lonely country road near the studio, and then his posture perks up and we know he has shrugged off the loss of his sweetheart and is heading for a new adventure. As trite as it seemed, that scene brought tears to the eyes of countless audiences.

There were also tears in Edna Purviance's eyes, but for quite a different reason. The Louse was making her miserable with his constant criticism, which now continued into the production of Chaplin's next project, a one-reeler called BY THE SEA. In an effort to cheer her up, I suggested we go for a drive one evening, but Edna said she would rather just go to my house and relax in privacy.

As things turned out, Edna spent the night with me, but everything she did and said seemed strained. The Louse was successfully lousing things up without even being there.

The next day Gilbert Anderson gathered several of his top production people for a meeting. It seems many of Essanay's contract players were threatening to walk out if something wasn't done about Chaplin. Their complaint was that The Louse's projects were dominating the studio's facilities and other films were either taking much longer to produce or not being made at all.

We all knew the facts of life when it came to the motion picture business. In this case, Chaplin was the goose that lays golden eggs, and from overheard comments reported to Anderson it was seeming less and less likely that Essanay would be able to match offers anticipated from bigger Los Angeles studios to lure Chaplin down there when his one year contract with Essanay ended in December.

That left us with two options. One was to let the other actors walk out and make hay with Chaplin projects while he was still under contract. The second option was to reign Chaplin in and shift more of the studio's resources to making pictures with the unhappy contract players.

The real purpose of our meeting was to inform us Gilbert Anderson and his partner, George Spoor, were sticking with Chaplin as long as they held his contract, and to hell with everyone else. I, along with most of the other men in the room, knew that choice sounded the death knell for Essanay. Sure, none of us would be unemployed for a while yet, but the handwriting was on the wall. Unless something changed, Spoor and Anderson would bank the huge profits The Louse brought in and let Essanay go the way of the dodo bird.

The other shoe dropped that evening when Edna showed up at my office wearing a very sad face. Her news was she'd decided to go back to The Louse, so it would have to strictly business between us from then on. It seemed strange she felt that way when Chaplin chased skirts no matter who he was "seeing." I wished her luck and meant it.

## November 17, 1927
## Warner Brothers Pictures, Hollywood, California

Everybody at Warner Brothers Pictures, my current employer, was walking around with their fingers crossed. So far our Vitaphone talkie, THE JAZZ SINGER was doing a land-office business, but the studio risked everything to produce the film, so it had to keep going as a top box office draw a lot longer to break even.

Trying to take my mind off of the pins and needles I was on, I spent the afternoon catching up on the motion picture industry news as reported in a half-dozen trade journals I'd been neglecting while working as a second unit director on THE JAZZ SINGER. That's where I ran across Edna's name in an article about the release of a French film in which she played a role. The main subject of the article, however, was her announced retirement from acting.

Prior to making the French film Edna was still working for The Louse. Counting the films she made at Essanay, Mutual, and First National, Edna appeared in 33 films with Chaplin between 1915 and 1927. One of those was Chaplin's biggest hit to date, THE KID.

Interestingly, Chaplin had married twice since 1915. Since both of his wives were actresses, but neither was named Edna, I had to wonder if she went back to Chaplin in 1915 because she loved him or because he told her she had to play the game his way if she wanted to keep making films as his leading lady, or both. Remembering her face when she came into my office that afternoon in April of 1915—and yes, I remember her face and that final meeting very well—I suspected The Louse still expected a lot more than acting from her for the paychecks he signed.

The article about her retirement mentioned Edna had never married. For a moment I thought about tracking her down and sending a note. When I thought about it further, though, I decided to let sleeping dogs lie. Edna Purviance made a choice twelve years ago and she was living with the consequences.

As for The Louse, I hoped his comeuppance would catch up with him someday, but it seemed unlikely. According to Variety Charles Spencer Chaplin was thought to be the richest man in the world. Still, money isn't everything.

## THE END

# C'est La Guerre

9:35 A.M.–Saturday, November 9, 1918
Above Northern France

From my assigned patrol altitude of 5,000 feet, the Albatross D-III appeared as little more than a tiny black cross against the dark green farmland west of the German airfield at Ars-sur-Moselle. In fact, it was not the aircraft itself, but the dark shadow following along on the ground behind it that brought the Boche ship to my attention.

ALBATROSS D-III

We were traveling in opposite directions. The Albatross was headed east at an altitude of about a thousand feet and at what seemed a leisurely speed. I speculated that the German flier might be completing his morning patrol and returning to one of the Jasta aerodromes around Labry. Such speculation, however, mattered little for, regardless of his reason for being on our side of the front lines, I intended to rid the skies of this Boche menace.

When I first saw the enemy pilot he was heading about a mile ahead of me and a mile to my right. Now, less than thirty seconds later we were abeam each other and I watched him for any sign that he saw me. Seeing no such indication, I planned my attack.

Lowering the nose of my Spad S.XIII slightly to gain some airspeed and lose some altitude, I held my westerly course for another minute. I used that time to give the skies around me a thorough perusal. It was a common tactic of the Boche to send a lone flier out as bait while his comrades lurked nearby waiting to ambush the unwary French, British or American pilot who went for the bait like a big stupid fish.

15

SPAD S.XIII

The skies on this particular morning, though, were clear and I put my plan of attack into motion by beginning a wide descending turn to the right. When I leveled my wings again, I was about three miles behind the Albatross and roughly two thousand feet above it. From the airspeed indicator attached to my port wing, I calculated my speed at around 190 kilometers-per-hour—a speed of about 120 miles-per-hour in American terms. The Boche continued at his leisurely pace as if oblivious to my presence. I would soon give him reason to regret his lack of vigilance.

During the next three or four minutes I continued to close the distance between us, all the while keeping a close watch on the sky above and behind me for other enemy aircraft. At the same time I made small adjustments to my glide path so I would end up slightly above the Albatross when the distance between us was reduced to one hundred yards—the perfect spot from which to rake the Boche ship from nose to tail with deadly fire from my twin thirty-caliber Marlin machine guns.

When I reached the position from which I would begin my attack, I pulled the cocking lever to clear my guns and gave the sky around us one last look. Then, with my hand on the firing lever, I turned my attention back to my target. The Albatross had disappeared into thin air!

Mere seconds later I felt the impact of machinegun bullets ripping into the underside of my Spad and realized I had just fallen for one of the oldest tricks in the book. The Boche pilot spotted me somewhere along the line, perhaps even before I saw him, and he had patiently waited for me to close into firing position. Then he pulled his power completely off and lowered his nose, causing me to fly right over the top of his rapidly slowing ship. From that point he went to full power and raised his nose, putting my Spad directly in his gun sight.

Cursing the overconfidence that blinded me to the possibility that, by such a simple ruse, I could quickly become the hunted rather than the hunter, I did three things simultaneously. Slamming my throttle wide open, I stomped on my right rudder pedal, and yanked the control stick back and to the right.

My Spad responded by instantly rolling into a tight, climbing turn to the right and, hopefully, out of my foe's line of fire. Feeling no more hits from the Boche's guns, I knew I had gained a momentary reprieve, but I fully expected the German to press his advantage by following me into my turn. When I turned to look back, however, the Albatross was again nowhere to be seen. Now what was he up to?

I lowered the nose of my ship, but stayed in the right turn until I had completed a full three-hundred-sixty degree circle. Then, leveling my wings, I scanned the sky above and below for the Boche. I spotted him nearly a mile ahead of me and running to the east for all he was worth. He had also dropped to tree-top level, using the descent to increase his speed and make himself harder to see against the ground.

In level flight, my S-Thirteen had a speed advantage of about twenty miles-per-hour over the Albatross. I would add to this advantage during my descent. Thus, I knew I could overtake the Boche before he reached the front lines ten miles to the east. Given the skill he demonstrated by suckering me into his trap, however, getting the Albatross into my gun sight again might be another matter entirely.

With the throttle still wide open, I aimed my nose at the rapidly fleeing Albatross and began closing the distance between us again. I saw the German pilot look back at over his shoulder, and when I closed to within firing range again, he took the only evasive action left to him. He pushed his left rudder pedal to the floor and the Albatross skidded left out of my gunsight.

I did exactly the same thing to bring my nose back on his tail. Just as that happened, he reversed the procedure and skidded to the right. Again, I followed his maneuver, but this time I kept my nose to the left of the Albatross so when he skidded back to the left a moment later, he flew directly into my line of fire.

Without hesitation, I fired and watched rips appear in the fabric along the left side of the Boche ship. Almost instantly a thin line of black smoke streamed from his engine and the Albatross slowed. I had hit something critical and I had him.

Reducing my speed, I centered the damaged Albatross in my aiming reticule and again opened fire. Pieces of the damaged machine flew off into the slipstream and I saw the D-Three's right wings sag. A split second later the Boche's nose came up and the ship shuddered on the verge of a stall.

To avoid a collision with the Albatross, I opened my throttle and pulled around into a climbing right turn. Suddenly my windscreen was filled with a long line of evergreen trees I failed to notice while attacking the enemy ship. I pulled the stick back as far as it would go and my trusty Spad hopped over the tree tops with just a few feet to spare.

After clearing the trees, I resumed my turn to the right, intending to set up another firing pass on the Albatross, but when I spotted the Boche ship, I knew the fight was over. As I watched, my worthy foe and his ship became a smoking pile of rubble alongside a roadway.

DESTROYED ALBATROSS

Even though I knew the German pilot would not have hesitated to do the same to me, I experienced a wave of sadness. A brave man had just lost his life in the service of his country. I wondered what he would say if I could ask him whether or not the honor of Germany was worth the price he had just paid for a very small piece of it.

The French seem to have an expression for every situation in life and this occasion was no exception. The appropriate phrase is, "C'Est La Guerre." It means such is war. Indeed.

Looking down at the wreckage again, I saw two farmers running toward the crashed Albatross with pitchforks in their hands to be used as weapons in the event the German pilot had survived the crash of his ship. They had no need of their makeshift weapons. The men waved enthusiastically as I passed over their heads. I am sure they felt no great loss at the death of a German pilot.

I climbed to about a thousand feet in a tight spiral over the wreckage. From that altitude I could see that the road alongside which the German ship had crashed intersected a major north-south road about a mile further east. About five miles north along the north-south road lay a French village I recognized as Abaucourt. I made note of these landmarks so our ground troops could locate the Albatross's wreckage and confirm my sixth and, as the fates would have it be, final aerial victory of the Great War

Then, also noting the position of the indicator on my ship's fuel gauge below the one-quarter mark, I turned southwest toward home, keeping a wary eye on the skies around me as I went. Home at that particular time was the airfield near Rembercourt where my unit—the First Pursuit Group of the Twenty-Seventh Aero Squadron—had been stationed for the past three months.

## 7:00 A.M. – Sunday, November 10, 1918
## Rembercourt Aerodrome, France

The next day, Sunday, 10 November, we awoke to a thick overcast of fog which kept our ships firmly anchored to the ground until mid-afternoon. Just as the sun appeared and patrols assignments were made, however, we received a dispatch informing us that an armistice had been agreed to by all parties and the hostilities were to officially end at 1100 hours the following day—the eleventh hour of the eleventh day of the eleventh month of 1918. Since neither I nor any of my comrades were eager to tempt the fates and risk becoming our group's final fatality of the war, we flew only casual patrols close to home that afternoon and during the morning hours of Monday, 11 November.

## THE END

# Tomboy

## Saturday, June 7, 1930—Santa Catalina Island

Somewhere in this country there is a depression going on, but not on Santa Catalina Island. Everyone here, rich and poor alike, is having a grand time this weekend. All of Avalon's hotels are full to overflowing and the new Avalon Casino is jumping with Sheilas and Sheiks who one might suspect were a trifle ossified if prohibition were not the law of the land, especially at William Wrigley's grand pleasure palace.

AVALON CASINO

The most intoxicating items served at the casino's Marine Bar are the maraschino cherries topping their Neptune Sundaes. It's a soda fountain, for cryin' out loud!

On the other hand, Wrigley has some good reasons for running a tight ship. For one, his Avalon Casino is the only dance venue in the county approved by the Los Angeles Unified School District for their teachers to attend. That honor is due to several factors, including a strictly enforced dress code requiring gentlemen to wear ties and sport coats, both of which may be rented at the ballroom entrance by those who are ill-prepared.

Another cause for the casino's high rating with the school district is an even more strictly enforced behavior code. I've heard it said that the ballroom manager actually walks around the dance floor with a stick to measure the space between dancers.

These and other fascinating peculiarities of the Avalon Casino were the reasons I was on the island with LOS ANGELES TIMES photog, Nettie Brewer. Our boss, TIMES Publisher, Harry Chandler, is a firm believer in downplaying negative news and shouting the happy news from the rooftops. The Avalon Casino and Catalina in general were about the happiest news around these days, so off we went aboard the Great White Steamer, SS CATALINA, on an all-expense-paid weekend to write happy words and snap happy pictures of happy people being happy on Wrigley's happy island.

Most reporters would jump at such an opportunity, and so would I, except for one small detail—a detail that goes by the name of Nettie Brewer. Now, before I say anything else about Nettie, I am obligated to tell you she is a very talented photographer. Proof of that is the fact she is the only woman on the TIMES photo staff. For that matter, Nettie is one of only two or three full-time women news photogs on the west coast. Now, having said that, I will say working with Nettie is just about my least favorite thing to do.

NETTIE BREWER

Nettie's problem, or more accurately, my problem with Nettie is she is a consummate tomboy. Worse, she doesn't come by that quality naturally. I don't know what makes her think she needs to act like a guy to get along with guys, but she works at it constantly. Nettie is always talking about guy things, like sports and automobiles. She also tells a lot of guy jokes, some of which are quite risqué.

She is so intent on behaving like a guy, it would not surprise me in the least to see her coming out of the men's room. I feel duty bound to also say I have seen no indications that Nettie is lavender. She clearly prefers the company of male employees at the TIMES to the females.

Anyway, there we were late Saturday afternoon gathering stories and photographs about what the frolicking tourists were doing on Catalina Island. Nettie photographed folks on the beach at sunset, riding bicycles through the little town of Avalon, and strolling along the Via Casino walkway en route to Wrigley's pleasure palace.

We talked to visitors waiting to enter the Casino's motion picture theater on the ground floor. The picture they waited to see was a new movie about the Great War, ALL QUIET ON THE WESTERN FRONT, staring Lew Ayres and Louis Wolheim. I wished the folks were going to see a happier movie. Our boss would not be pleased about such an unhappy movie in our story.

Around six o' clock, I figured we had earned a dinner break and steered Nettie past the casino to Descanso Canyon, the location of Avalon's best hotel, the Saint Catherine. The place was packed, but the maître d' quickly found a table for two highly placed members of the fourth estate such as we.

After we were seated and our waiter was advised of our menu choices, Nettie put on a serious expression, looked me in the eye for a moment, and then said, "Chet, would you answer a question for me?"

Her seldom seen serious expression had me wondering what was coming, I said, "Sure, if I can."

"Why don't you like me?"

Talk about being on the spot! I said the only thing I could think of. "I like you fine, Nettie. What makes you think I don't?"

She shrugged. "Just the way you act around me. You aren't . . . I don't know . . . as friendly as you are with other people we work with."

Still trying to dig myself out this hole she had me in, I said, "Gosh, if I treat you differently, I don't do it intentionally. You're a nice person, I have no reason to dislike you."

"I think you do. Is it that I'm not as feminine as you think I should be?"

She had the goods on me there and my face must have betrayed that, because Nettie said, "That's it! I can tell that's it! I don't act all silly like other women in the office. Well, Mister, I'll have you know there's a darn good reason for that!"

Trying to get back on my feet after a good swift kick in the kiester, I said, "I'm sure there is, Nettie, and that's your business. I just . . . ."

"Do you want to know why I act like a tomboy?"

I started to shake my head in the negative, but she was going to tell me anyway. "I don't act like the silly girls because I work with guys who go all gaga over silly girls—the brainless flapper types—and by acting the way I do, I don't have to constantly fend off a bunch of randy reporters whose egos get bruised if a girl doesn't fawn all over them and make them think she wants to jump right into bed with them. That's why!"

Nettie was so vehement in her tirade, she attracted the attention of a few diners at nearby tables. Besides being embarrassed, I was thoroughly irritated with her for making a fuss and putting me on the spot.

Speaking in a loud whisper, I said, "Okay, you've got it all figured out, and that's fine with me because I assure you I have no desire to jump into bed with you, Miss Brewer. I will admit to being curious, though; just exactly how would you act if you did want to jump in bed with a guy? I bet you don't have any idea about that, do you?"

Nettie looked at me, but said nothing right away. About the time I noticed something that looked a lot like a tear begin to roll down her cheek, she said softly, "Yes, I do have an idea about that. I would ask him why he didn't like me."

If I had any doubts about Nettie having a female side, she was eliminating them with one of the oldest ploys in the Modern Women's Guide To Conquering Men, and it was working. Even if I thought she was faking the tears, I would have felt just as badly.

I began an apology, but she didn't let me get very far. Nettie jumped up, made a weepy apology of her own, and dashed off in the direction of the powder room. A few diners at nearby tables, especially women, glared at me for upsetting the darling little sweetheart at my table. Phooey on them!

Our dinners arrived and Nettie followed them to the table a few minutes later. While I stood and held her chair, Nettie said something about how good her roasted white sea bass looked, marking an end to our previous conversation. I was both happy and unhappy about that.

I was happy to be discussing dead fish instead of my liking or disliking Nettie, but I still wished our talk had ended on a happier note. I was beginning to understand why Harry Chandler preferred positive stories over negative stories.

Then, I realized there was something else going on way in the back corner of my mind. Nettie all but said she wanted to be intimate with me. That idea was as alien to me as someone offering me a free trip to Mars. Now, though, some part of me was wondering what an intimate relationship with Nettie would be like.

Physically, she was somewhat plain with a straight up and down figure, and she went out of her way to avoid the current fashion styles of bobbed hair and overdone makeup. Her hair was red, long, and a little wild. Her smile looked great without painted cupid bow lips and . . . well, quite honestly, Nettie was a long way from unattractive.

Try as I might, I couldn't banish those thoughts from my mind. They lasted all through dinner, including my Peach Melba dessert, and they were still bouncing around in my head when we left the Saint Catherine's dining room and set out for the casino ballroom.

We had an appointment with the Ballroom Manager to interview and photograph a few carefully selected smiling, happy guests. On the way to the ballroom entrance, I removed a slightly wrinkled tie from my sport coat pocket, wrapped it around my neck, and gave it a Windsor knot.

Nettie stopped walking when I was done with the tie, handed me her camera bag to hold and precisely squared the tie with my shirt lapels. She then gave me reassuring nod and up to the ballroom we went. It was a simple gesture and I enjoyed it. I'm not sure why.

From halfway up the switchback entrance ramp we could hear the orchestra playing a rousing version of version of Get Happy. Harry Chandler would approve.

The orchestra we were hearing was that of Buddy Rogers. Rogers was making quite a name for himself lately. Not only had he played a leading part with Clara Bow in the hit movie WINGS, his orchestra was one of the most popular on the west coast. He billed himself as "America's Boyfriend," a reference to his role in WINGS.

BUDDY ROGERS · ORCHESTRA    CATALINA ISL.

We spent the next hour or so interviewing four couples the Ballroom Manager lined up for us. They were very happy to be having so much fun in Mister Wrigley's casino. When I completed the interviews, we led the couples out to the exterior balcony around the ballroom. Nettie photographed the couples in dancing poses out on the balcony in front of double doors that opened into the ballroom.

Nettie assured me that, with the doors open, the photographs would look just as if they were taken inside the ballroom, but anyone on the dance floor who might not wish to appear in the LOS ANGELES TIMES Metro Section would be unrecognizable.

The Ballroom Manager insisted on that precaution. The casino staff was the heart and soul of discretion.

Pictures completed, we stopped in at the Marine Bar for two Cokes we took back out to the balcony so we could look at the lights of Avalon reflected on the water in the harbor. The sky was clear enough that we could even see a few lights over on the mainland, 20-some miles away. I took a deep breath. The air was mild and fresh with the faint sweet smell of orchids floating on it. Then I realized Nettie was supplying the orchids.

We were side by side leaning against the balcony railing and I was suddenly very aware of her presence. Those thoughts I was having earlier about Nettie were back in force. That made me decide to test the waters.

"Nettie?"

"Yes, Chet?"

"Would you like . . . I mean would you care to dance, I mean as long as we're here and everything?"

She made me wait at least half a minute before answering. "Sure. I mean as long as we're here and everything."

I looked at her face to see if she was mocking me. Nothing in her expression said so. Nettie was simply smiling a soft smile, although I thought I might have detected a faint hint of victory around the edges of that smile.

We deposited her camera case and our Coke glasses on an empty table, and then I escorted her to the dance floor. Rogers' band was playing a romantic arrangement of EMBRACEABLE YOU. Now, understand I am no Fred Astaire by any means, but when I took Nettie in my arms, we seemed to float across the dance floor as if on air. She was such a good dancer, she made even me look good. Nettie was just full of surprises tonight.

I managed to make to the end of EMBRACEABLE YOU without stepping on her feet, and the band went straight into another ballad. I looked at Nettie and smiled. She raised her arms and we kept right on dancing.

The band was playing EXACTLY LIKE YOU. The lyrics seemed very apropos to the moment:

*I know why I've waited.*
*Know why I've been blue.*
*I pray each night for someone*
*Exactly like you.*

When the music stopped we just stood there for a moment with Nettie leaning into my arms. Glancing over Nettie's shoulder, I noticed the Ballroom Manager looking at us and gently slapping the palm of his hand with a short ruler. I said, "Oh, oh. I think we'd better take a break. The Ballroom Manager has his measuring stick out and he's looking in our direction."

Nettie stepped back and said, "That man really knows how to spoil a party."

We went back out onto the balcony, and looking me straight in the eye, she said, "I didn't say that right. The Ballroom Manager didn't spoil the party. I've never been so happy as I am right now."

I rested my hands on her waist. "That goes for me, too." I gently turned Nettie and led her to a column that hid us from the ballroom.

We had the balcony to ourselves and I stood there for a moment looking at the radiant woman before me and working up my nerve. As usual, Nettie was way ahead of me. Grinning, she said. "Darling, if you intend to kiss me, I suggest you do so before that nasty man with the measuring stick shows up."

That broke the ice, so to speak. I grinned back at her and we kissed a sweet kiss that fit the mood perfectly. When the kiss ended I held Nettie close to me for a long moment, and she whispered in my ear, "I'm sorry if that was too forward of me, but I've waited a lifetime for that kiss. I didn't want the moment to get away from us."

I looked at Nettie. "A lifetime?"

"Yes, I've been waiting my entire life for someone, like the song says, 'exactly like you.'" After a pause, during which I said nothing because I didn't know what to say, she frowned a little and asked, "Is that all right?"

"Yes! I mean, it's fine . . . wonderful! It's just this has all happened so fast and I'm still trying to catch up."

The little frown was still on Nettie's face. "Oh, gosh, you think I've been too brazen, don't you? I'm sorry, Chet, I . . . I just . . . ."

In a firm voice, I said, "Oh, stop it! I don't think any such thing. For me, this is like finding a really special treasure. I have to think how to protect it and keep it safe. I don't want to mess everything up."

Nettie was smiling again, "Oh, what a sweet thing to say. I can tell there are advantages to falling in love with a journalist."

Her words, "falling in love," hit me between the eyes. I hadn't thought of what was happening in those terms yet. She was right, of course, we were falling in love. That both delighted me and scared the hell out of me. I mean a couple of hours ago I was trying to think of ways to avoid tomboy Nettie, and now we were holding hands as we walked from the casino to the Saint Catherine Hotel.

We walked in silence, and that silence finally got the better of Nettie. With a sincere note of panic in her voice, she said, "Chet, you're scaring me. You keep not saying anything and I can't tell what you're thinking."

Despite her forwardness, Nettie was clearly as befuddled about our situation as I was. She had decided to put her feelings about me out into the open, and now she realized she was vulnerable and not so sure she'd done the right thing. I wanted to set her mind at ease, but at the same time, I knew doing that would be tantamount to making a commitment. I felt backed into a corner, yet being in that corner with Nettie also felt swell.

As is usually the case in such debates between my heart and my brain, my heart won. "Nettie, I certainly don't intend to scare you. I'm afraid I'm kind of new to this love stuff, so you'll have to forgive me if I occasionally violate the rules of the game."

Nettie replied, "I'm not sure there are any rules. Well, maybe one. A very smart man whose name I cannot recall once said, 'Love without conversation is impossible.' I believe that."

We said goodnight in the hallway outside Nettie's room and shared a short, sweet kiss. When I walked down the hall to my room, I'm not sure my feet ever touched the floor. Love finished its job on me overnight. I know this because I found myself singing EXACTLY LIKE YOU to the mirror while I shaved the next morning.

Sunday morning, as we rode the SS CATALINA back to San Pedro, I told Nettie I felt like we were setting off on a voyage of adventure that was already changing our lives and would continue to do so as long as we lived.

Nettie said she felt the same, and that began a discussion about the details of our voyage of adventure. The answers to the questions we raised would be the decisions that would bring about those big changes in our lives.

We talked about some of those changes like our jobs at the LOS ANGELES TIMES; and if we got married, where we would live; and how many kids we ought to have; and on and on. There was one fact, though, about which there was no question in my mind: Nettie the Tomboy was definitely not aboard the SS CATALINA that morning. In fact, I never saw her again.

THE END

# A Visit From Benny The Bug

August 16, 1939—Santa Monica, California

This whole predicament comes about when Faces O' Shaughnessy sees Benny the Bug on the REX. Now, Faces has this special kind of talent for rememberin' people he sees, and he has seen all the unreputable mugs out here on the west coast who is known for causing trouble. You might say Faces is like a walkin' mug book.

That's why my boss, Tony the Hat, has Faces around on the REX all the time. The boss, he runs a strictly legit operation and he don't want nobody makin' trouble that might louse up the action. The way it is, casino gambling is illegal in California, and the boss figured out this swell racket where he anchors this big old boat, the REX, outside the three-mile limit where the cops cannot touch him and sets up a gambling casino.

The suckers come out to the REX on these little boats they call "water taxis" so they can play the games, and Tony does it up brown for 'em with a ritzy restaurant, only top-shelf booze in the bars, and all the stuff that makes the high-rollers think they are really living it up while they are dropping bundles of cash at the tables. Like I said, it is a swell racket.

THE REX GAMBLING SHIP

So anyways, Faces sees Benny the Bug on the REX, and he sez to himself, he sez, "What is this mug from the Dago outfit doin' on our turf?"

He sez that because Benny the Bug works for Big Al Franco, the top guy in the San Diego outfit. Now, Big Al ain't exactly competition for Tony the Hat because our operation is strictly legit and Big Al, he works the shady side of the street— pony parlors, gals, and all like that. Even so, the boss does not want mugs like Benny hanging around the REX because it is bad for business. The suckers do not like associating with low-brows such as Benny.

Knowing how the boss feels about such things, Faces goes and tells the boss he seen Benny the Bug and the boss sends for me. The boss does this because I am his fix-it guy, meaning that whenever there is anything going on the boss do not like, he tells me to fix it. Now not meaning to brag, but I am very good at what I do and the boss knows he can count on me to make it right—whatever it is that needs fixing.

So I hot-foot it down to the boss's office on the REX and he sez, "Faces tells me there is a mug from the San Diego outfit on the REX tonight—some jamoke who is called Benny the Bug. You know of this fellow?"

I sez, "Yeah, I seen him around here and there—funny little guy, always cracking jokes. He is a sharp dresser, too. Benny is what you call an all-purpose hitter—he does whatever there is that needs doing."

"Well," sez the boss, "I want you should find out what this bug is doing on the REX, and if you figure he is up to no good, make sure he does not come back."

"Okay, Boss, consider it done."

"But if you must run him off, do not do it here on the boat in case he makes a fuss. Follow him back to the dock and explain things to him there. Understand?"

"Sure thing, Boss."

So I go back up to the main casino deck and Faces shows me where this guy, Benny the Bug, is. Even if I did not know what Benny looks like, he would be hard to miss dressed like he was, in a snazzy suit, white shoes, and a bright red shirt. Like I was saying before, he is a sharp dresser.

So I watch Benny a while to see what he is doing, and what he is doing is nothing. I mean he is just walking around watching the suckers lose their dough. Then, after he does nothing for another hour or so, Benny takes himself down to boarding ramp where the water taxis load and he gets on the next one that shows up. I wait 'til the last minute before the water taxi shoves off and jump aboard myself.

All this time Benny the Bug is acting perfectly natural; he does not do a single suspicious thing, which is very suspicious for a guy like Benny. When the water taxi docks at Santa Monica, Benny gets off and starts walking casual-like toward the street end of the pier. I follow him and when we get near the street where there ain't so many people around, I catch up and sez, "Hey, Benny, wait up a sec."

Benny turns around, and when he seen who I am, he gets this big slop-eatin' grin on his face and sez, "Why, hello, Jimmy. Fancy meeting you here."

"Yeah," I sez, "Fancy that. The boss and me is wonderin' what you are doing here."

"The boss? Oh, you are still workin' for Tony the Hat?"

"Yeah, I am still workin' for Tony the Hat. So what is it that you are doing here, Benny?"

Grinnin' some more, Benny sez, "Big Al gave me a few days off, like for a vacation, so I come up to the big city to see the sights."

"I meant, what was you doin' on the REX, wise guy."

"The REX is one of the sights to see in LA. Is that not so? I never seen a gamblin' boat before, so I wanted to see what it was like. That is a swell boat Tony has—really swanky."

"Yeah, and the boss wants to keep it that way, by which I mean he don't want no trouble makers around gumming up the works."

Benny the Bug gets this look on his face like I hurt his feelings and sez, "Trouble maker? Me? Heck no, Jimmy, you got it all wrong. I am not here to make no trouble. Like I said, I just want to see the sights."

Benny sure sounded like he was on the level, which puts me on the spot. If things was like he said—if Benny was really just on a vacation—and I run him off, such a lack of hospitality is likely to get the Dago outfit all riled up. The boss would not be happy if that happened because he likes everything to be quiet and peaceful like. Besides, I got nothing personal against Benny and I was starting to feel bad about rousting him.

So I sez, "Okay, Pally, I am going take your word on that, but you better be on the level."

## August 17, 1939—Aboard The REX

All that was last Wednesday night, and the next night, Faces comes down to the Frenchie restaurant on the REX where I was having some dinner and sez Benny the Bug is back again.

I sez, "What is he doin'?"

"He was playing the cheap slots when I come down to get you."

"All right, keep an eye on him while I finish dinner, then I will come up and see about him."

So I finish my bully-base—that is kind of a French fish stew—and takes myself up to the casino, where I find Faces leaning against a wall near a row of one-armed bandits. He sees me comin' and nods toward the row of one-armed bandits, where I see Benny throwing nickels down the coin slot of a fruit spinner.

CRAPS ABOARD THE REX

I nod at Faces to let him know I see Benny and Faces nods back, and then wanders off to look around for any other bad apples that might have dropped into the barrel. Well, I am watchin' Benny and the only thing about him that's different since last night is he's wearin' a yellow shirt instead of a red one.

After I am watching him a while, though, I am noticing something else different about Benny the Bug. Tonight he is acting slightly nervous—nothing real obvious, but he is lookin' around the room every once in a while like he's watching for someone or something.

I am still trying to figure out what Benny might be up to when Tiny, one of the boss's errand boys, comes up and taps me on the shoulder, which is difficult for Tiny to do because I'm over six foot and he is hardly five. He sez, "J-J-Jimmy, the b-b-boss wants to see you. He sez right now c-c-cuz it's a 'mergency."

Now, in all the time I work for Tony the Hat, I do not ever remember him ever saying anything was a 'mergency. That is not his style. So I tells Tiny thanks and take off for the boss's office on a dead run. When I gets there, he sez, "Jimmy, we got us a big problem. Somebody in the casino is passing funny money."

"Who is it, boss? I'll . . . ."

"That is just the problem. We do not know who is doing this. The bogus bills is twenties and fifties—real good quality—and they are coming in from all the cashiers. Marty, the head cashier, spotted a bad fifty, and when he started lookin' close, he found bad bills in the receipts from every window in the joint!"

"No kidding?"

The boss looks at me like I have said something nonsensical.

"This is not something about which I am likely to be kidding, Jimmy. So far they're into us for about two Gs!"

"Do not any of the cashiers know who is passing the bogus bills?"

"No, they do not. Marty has been talking to the cashiers, even the pit bosses, and ain't nobody seen a thing because they did not know there was anything going on. They sure do now!"

"But how are the passers working it so they make any money, instead of just taking their chances at the tables?"

"They must be buying chips, playing a few hands or betting on a few spins of the wheel, and then cashing in their chips. Then they must be buying more chips at another cashier station with the bogus bills."

"Clever fellows."

"This sort of clever fellows we do not need aboard the REX. Now get yourself up there and find out who is being so clever before they rob us blind. I do not want to shut the casino down, but I will not have any choice if this should continue."

"Okay, Boss, I'm on my way."

Back on the casino deck I find Faces and tell him what is going on because two sets of eyeballs is better than one. Faces sez he ain't seen nothin' fishy, but he'll start looking closer.

I sez, "We are looking for a high-roller . . . somebody buying a lot of chips. You take that side over there and I'll take this one here. Meet you at the other end."

Faces nods and we set off to find our paper hanger. I was almost to the far end of the casino deck when I am noticing that Benny the Bug is no longer playing the cheap slots. In fact, he is nowhere to be seen.

At the far end of the room I meet up with Faces and I mention this sudden absence of Benny the Bug I have observed. Faces sez he did not see Benny too. That got me remembering the way Benny was acting funny—looking around and all. I sez, "I got me a suspicion maybe our pal Benny knows something about this funny money."

Faces shakes his head. "Benny sure as hell was not passing no phony bills. He was playing the cheap slots."

"Yeah, but he might be working with somebody else. Maybe he come in to case the place last night—you know, to see how we operate—and brought someone we would not know back with him tonight to do the paper hanging."

Faces thought a minute and sez, "I guess that might be, but where is he now?"

"You keep looking around here and I will check the taxi boats. Maybe a boat driver has seen him coming or going with someone."

I was just heading for the boat deck when two of the boss's muscle guys walk by dragging some jamoke between 'em. I stop the guys and sez, "What do we have here?"

Slugger, the bigger one of the two who has a busted nose that never got fixed right sez, "This here is the guy who was passin' the funny money. The cashier at Cage Two rang his alarm button and we get there just in time to grab this guy."

The paper hanger was an average looking Joe with a pair of them horn-rim glasses and a gray plaid fedora on top of his head. He is also looking kind of familiar, like maybe he is a regular customer on the REX.

While I am looking him over, the guy sez, "You guys got it all wrong. That was not my money . . . I mean I found that wallet on the floor and was just buying some chips as a reward for myself before I turned the wallet in. Honest, that is the truth."

The guy's story sounded goofy enough to be true. Besides that, he is shaking like a leaf. Nobody that scared is gonna be making up stuff that made him look almost as bad as what we already caught him doing. I sez, "Okay, Pally, let's go down and see what the boss thinks about this malarkey you are trying to feed us."

Tony listened to what the jamoke had to say and shook his head. "I ought to have the boys feed you to the sharks. That is what I ought to do."

Now the guy is not just shaking, he is also white as a ghost. He sez, "But no harm was done. All of the money is still in the wallet. Couldn't you just let it slide this time? I promise I'll never do anything like this again. I knew it was wrong, but all that money . . . it just made me crazy."

Tony looked at me and raised one of his eyebrows like he was asking if I thought the guy was on the level. I shrugged my shoulders, meaning I do not know if he is on the level or is not.

The boss turned back to the jamoke and sez, "All right, I am going to let you off the hook this time, but do not ever show your ugly mug on the REX again or you are going to be fish food. You understand my meaning, Pally?"

34

The guy nodded so hard I thought his head would surely fall off, and the boss, he sez to the muscle guys, "Okay, take this jamoke out of here and put him on a water taxi. And if you ever see him on the REX again, do not ask no questions, just feed him to the sharks."

After they leave, Tony sez to me, "What do you make of that, Jimmy?"

I have been deliberating about what is goin' on, so this time I have an answer for the boss. "I'm betting the real paper hanger somehow figured out we was wise to him and ditched the rest of his funny money in that wallet. He probably also figured some shmuck would find it and think he was in the chips, and then we would catch the shmuck and he would take the rap, which is almost the way it turned out."

"Yeah, that sounds right. We got plenty lucky tonight. There is another two Gs in this wallet. If they had passed it, we would be out four Gs total."

"I guess so, boss, but it burns me up that they got away with anything at all, and it is not likely we are ever gonna know who done this foul deed."

Then the boss sez something that sounded kind of philosophical. "Yeah, Jimmy, but this here is a risky business even if it is legit. Think of it like this, we paid two Gs to get learned a lesson tonight. We just got to make sure we learned that lesson real good. Now go on home and get some rest and we will start fresh in the morning."

Half an hour later I am walkin' up the pier to where my car is parked when a snazzy red convertible car with the top down rolled by on the street. It slowed and even in the dark I saw that Benny the Bug was behind the steering wheel. He waves at me and hollers, "Hey, Jimmy, thank Tony the Hat for his hospitality. He has got himself a real nice boat there."

Then he laughed and drove off so fast the tires squealed. His car went under the streetlight at the corner, and that is when I got a look at the guy with Benny. I might be wrong, but I would swear the guy was wearin' a gray plaid fedora and horn-rim glasses.

## THE END

# The Horn Man

## 1939—The San Francisco Bay Area

According to my old man, playing a musical instrument is strictly for sissies and all musicians are bums. Despite his opinion—or maybe because of it—I became a musician.

Squirreling away every dime I made delivering newspapers and doing odd jobs, I finally saved enough to buy the slightly dented silver cornet Mister Alperstein was "saving for me" in the front window of his pawn shop on Mission a few blocks from my folks' house on Citrus Avenue in Daly City. To use one of my old man's favorite expressions, I was in hog heaven as I sat on my bed and impatiently ripped away the butcher paper Mister Alperstein used to wrap my purchase.

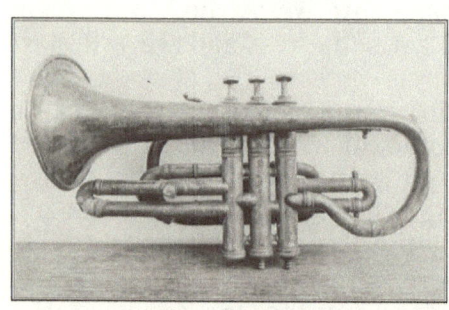

I won't bore you with the stories about how I kept the neighbors. and especially my father, awake practicing long into the night, but I did. Things got better for our neighbors, though, when I saved enough to take some lessons from Mister Martinelli who owned the little music store in the middle of the block on Mission between Eastlake and Como.

Skipping ahead through my musical career to my senior year of high school, four of my buddies and I formed a band we were sure was the hottest thing to come down the road since Ben Pollack. Better yet, we were good enough to actually land some gigs.

The Frisco Bay Jazz Orchestra, as we called ourselves, performed Sunday afternoons at the Seven Mile House near Brisbane. We had to lie about our ages because the place served alcohol, and we only made two bucks each for a three hour performance, but we were a working band. That's what mattered.

As Summer, 1939 arrived, I graduated from Jefferson Union High School and the fun and games came to an abrupt halt. First, my old man laid down the law. If I was going to continue living under his roof, I had to contribute ten bucks a month toward family expenses.

Next, the Seven Mile House got wise to our ages and fired us on the spot, which meant I was already ten bucks a month in the hole. I needed to find a job, and from the sound of my father's ranting and raving about his no-good son, I had to do it fast or start sleeping in the park.

That's when a little luck came my way. The papers were full of news about the Golden Gate International Exposition on Treasure Island in the Bay. To me the best part of the exposition was there were jobs to be had. True, the jobs were temporary, but some of them paid pretty well.

I found out just how well they paid by riding the municipal trolleybuses to the Ferry Building at the foot of Market Street, and then taking a ferryboat over to Treasure Island. If I owned a car, I could have driven the trip in about 30 minutes. Public transportation stretched the trip into a little more than two hours.

It turned out, though, that my travels paid off handsomely. The exposition opened the previous February and was just hitting its stride by June. They even had an employment office set up at the administration building for directing applicants to available jobs. The list of jobs was long, but I spotted the one I wanted right away: "Street Musician."

Without any idea what was expected of an exposition street musician, I talked to a cigar-chomping fellow in a derby hat who took my word for the fact that I could actually play the trumpet and gave me instructions to show up the next morning at nine. I got up at six-thirty and made another two hour journey to Treasure Island.

Once there, it took a few minutes to figure out where I was supposed to be. Then it took a little longer to get into my costume, a fluorescent pink and black Mexican Mariachi shirt with ruffled sleeves. Finally, I headed out into the exposition proper with another cornet player and two guitar players and we spent the day playing songs from a little book of what was apparently Mariachi music, but you couldn't prove it by me.

We were paid daily, so at the end of the day, I headed back to Daly City with six crisp new one dollar bills in my pocket and a promise of the same for the next day. That routine continued through July, and then fortune smiled at me again in the form of a tall, slender Negro fellow in a tight-fitting six-button double-breasted jacket with a straw boater on his head.

He was waiting for me outside the employees' changing building when I came out after my shift. The fellow stopped me, saying, "S'cuse me son, can I talk with you for a minute?"

I guessed from his outfit he might be a performer of some kind. "Sure, what's up?"

"I heard your horn out there earlier and went lookin' to see who was playin' it. You got you some fine chops, kid."

"Thank you, Mister."

Offering his hand, he said, "The name is Billy Davis. Maybe you heard of me?"

Actually, I had heard of Billy Davis. He was a piano man who worked with a small band that mostly played in the colored bars and dancehalls around the Fillmore. He was known for playing what local music lovers were starting to call "San Francisco Jazz." He also made a few records and I owned one. It had MOOD INDIGO on one side and ONE O' CLOCK JUMP on the other.

Shaking his hand, I said, "Yeah, I've heard of you, Mister Davis. I even have one of your records. I'm Dex Engel."

He grinned a toothy grin. "Cool! So you're hep to our kind of jive?"

"I sure am."

"Then maybe you'd like to sit in with us, sort of like an audition?"

My heart rate doubled as I said, "That would be swell, but I'm nowhere near good enough to play with you fellows. I'm still new at this."

"How 'bout you let me be decidin' if you're good enough, Kid. Anyplace else you got to be for the next hour or two?"

"You mean now?"

"Yeah, we're playin' over in the Gayway, and our horn player . . . well you might say he ain't in no condition to play no more . . . permanently."

EXPOSITION GAYWAY

I was so excited at the prospect of sitting in with a real top professional band, it never occurred to me to ask what happened to the band's horn man. I'm not even sure the fact that he was stabbed to death in some kind of argument over a woman would have made any difference.

"Sure, Mister Davis, if you think I can cut it, I'd love to sit in with your band."

"Then, come on, man. I'm late already. And for heaven sake, call me Billy. I ain't no 'Mister.'"

When we got to the little Gayway dancehall and bar called the Squeeze Inn, I was introduced to five fellows who were waiting impatiently on the stage behind the curtain. They treated me with respect and sincerity, as if they were actually pleased to meet me. Apparently, if Billy Davis said I was okay, I was okay. I couldn't help wondering how things might have been if the tables were turned and I was a Negro meeting members of a white band.

With introductions made, Billy took me aside and said, "Now, you just kinda listen to the songs we play and how we play 'em. When you think you've got the hang of it, just join in."

That confused me. "You don't use printed arrangements?"

"Hell, no, kid. All you gotta do is learn the melodies and chords. After that, we improvise. That's how you make music that comes from your soul."

On that note, Billy went to give his band the list of songs he wanted to play during their first set. I just stood there feeling like I was in way over my head.

Billy's band consisted of seven pieces: clarinet, tenor sax, trombone, and a rhythm section made up of Billy's piano, a guitar, bass fiddle, and drums. When everyone was set, Billy bobbed his head to the tempo he wanted and they took off on TEA FOR TWO in a style slightly reminiscent of Art Tatum. I watched Billy in awe, trying to understand how only two hands could play so many notes.

The group's second song was STAR DUST, which Louis Armstrong recently recorded. With no trumpet in the band, though, the clarinet play took the lead. The beat was solid—I knew that was a requirement for dance music—and the solos were conservative, but bouncy so each tune took on a little extra life.

I looked out into the audience, which added up to maybe thirty people equally divided between Negros and whites. While a few were dancing, most were just listening, but even the watchers were into the music. You could tell that by their expressions and tapping feet.

After STAR DUST I wanted to join in so bad I could hardly stand still. When Billy played a Ferdie Grofé style intro to a novelty number called MAKIN' WHOOPEE we used to play at the Seven Mile House, I took a deep breath and dove in.

I began playing a kind of counter melody to the sax solo, and at the end of 32 bars, Billy looked across the stand and said, "Take one, Kid."

Staying fairly close to the melody with just a few embellishments here and there, I took the lead. I was playing what I considered a "safe" version in case the audience didn't want too much jazz. Coming to the end of the 16 bar chorus, I heard Billy said, "Take it around again, Kid, and make it jump."

I did and got some applause from the audience. I also got a nod and a big grin from Billy. From that point on I had a ball. When we finally ended the gig around nine, Billy cornered me and said, "Kid, the job is yours if you want it. The pay is fifteen a night when we're playin' in the clubs on Fillmore, and ten a night for three hours on Wednesday nights here."

"You've got yourself a horn man, Billy."

"Swell. I was hopin' you'd stick around. Meet us tomorrow night at Elsie's on Fillmore between Sutter and Post. We kick things off about seven on weeknights. That jake with you, Kid?"

I said it was jake with me, but my father strongly disagreed. I should have kept my big mouth shut when he demanded to know why I was just getting in at midnight, but I was excited about my new job with Billy Davis. My old man got excited about it, too.

"You ain't playin' jungle music with no nigger band while you're livin' under my roof!"

Of course, I replied, "Then I'm not living under your roof."

The next morning I packed a bag and said goodbye to mom. She was upset, but didn't make a fuss because dad was in the next room.

Then, with a grand total of thirteen bucks in my pocket, I headed for Mission Boulevard to catch a trolley into The City. I rented a room with bath privileges at 2121 Bush Street, just a block south of Fillmore. Best of all, the rent was only ten dollars a month. I was back in hog heaven.

My life seemed just about perfect. The Billy Davis Band was

becoming a big attraction even with white folks, so the clubs kept us working every night. On Wednesdays, Billy even got the exposition to move our start time on the Gayway up so we could work another gig afterwards, making Wednesday a twenty-five dollar day for me.

The money was rolling in, and despite temptations, I did my best to spend it wisely. My first big purchase was a brand new cornet from Golden Gate Music. After trying out several of the horns they had, I decided on a Besson from England. It cost a little more than the others—a C-note—but the sound I made come out of it was exactly what I wanted.

1934 CHEVROLET COUPE

My second big purchase was a used 1934 Chevrolet Master Coupe for $400 from a car dealership on Van Ness at Bush. The Chevy was dark blue and in beautiful condition. It was a little scary spending that kind of money, but it was worth it so I could get around without relying on the Muni . . . back in hog heaven again.

In fact, I didn't know how things could be any better, and then I met Jacqueline, or Jackie as I came to call her. It was another one of those times when good fortune snuck up and tapped me on the shoulder when I was least expecting it.

JAQUELINE DUMONT

The band was taking a break and I was drinking a Coca-Cola at the Squeeze Inn when I first noticed the woman, and the first thing I noticed about the woman was her hair. At a time when short and medium-length styles were in vogue, Jackie's dark auburn hair was long with just a few soft swirls.

Then, she glanced in my direction and I noticed her eyes. Jackie's eyes were big and green, with a sense of wonder in them, as if she was perpetually curious about everything she saw. Then she smiled at me and I was hooked. Jackie's lips were full and soft, making her smile wide and as real as a smile could be.

Now, you have to understand that, being a musician, I never

had much time for girls in high school, or since then for that matter, so even though I was looking at the most beautiful woman in the world and she was looking back at me with an encouraging smile, I had no idea what to do about the situation.

Of course, at that point Billy and Roger, our bass player, walked by and Billy said, "C'mon, Kid. Time we be gettin' back to work."

I looked back at the pretty woman and made a horn playing gesture with my hands. She nodded and I said a small prayer that she would still be around when we got off in about half an hour.

The first song on Billy's play list for the last set was the Jimmy McHugh standard, EXACTLY LIKE YOU. When my turn to solo came along, I looked straight in those gorgeous green eyes and played my heart out. That special smile crossed her lips and stayed there until I'd done two choruses of the best horn playing I ever did.

When we ended our final song of the last set—PUTTIN' ON THE RITZ—I hustled backstage to put my horn away. If I was going to meet my dream girl, I had to hurry. We were due at our Fillmore gig at Jack's Tavern in less than an hour. Then Billy slowed me down some. With a grin, he said, "Kid, you tell that little gal in the black dress if she can make you play like that all the time, I'll put her on the payroll."

It took me a minute to realize who he was talking about because I was so busy looking at the rest of her, I actually hadn't noticed she was wearing a black dress. When I finally got out into the audience, though, I got a big letdown. My new love, whose name I still did not know, and her friends—two other girls and a fellow of about the same age—were gone.

Disappointed didn't begin to describe how I felt. Dang Billy! If he hadn't slowed me down I probably would have caught her before she left. Now the only thing I could hope for was she would come back next Wednesday, but next Wednesday seemed like ten years away.

Jack's Tavern is kind of historic. It was the first joint on Fillmore to cater specifically to Negro audiences. Jack's had a house band, the Saunders King orchestra, but they were off Wednesday nights, so we filled the gap. The music at Jack's was truly San Francisco Jazz—smooth, cool, and conservative enough to attract more sophisticated audiences who didn't like what they called "jungle music."

I said Jack's catered to Negro audiences, but there were often a few white faces scattered throughout the audience. That night I was overjoyed to see one particular white face in the audience. There she was, my brunette with one of her girlfriends I saw at the Gayway show. I couldn't believe my eyes. She had to be a true music lover to know Billy Davis played at Jack's on Wednesday nights. She also had to be somewhat fearless. While they were perfectly safe at Jack's, two white girls by themselves at night were an uncommon sight in the Fillmore.

Billy noticed her, too. As he called out the first few songs from a list on the piano's music rack, he nodded at me. "Looks like you got yourself a fan, Kid. Any special requests?"

I thought for about half a second, and said, "How 'bout IT HAD TO BE YOU?"

"You got it, Kid. Top of the list."

IT HAD TO BE YOU was a popular little ballad written and made popular by Isham Jones a few years back. It seemed like the perfect song for the occasion. I played it sweet and cool to the accompaniment of muttered remarks about "schmaltz" from my fellow band members. I could tell my dream girl liked it, though, and by her smile, I could tell she knew I played it for her.

When the set ended, I wasn't taking any more chances. I set my horn down on top of Billy's piano and went straight to her table. On my way, however, it occurred to me I had no idea what to say when I got there. That, however was not going to stop me, so I improvised.

"Ah . . . Hi, my name is Dex Engle and . . . I think I saw you earlier tonight at the exposition, and . . . ah . . . I play cornet in the band . . . and . . . ."

The girl with her thought I was hilarious and was barely able to contain her giggles, but my dream girl took the hand I offered and shook it. The sensation of her skin against mine was electric. To the accompaniment of a beautiful smile, she said, "Good evening, Dex. I'm Jacqueline, or Jackie to my friends. Yes, we enjoyed hearing you at the exposition, so we came in to hear more. Oh, this is my roommate, Betty."

I didn't want to let go of Jackie's hand, but I had to be polite, so I shook Betty's hand. Feeling a little more at ease, I said, "I'm curious, Jackie, how did you know we were playing here at Jack's?"

Still smiling, she said, "Oh, that was easy. A young boy was passing out fliers with the band's schedule on them in front of that little place on the Gayway. You fellows must get a lot of fans who never heard of you before that way."

About that time I saw Billy climbing up on the bandstand.

"Gosh, it looks like I have to go back to work. Ah . . . will you be here for a while."

Laughing, Betty said, "Yes, we'll be here. I don't think I could drag Jackie out of here if the place was on fire."

Jackie looked at her friend with a feigned expression of exasperation. "Oh, you! Stop that!"

I said, "That's good. I . . . ah . . . would really like to talk with you more."

And that's how the evening went along until we finished our last set about midnight. I went back to Jackie's table to find her and Betty putting their coats on. Betty was saying something about catching the Muni.

I quickly said, "Oh, you don't need to take the Muni. I have a car. I would be happy to give you a lift home."

Betty looked at Jackie. "What do you think? Can we trust him to be a gentleman?"

Jackie glanced appraisingly at me, and then turned to Betty with a grin. "More to the point, can we trust you to be a lady?"

Outside, we walked half a block to where I parked my Chevrolet coupe. We all slid in and Jackie said, "We don't live far, just up on Jackson near the Presidio."

It really wasn't far, which was a little disappointing because with all three of us on the front seat of my little coupe, I could feel Jackie close to me and I liked that feeling. We got to their apartment building and Betty had her door open before I even got the car stopped.

"It was nice to meet you, Dex. As usual, Jackie's taste in men is flawless. I'm going to run upstairs now and give you two some privacy, but don't sit down here talking all night. Remember, Roomy, we have to work tomorrow, which by the way, is already today. Goodnight."

Jackie and I both laughed at Betty's speedy departure. Jackie said, "I apologize for Betty. It seems like she's always in a hurry."

LEGON OF HONOR MUSEUM

"Well, if you have to work in the morning, I don't want to keep you from getting your sleep. I'm curious, though. May I ask where you work?"

"Of course you can. We both work up at the Palace of the Legion of Honor fine art museum. Betty is a docent and I work in the collection

44

catalogue department."

"Wow! That's something! You must really know your art then."

Still grinning, Jackie said, "I know a lot less than I should know, but I'm learning. Now, may I ask you a question?"

"Go ahead."

"I was just wondering how you came to be playing with Billy Davis. I mean . . . ."

"You're wondering what a white guy is doing playing with a Negro band, right?"

"Well, sort of. Not that I think there is anything wrong with that. It's just a little unusual."

"You're right, it is unusual. To be honest, I'm not sure how Billy picked me. He lost his cornet player and heard me playing street music out at the exposition. I guess he liked what he heard, because he asked me to sit in and audition. The next thing I knew, I was Billy Davis's horn man."

"For what it's worth, I think he made a very good choice. I actually had shivers running up and down my back when you played IT HAD TO BE YOU tonight."

Hearing her say that made me feel like a million bucks. "Well, I guess that was sort of the idea. I'm really glad you liked it. Now, I'd better let you go in or Betty will be down here giving us both the dickens."

I held the door while Jackie slid across the seat and stepped down from my Chevrolet. As we walked to the front door of her apartment building our hands brushed and suddenly I felt her hand in mine. At the door Jackie said, "Gosh, Dex, it's been wonderful to hear you play and talk with you tonight. I hope we can do it again soon."

"Ah, would tomorrow be too soon?"

Jackie gave me her wonderful smile. "I get off work at five."

"Could I pick you up at the museum and take you to dinner before we play?"

Squeezing my hand, Jackie said, "I would love that!"

A minute later I watched the apartment building door close behind her with what was probably a very silly smile on my face. I'd never been in love before, but if that's what was happening to me, I liked it. I liked it a lot.

During the next couple of weeks Jackie and I saw a lot of each other. We went out to dinner or did something together just about every other night. We were enjoying just getting to know each other, and I discovered there was a lot to learn about Jackie. For example, I learned that her father was J. Charles Dumont, a prominent San Francisco businessman, who was said to be one of the wealthiest men in town. Of course, I told her about my folks and where I came from, which was nothing to brag about, but I didn't want there to be any secrets between us.

Then things began changing. More and more often she had some other commitment and wasn't able to meet me. I felt terrible about it, as if I'd done something to make her unhappy, but I couldn't imagine what it was. I was really down about it.

Billy noticed my mood and had something to say about it. "What's got you in a funk, Kid? You and that little girl have a falling out?"

I nodded a gloomy nod. "Yeah, and I can't figure out what I did to upset her."

"Hell, Kid. I can tell you what you did."

I looked up at him. "You can? What'd I do?"

"You joined up with this ragtag nigger band, that's what."

"No, it can't be. She's never said anything about that."

"That's cuz it ain't her who's got a problem with the color of our skin. I've seen this before, Kid. It's her family. They're the ones with the problem. That girl is Nob Hill all the way to the bone, and on Nob Hill, Negros ain't people, they're servants."

I tried to argue the point with him, but Billy was adamant. He said, eventually, I would have to choose between Jackie and the band. I told him he was nuts and walked away shaking my head. I was also wondering if he could be right.

The Wednesday following my conversation with Billy, I was surprised to find Betty waiting for me outside the Gayway dancehall. I was also sad to find Jackie was nowhere in sight. Betty took my arm and suggested we go somewhere we could talk. Sitting at a table in a doughnut shop, we ordered coffee and Betty said, "First of all, Jackie doesn't know I'm here and I don't want her to know. That okay with you?"

I shrugged. "I guess so. What's this all about?"

She put her hand on mine and said, "This isn't going to feel good, but the plain and simple truth is Jackie's father has made it very clear to her she is not to see you anymore."

I was more shocked than surprised. "Why?"

Looking me in the eye, Betty said, "I think you know why, but I'll spell it out for you. Her father doesn't want her around anyone who associates with Negros."

"But she's an adult. He can't tell her what to do."

"Dex, with his money and power he can do any darn thing he

wants. He even has one of his men following her around so he can 'convince you' to stay away if you show up at the museum or our apartment.

"She is like a prisoner in her own home, and her father told her if there is any trouble about it, he will move her back into the family mansion and lock the door."

I couldn't believe what I was hearing. Billy had no idea how right he was when he told me why Jackie stopped seeing me. I sighed.

Betty lowered her head. "I'm sorry, Dex, but that's how it is and I thought you ought to know the truth. Jackie would tell you herself, but she's afraid that man following her will hurt you if she tries to see you."

"What does Jackie say about all this?"

"What do you think she says about it? Dex, even though you've only known each other a short time, Jackie is in love with you and she's miserable."

I sat back in my chair and took a swallow of lukewarm doughnut shop coffee. "Any ideas about how I can fix this?"

Betty shook her head. "Short of kidnapping Jackie and taking her somewhere her father can't find you, I don't think it can be fixed. I don't know Jackie's father very well, but she's told me enough about the man to know once he makes up his mind about something, he never changes it."

A thought occurred to me. "I know you weren't serious about kidnapping Jackie, but do you think she would go away with me? I mean to someplace where her old man couldn't find us?"

"I don't know. She's desperate, so she might, but you would both be giving up a lot if you did that. She has no brothers or sisters, so she stands to inherit a huge fortune, but her father would surely disinherit her if she did what you suggest. He would do that just to be mean. And you have a good start on a musical career here. You would lose all that. And besides, Jackie's father has that guy following her around. He would put a quick stop to anything you tried."

I looked at the wristwatch I bought just so I wouldn't keep Jackie waiting when we went out. I was already late for our Wednesday night gig at Jack's. I thought Billy would understand, but there was no sense to pushing my luck.

"Betty, I have to go. I really appreciate you coming down to talk with me about all this. Can I give you a lift home?"

"No thanks. I don't think it would be smart for you to be seen in our neighborhood. I'm sorry I couldn't bring you better news.

This is all very sad."

I nodded. "Yes, it is, but I am not going to take it sitting down. Is there a way we can talk again without making the situation worse?"

Betty thought for a second. "Where do you play Friday night? Maybe I could just come hear you play."

"We're at Elsie's Breakfast Club. It's on Fillmore between Sutter and Post. We go on at nine. I could meet you there early so you don't have to be out late."

She nodded. "Yes, I'll be there by seven-thirty."

"Thanks, Betty. I can't begin to say how much I appreciate you helping us this way."

"I just wish I could do more. Jackie's my best friend. I hate to see her hurt and I think you're a very talented guy and you treat Jackie right. You two deserve a life together."

Later that night, after our last set at Jack's, I told Billy what I learned from Betty.

Billy was entirely sympathetic. "You're gettin' a bum deal, Kid, but in the white folks' world it's always about the golden rule. Them what's got the gold rule. Whatcha gonna do about it?"

"I don't know, Billy, but I have to think of something."

"You want to know what I'd do if I was in your shoes?"

"Yeah. What would you do?"

"First, you got any long green?"

Nodding, I said, "Yes, I've saved up a few hundred."

"Good. I'd use that for travelin' money and take that little gal way away from here."

"But where could we go? And how the hell can we go anywhere with that bodyguard or whatever he's supposed to be following her?"

"One question at a time, Kid. First, would your little gal go with you if you asked her?"

"If we could do it safely and there was a good chance of giving her old man the slip, I think she would."

"Good. You ever been down by Los Angeles?"

"No. Why?"

"'Cause things is really jumpin' in jazz down there, mostly along Central Avenue. That's downtown. Some really heavy hitters are inventing a whole new kind of music down there, guys like Wardell Gray . . . Teddy Edwards . . . Charlie Mingus . . . Buddy Collette . . . cats like that. They're playin' west coast sounds like us, only bigger and better."

"Really?"

"Really, Kid, and I know guys down there who'd put you on the 'roll just 'cause I said so. Now, understand, I don't want to lose you, but getting' you and your little gal straightened out is more important."

"Thanks, Billy. It might work. The trick would be pulling it off without Jackie's old man getting wise."

"Don't get ahead of yourself, Kid. First thing you got to do is see if your gal agrees with the plan. If she say so, I might be persuaded to help some, but it'll cost you."

"I will get word to her tomorrow. What's it going to cost me, Billy?"

He beamed his bright white smile and said, "We've got a record makin' session on for tomorrow. My help is going to cost you a reprise of that solo you did for your gal on IT HAD TO BE YOU."

I grinned back at him. "Deal!"

Thursday evening Betty walked into Elsie's just when she said she would. We sat down, ordered something to eat, and I laid out Billy's idea for her to take back to Jackie.

Betty listened carefully, and then said, "That's awful risky. I hope you know what you're doing."

"I don't know if I know what I'm doing or not, but I do know I can't go on missing Jackie like this."

Nodding, Betty said, "I understand, Dex. I'll give your message to Jackie when I leave here. If she says yes, I'll come back later and let you know."

"I hate to make you go out twice tonight, but that would be swell, Betty."

She smiled. "Well, I can't make you wait for her answer, now can I?"

I leaned over and kissed her cheek. Betty grinned. "Careful, there, Mister Dex. I'm no more immune to your charms than Jackie."

As good as her word, Betty returned about nine. From the stand I saw her flash me a smile and a thumb-up gesture. Of course I rushed down to hear what she had to say as soon as we took a break.

"Jackie cried when I told her you were going to rescue her like a knight in shining armor."

"But she agreed to go with me?"

"Yes." After a short pause, Betty added, "I did embellish the offer you made a little, though."

Puzzled, I asked, "In what way?"

"Well, I told her your plan included marriage. I knew that was the only way she could say yes. That is what you meant, isn't it?"

"Honestly, I hadn't thought that far ahead yet, but yes. If Jackie will have me, I'd be proud to be her husband."

Betty winked. "I knew that's what you had in mind. Now, what's the plan and when is all this going to happen?"

That was a darned good question. All I had was a general idea of a plan, but I didn't have any details about how I was going to do it. I said, "I've got to work some of that out. I wanted to be sure Jackie was willing to go with me before I made any commitments. Can you meet me again Monday night? I will have everything figured out then."

Frowning slightly, Betty said, "Can I tell her how soon all this is going to happen so she can get ready?"

I didn't know that either, but I improvised. "Yes. Please tell Jackie we'll be leaving before the end of next week."

As it turned out, I was able to keep that promise. With Billy's help we had a plan in place by Monday so I could tell Betty what Jackie needed to know. Actually Betty needed to know some of it, too, because she would play a key role in the "great escape," as I began thinking of our scheme. The date was set for the following Friday.

The weather gods were with us and a rain storm moved in Friday morning. That was a good thing because Betty could bundle up in Jackie's coat and use her umbrella, which made it harder to tell she wasn't Jackie. That was important because we needed to fool Jackie's bodyguard into thinking it was Jackie who was taking a taxi, driven by a friend of Billy's, from the girls' apartment that morning.

While Jacqueline peeked from her second-floor bedroom window, Betty climbed into the yellow and red DeSoto taxicab and it drove off. Then Jackie held her breath waiting for the bodyguard to follow in his business coupe. He did. So far the plan was working, but it had a long way yet to go.

The next step was carried out by Billy, who pulled up in front of Jackie's apartment at 3445 Jackson Street in a borrowed Lincoln limousine. He escorted Jacqueline from her front door to the limo and put her bag in the trunk. The idea was a Negro in a chauffer's outfit driving a limousine was nothing unusual and would throw anyone who came around asking questions in the neighborhood off the scent . . . we hoped.

Without delay, Billy drove the limousine straight across town to Pier 35 on the Embarcadero, where the Matson luxury steamship SS LURLINE was minutes away from leaving on the final leg of a trip from Hawaii to Los Angeles via San Francisco. Billy saw Jackie to the gangplank where she quickly boarded as a last-minute passenger, using the ticket I bought for her and Billy gave her during the ride to the dock.

Moments later, as the LURLINE's gangplank was rolled away, a steward escorted Jacqueline to First Class Cabin 126, where her future husband was anxiously awaiting her arrival. After I tipped the steward and closed the stateroom door, Jackie and I embraced as if we hadn't been together in years. Then we just stood there staring at each other for a long time.

Despite her smile, Jackie also wore a nervous frown. Finally, she said, "Did we make it, Dex? Really?"

"I think so, Jackie. If there was any doubt about that, Billy would not have brought you to the ship. We had an alternate plan."

Jacqueline moved to one of the two portholes in our cabin and looked out. It was an exciting moment. Through the portholes we could see the new Golden Gate bridge and the Pacific Ocean beyond it. We felt the deep throb of the LURLINE's engines as they propelled us to a new life. We heard the throaty rumble of the big ship's fog horn as she cast off the last lines connecting her and us to San Francisco.

Jackie said, "I can hardly believe it. For the first time since the day I was born, I'm really free, and I owe it all to you. Thank you, Dex, thank you with all my heart. I'm going to be the best wife you can imagine. Honest, I am."

I couldn't help grinning at her enthusiasm. "I hope you're going to do that because you love me, not just because I rescued you from your father."

Jackie turned to look me in the eye. "Can't I be grateful and love you at the same time? I hope I can because that's what I am."

"I don't guess there are any rules that say you can't."

Sitting on the edge of one of the twin beds in the cabin, looked up at me demurely. "You know something else?"

"What?"

She ran her hand slowly over the bed's comforter. "This is the first time since we've known each other that we've been alone together in the same room. That feels strange and exciting at the same time."

She was wearing the black dress she wore the first time I saw her at the Squeeze Inn. It was short, so her legs were exposed clear up to her thighs when she sat. I was looking at her legs, which though crossed modestly drew my eyes, even though I tried not to stare.

Almost immediately, I felt ashamed because I was sure Jackie noticed me staring at her legs. I said, "I'm sorry. I didn't mean to put you into a compromising situation. This just seemed like the best place for us to hide out until . . . ."

Interrupting my apology, Jackie said, "Did you think I was complaining about being alone with you?"

My level of embarrassment climbed. "Well, no, but . . . ."

"Dexter, do you plan to become my husband?"

"Yes! I made arrangements with the purser for Captain Berndtson to perform a shipboard wedding ceremony this afternoon when we are in international waters."

Jackie stood and walked into my arms. Then we kissed again, this time with a lot more passion. When our lips parted, she looked up into my eyes. "Then we are only fudging on the rules by a few hours. Is that right?"

"Yes, but . . . ."

Jackie smiled her wonderful smile and said, "Good! I won't tell if you don't." She punctuated that promise with another steamy kiss that left my legs quivering a little.

Looking nervously at my wristwatch, I said, "Jackie, you must be hungry. Maybe we should go to the dining room and have lunch. On this leg of the trip from Hawaii it's open seating and . . . ."

Placing her hands gently on my face so we were looking each other in the eyes again, and her expression changed to one I can only describe as curiosity. "Dexter, we have no secrets from each other, is that right?"

Nodding, I said, "Yes, of course."

"Then I want you to give me a very honest answer to an important question."

Fearful of what her question might be, I gulped. "Okay."

"Dex, have you ever . . . been . . . been with a woman?"

I found myself staring into her big green eyes and speechless. Jackie said, "Your answer will be okay with me no matter what it is, but I think it might help us get off to a good start. At least, that's what Betty thinks."

Knowing that Jacqueline discussed our intimacy with Betty left me completely flummoxed. Still staring into my eyes, Jackie encouraged me. "Come on, Dex. Tell me. I'll tell you, too."

Seeing no other way out of my dilemma, I blurted, "No. I've never been . . . done anything with . . . ."

Jackie kissed me again, and then with her grin as wide as I ever saw it, she said, "Good! I've never been with a man, either. We will learn all about sex together!"

The rest of our overnight cruise from San Francisco to Los Angeles was a wonderful blur of sounds, and textures and the most amazing moments I ever experienced. Some of those moments were full of passion and others were as tame as standing at the LURLINE's railing and watching the small diamond in Jacqueline's new ring sparkle in the sunlight.

I felt a little sad when I heard the announcement over the ship's public address system that we would be docking in San Pedro around one-thirty on our second day out. Still, it was time to get on with our lives, so my bride and I studied the crowd at the steamship dock from the top deck, and not seeing any faces we recognized or needed to be concerned about, Jackie and I strolled down the LURLINE's gangway bold as brass.

For our first few minutes ashore, I was worried the next phase in the plan had gone wrong, but then I spotted a heavyset fellow at the edge of the crowd with a small sign in his hands. He was bald and wore a vest over a tie decorated with whatever he had for lunch, but the important part was his sign. It said: ENGLE.

I pointed him out to Jacqueline and we wove our way through the crowd to where the guy was standing. I said, "Are you Weaver?"

Hearing me say his name surprised the fellow. He turned to look at me with a confused expression. "You Engle?"

"Yeah."

"Well how about that? I was expecting a Negro. That's why I was over here where the crew gets off." He gestured and added, "C'mon. My car is over here."

I noticed he didn't offer to help with our bags. We had four all together, a large suitcase with my clothes in it, a medium sized case for Jackie's stuff, my horn case, and Jackie's large handbag, in which she packed last minute essentials she brought along.

As we walked he asked, "So how is it Billy got himself a white boy to play in his band?"

"He was hard up so he had to settle for me."

The guy looked at me like he was trying to figure out if I was kiddin' him or not, but he had nothing more to say. Finally, we came to a nearly new Buick sedan. He opened the doors and we all climbed in.

The fellow Billy arranged to meet us at the dock was Eddy Weaver, a used car dealer in nearby Wilmington. It seems the guy used to have a dealership up in San Francisco, but he got himself in trouble up there somehow and headed south. Despite his past, Billy said the guy would sell us a reliable car for a fair price.

Weaver's used car lot, Harbor Motors was at the west end of Anaheim Street, which turned out to be Wilmington's main drag. The lot was nothing fancy, but the cars he offered for sale were clean and seemed well cared for. The specific car Weaver picked out for us based on the information Billy gave him was a light gray three-year-old Plymouth coupe.

As we walked around it, Eddy Weaver told us of the car's many virtues. "She's the P4 model. That's the top of the line with a six-cylinder 82-horsepower motor. This little beauty will take you anywhere you want to go. The transmission is Chrysler's new fully synchronized quiet model. It so easy to shift even little Missy here can drive it without effort. The Plymouth also has fully hydraulic breaks, a heater, and she burns regular gas, so she's cheap to operate."

I said, "How much?"

"Well since you're a friend of Billy Davis and all, I'll make you a special price of four-hundred-fifty dollars, and she's got a full tank of gasoline to boot."

1934 PLYMOUTH COUPE

Looking Weaver in the eye, I shook my head and said, "Didn't Billy tell you we can only afford four hundred?"

Smiling, Weaver said, "I think he might have said something about that, but this car is well worth the extra fifty bucks." Looking toward Jackie, he said, "She's a beauty, isn't she, Missy?"

Jackie gave Weaver a disdainful smile in return. "For four-hundred she's a beauty. For four-fifty she's overpriced. Besides, I think it would be a nice wedding present if you sold us the car for the price you told Mister Davis."

Weaver looked at me and back at Jackie. He must have seen a sale about to fly away, because he said, "All right, Missy, four-hundred as a wedding present."

Inside Weaver's tiny office, he gave me some forms to fill out in exchange for eight fifty dollar bills. "Billy said you two . . . ah . . . wanted to be invisible for a while, so here's the deal with the auto registration. If we register the car in your name now, your address and all will be in the public records within a few weeks.

"Right now, the car is registered to Harbor Motors—that's me—and the registration is paid up through the end of the year. That gives you about four months before you get in trouble with the Department of Motor Vehicles for not registering the car. If anyone notices, we just tell them it was an oversight, and you'll have the bill of sale to prove you paid for the car. After December, though, you're on your own."

With our luggage in the Plymouth's trunk and written directions to our next stop, the Dunbar Hotel in what Billy called "South-Central Los Angeles," we headed north on a wide, busy street called Figueroa Boulevard. As we drove, I gave Jacqueline a grin and said, "Well, Missy, what do you think of Mister Weaver?"

"I think he's creepy and he tried to steal fifty dollars from us."

Feigning shock, I said, "Mister Weaver? You think a nice fellow like him would try to cheat us?"

"Nice fellow? Ha!"

"Then I'm sure glad you were along to keep him honest."

"I swear if he called me 'Missy' once more, I would have kicked him right where it would hurt the most!"

Our destination, the Dunbar Hotel, was an elaborately decorated four-story brick and concrete building that filled the northeast corner of South Central Avenue and East Forty-Second Street. I knew the Dunbar was a Negro hotel, but you would never know that to look at it. It looked as swanky as any other downtown hotel in any other city. The neighborhood, however, was a different story.

We parked near the Central Avenue entrance to the Dunbar and Jacqueline took stock of her surroundings. "Gosh, this reminds me of the Fillmore district back home, only this neighborhood . . . ."

Jackie stopped mid-sentence and turned to face me. "I'm sorry, Dex. I'm not complaining; really, I'm not."

"I know, Jackie." Looking for something positive to cheer her up, I added, "The hotel looks nice, though."

"Yes, Dex, it really does."

The Dunbar also looked as if it ought to have a doorman, but if it did, he was on a smoke break. As we carried our bags into a spacious Spanish-style lobby, the fellow behind the registration counter watched us a little warily. He apparently wasn't used to white folks in his lobby. A man and a woman seated in a couch also eyed us.

Setting our bags down near the counter, I said, "Good afternoon. We have a reservation. The name is Engle."

Frowning, the clerk asked, "You sure you folks is in the right place?"

I smiled. "Yes, I'm sure."

The clerk then thumbed through a stack of what I guessed were reservation cards and stopped at one. "Yes, sir, I guess you is. Says here you gonna stay for a week, that right?"

"Yes. We might even be here a little longer."

"Yes, Sir. We have reserved a dee-luxe room with a bath for you. The rate is nine dollars a week or one-fifty per day if you stay less than seven days. Please sign this here card."

As I signed the registration card, he said, "Ah, that will be nine dollars for the week . . . in advance."

Now it sounded as if he had us figured for poor white folks who might stiff the hotel if he didn't get the room rent up front. He seemed to relax a little when I laid a five and four ones on the counter.

"Thank you, Sir." Over his shoulder, he shouted, "Front."

A kid in a maroon jacket and a spiffy bellboy cap came trotting out of a room behind the counter and stopped so short he almost fell flat on his face when he saw us. The clerk said, "Show the Engles, here, up to two-ten."

Looking at the counter man like he was off his rocker, the kid said, "I surely will." Picking up our suitcases, the bellboy said, "This way, folks."

As we followed him up a stairway to the left of the registration counter, I glanced back toward the lobby. The folks on the sofa were still watching us like we were two-headed creatures Orson Welles dreamed up for a radio show.

At the top of the stairway we followed him along a mezzanine walkway with a dining room on one end and guest rooms lining the other three sides. He stopped at #210 and opened the door.

We were led into a nicely furnished room with bright yellow wallpaper. Our window overlooked the hotel entrance on Central Avenue. The bellboy set our bags on a pair of luggage stands he found in a closet. Next he pointed to a door next to the closet and said, "That there is the bathroom. The radio is over there on the dresser. To make a telephone call, you gots to dial 'O' and the hotel operator will make the call for you."

The boy glanced around the room as if trying to think of anything he forgot. Finally, he said, "Oh, and if you gets hungry, the dining room is at the other end of this floor. They opens up at five for dinner."

Along with my thanks, I tipped him fifty-cents. He looked pleased. Handing me the room key, he said, "Thank you, Sir," and sounded as if he meant it.

He closed the room door on his way out, and I looked at Jackie. There was a single tear track down her right cheek.

I held out my arms and she sort of fell into them. "What's wrong, Jackie? Are you okay?"

She nodded against my chest. "I'm okay, Dex. It's just that this place . . . is sort of . . . sort of overwhelming."

"The hotel? You've been in Negro clubs and businesses before. What's different about this place?"

Leaning back to look at my face, Jackie sniffed and said, "Those times I was on the outside looking in, now . . . ."

I finished her sentence for her. "You're on the inside looking out and it's kind of scary. Is that it?"

Jackie nodded again. "Yes. I mean I know these are good people and they're just like us, but I feel very out of place." After a short pause, she added, "Now I have an idea how Negroes feel when they are in the middle of a room full of white people."

I was pretty sure she couldn't begin to imagine what a Negro in a room full of white people feels like. Neither could I for that matter. I took a deep breath and said what I knew I had to say for Jacqueline's benefit.

"Jackie, I'm sorry this is upsetting you. Would you feel better if we put you on a train back to San Francisco?"

Jacqueline's eyes filled with tears and she stared at me in what I can only describe as shock. "You want me to go away?"

57

"No, Darling. That is absolutely the last thing I want, but the most important thing is how you feel. If being here scares you or makes you feel uncomfortable, that's no good."

"But you've invested everything you have in this plan to get away from my father so we can be together. If you send me away, what's the purpose of it all?"

Not knowing what to say to that, I shrugged. Almost angrily, Jackie said, "No, I won't go away! We're in this together. I am as committed as you are."

I put my arms around her again, but she pushed me back a little. "Dex, I want your promise that you won't send me away . . . that you'll let me see this through with you."

Smiling softly, I said, "You have that."

"No. I want to hear you say it."

"All right, I promise we'll see this through together."

"And you won't send me away?"

"Absolutely not."

She kissed me, and then said, "Good. Now help me unpack our bags and put things in the closet so the wrinkles will hang out. You have to look good tomorrow when you meet that bandleader."

That bandleader's name was Ray Anderson, a drum man who started out with Billy Davis in San Francisco, just like I did. Part of our plan to escape San Francisco was for Billy to call Anderson on the long distance telephone and tell him I was a good horn man. Bill did that, and Anderson told him to send me down with my horn so he could hear for himself.

Bringing Jackie with me for good luck and so she wouldn't be alone her first day in LA, I walked into the huge Club Alabam next door to the Dunbar on Central Avenue at ten the following morning—Monday morning.

Ray Anderson was pretty much what I expected from Billy's description: As big around as he was tall with a raspy voice and a pinky ring that was almost as big as he was. The most noticeable thing about Anderson, though, was his rhythm. The man seemed to vibrate with the rhythm playing in his head.

His band, which was larger than Billy's, included Anderson on drums, two saxophones, a clarinet, a trombone, a cornet, a piano, a rhythm guitar, and a bass fiddle. They were set up on the Alabam's stage, where they were having a practice session.

When Ray saw us watching I introduced myself. He said, "Oh, sure. You're that white horn man Billy Davis is so fired up about. Well, don't just stand down there. Break out your cornet and come on up here so we can hear what you got."

I did as asked, with a kiss for luck from Jacqueline. When I got up on the stage, Anderson said, "We doin' a Fats Waller thing up here this mornin'. You know AIN'T MISBEHAVIN'? Course you do. You take it right after the first piano chorus, and make it smooth. Fats gotta be played smooth or you're missin' the whole point of it."

With that, Anderson gave us a tempo and we were off. Mostly I watched the piano player during his chorus to get the key and the chord changes, a trick I learned from Billy back when we were playing at the Squeeze Inn. When my turn came, I stuck with the melody for sixteen bars and played it legato. Pointing one of his drumsticks at me, Ray signaled me to take another chorus.

During my second chorus I wandered around the melody a little, trying to expand on what Waller wrote in the first place. After my second chorus, Anderson waved us off.

When we were all looking at him, he said, "Well, saints alive, Billy was right! This white boy play that damn cornet like he was born to it." He looked over at his horn man, a fellow I later learned was called Buck Farmer, and said, "What you think, Buck?"

Farmer laughed. "All I can say is I wish I just played what he played."

The consensus of opinion was Ray Anderson should hire me to replace his other horn man, who recently moved away. I started Tuesday at twenty bucks a night and we played six nights a week. Suddenly, I went from unemployed to makin' a hundred and twenty a week.

Jacqueline figured out that was more than six grand a year. We felt like we were rich, but remembering a band gig can go as quickly as it comes, we opened a bank account and stashed away as much of my pay as we could every week so we would have something to fall back on when hard times came again.

CLUB ALABAM

After a few months, things also improved for Jacqueline at the Dunbar. She went to work with me at the Club Alabam every night and worked up her nerve to explore the hotel a little on her own during the day.

From those explorations, she soon gained two friends. One was Lena, who ran the hotel flower shop, and the other was a hotel guest named Caroline.

She was married to a Negro member of Artie Shaw's band. Many black members of mixed-race bands and their families stayed at the Dunbar because they couldn't stay in white hotels.

The most unfortunate part of our new lives in Los Angeles was the specter of J. Charles Dumont. He was always close to our thoughts, but we heard nothing from or about him, and that made matters worse. Jackie and Betty carried on a clandestine correspondence, being careful not to give our location away, but as far as we knew, her father's only attempt to track Jacqueline down was asking questions around the neighborhood right after Jackie disappeared.

Another part of our situation that bothered me was using my real name in Los Angeles. I was afraid using my name would make it easier for Dumont to find us, but Jackie and I discussed that on the boat down and decided it was necessary in order to capitalize on any leftover fame from my days of playing with Billy Davis in San Francisco.

Then there were nights when our biggest problem was getting to sleep. I typically got done working around midnight or one, although some nights we went to the Last Word, "The East Side's Smartest Sepia Night Club," for after-hours jam sessions with other Central Avenue musicians. On those nights we might be out until three or four in the morning.

On top of the long hours we kept, many nights the heat kept us awake. Los Angeles was going through a hot spell, and the Dunbar did not have "refrigerated air" in its rooms. The only way to get any relief on hot nights was to leave the window open and hope for a breeze.

I particularly remember one such occasion, but the heat wasn't what made the night memorable. As we lay there drenched in sweat and hoping for one of those rare breezes, Jacqueline gently laid her hand on my bare chest and softly asked, "Dex, are you awake?"

"Yeah."

"May I ask you about something I heard today?"

"Sure, what did you hear?"

"Caroline told me the word is out that Bobby Ross's trumpet man, Teddy Williams, left Ross to start his own band. She said it's an all-white band."

"I heard that, too. What about it?"

"I was wondering what you thought about trying for a job in his new band. Caroline said she heard the new band was going to play jazz and would be based out of Los Angeles."

"I could look into it. I don't know if Williams ever played jazz, but the guy in it with him, Jeff Mills, plays jazz in some of the best clubs around Los Angeles."

"Then you'll look into the new band?"

"Okay, but what makes you so interested in me getting with a new band. I thought you were getting along here pretty well now."

She rested her cheek on my shoulder. "I am, but . . . ."

"But what, Jackie?"

Propping herself up on her elbows, she said, "But I don't want our children to be born here."

That surprised the hell out of me. "Kids? Are you . . . ."

"No, silly, but Caroline is."

I jumped from shocked to confused. "What does Caroline being pregnant have to do with us?"

"She just got me thinking . . . I mean about our future and having children and that kind of thing."

The idea of leaving Ray Anderson's band didn't sit well with me at first, but I told Jackie I would see what I could learn about the new Williams-Mills band, so I did. What I learned was the band had some strong talent in it and a terrific gal singer, called Marion Haines. True, they were primarily a dance band, but their sound had a lot of solid jazz qualities about it.

I came to the conclusion that playing in this particular white band might not be as bad as I originally thought, so I let it be known in the right circles I was interested. That led to Jeff Mills showing up in the audience at the Club Alabam one night.

I didn't know Mills from Adam, but one of Anderson's sax men pointed him out. That of course led to much speculation as to what the bandleader was doing at the Alabam. Mills put an end to that speculation by approaching me at closing time. He suggested I stop by a Williams-Mills rehearsal the next day, and I should bring my horn.

LEIMERT PARK COTTAGE

A week later, on September Sixteenth, Jackie and I had a night of celebrations. For one thing, it was her birthday. For another, we celebrated my new job as lead horn man with the Williams-Mills Orchestra. We also had a new home to celebrate—a two bedroom house on a tree-lined street in a new housing development called Leimert Park.

Our new rented home was four blocks west of the Coliseum and about halfway between South Central and central Los Angeles to the north. It turned out renting the house actually saved us money. It cost us twenty-seven dollars a month compared to thirty-six bucks for four weeks at the Dunbar. At the same time, my weekly salary went up five dollars when I joined the Williams-Mills Orchestra. I was bringing home about $540 monthly; we could afford $27 of that for a nice home.

Another major event in our lives occurred that night, although we didn't know about until later. That event was the conception of our son.

While our future looked bright, but my last night with Ray Anderson's band wasn't a happy occasion. Ray understood why I was leaving, but several of the guys thought I was "selling out" and took my departure personally. In a way they were right, but when all was said and done, my responsibility was to Jacqueline and my unborn son.

Our son arrived a week early, on Friday, June 7, 1940, and he was our pride and joy. We named him William in honor of the man who made it possible for Jackie and I to be together, Billy Davis. Billy sounded delighted when I made a long distance call to let him know he had a namesake.

William had a pair of lungs that made me think he might someday follow in his old man's footsteps and become a horn man. If he did, though, it would be his decision.

June 7, 1940 was a special day for another reason. It was our first anniversary. Jacqueline and I agreed Billy was the most wonderful anniversary present we could possibly receive. She also received a gold Longines-Wittnauer wristwatch. Being able to give Jackie the sort of present she deserved made me feel wonderful. It wasn't so much the cost of the watch, but the idea that I could support my wife and child playing music. I wasn't the bum my old man always thought I was.

### DEXTER WALTER ENGLE
May 30, 1920 – June 12, 1940
By Jacqueline Engle

I found the words you have read up to this point on sheets of folded paper in Dexter's cornet case. More than once during our time together, I urged Dex to write about his life because I was sure he would be a celebrity one day and his fans would want to know all about him. I believe the pages we found in his horn case are the result of my prompting.

My purpose here is to pick up from where Dexter's account of his life concludes so you can know how his story ends. In many ways, though, Dex's story will never end. His music lives on the recordings he made with Billy Davis and Ray Anderson, and I have made sure his spirit will live on in young men and women who follow in his footsteps.

Finally, I have one more important reason for writing this ending to Dex's biography. I want our son, William, to know his father's story because it is an important lesson about what a person can do with their talent if they are determined.

The saddest part of Dex's story is the way in which he died. The Williams-Mills Orchestra was playing at the Café Trocadero on the famous Sunset Strip, and when my father came to Los Angeles on business, he happened to see a Trocadero newspaper advertisement in which Dex was mentioned.

By this time my father already knew we were living in Los Angeles, but he seemed content just to change his will and let my punishment for disobeying him go at that. Seeing Dex's name in the newspaper, however, apparently relit father's rage. As far as the police were able to reconstruct the events leading up to Dex's murder, father ordered the man who followed me in San Francisco to come down and "finish the matter once and for all."

That man shot Dex as he was leaving the Trocadero after playing there Wednesday, June 12, 1940. By some miracle, a Los Angeles County Deputy Sheriff pulled into the parking lot at that moment and witnessed the killing. A gunfight followed in which my father's gunman was seriously wounded. His loyalty ended when threatened with a death sentence, and my father was arrested for complicity in Dex's murder. Both were sentenced to life in prison without parole.

The man I was supposed to love because he was my father took the only man I ever really loved away from me, but his prison sentence meant nothing to me. No, he would pay dearly for killing Dex. I knew no amount of money would replace Dexter, but I conceived of a way in which my father's estate could help Dexter's spirit live on.

Hiring an attorney who was just as big a jerk as my father, I filed a wrongful death suit and went after everything J. Charles Dumont had with vengeance. And I got it, too. After nearly a year in court, my father's entire estate, including the physical property became mine.

During the year it took to settle the lawsuit my best friend, Betty, came down to Los Angeles and became "Aunt Betty" to help care for William while I worked at the nearby Los Angeles Natural History Museum to earn our living. However, when the lawsuit was finally settled, we made some changes.

First, Betty, William, and I moved back to San Francisco. We decided we would live in a home my father's sister had once owned near Sea Cliff, so I put the family's Nob Hill mansion up for sale. Whoever bought it got a good deal because I just wanted to see it and the evil memories it housed gone. The proceeds from the mansion along with a large part of father's bonds and stock holdings went into a trust fund I call the Dexter Engle Youth Music Scholarship Fund.

The idea was to make money available for young men and women of high school and college ages who demonstrated the desire and talent to pursue a career in music to attend the California School of the Arts in Berkeley. There, they are able to study a variety of musical styles from jazz to classical.

Dex was largely a self-taught musician, but he sometimes wondered aloud how far he could have gone with a formal musical education. Now, with Betty administering our fund, promising young musicians—black or white, men or women—have the opportunity to go as far as their talent and desire will take them. In that way Dexter's spirit will live forever in their performances.

THE END

# Night Train to Frisco

Union Station, Los Angeles—October, 1942

My cab turned off Alameda Street onto Union Station's palm-lined drive a few minutes before 6:00 p.m. That left me with more than an hour to kill before my train, the Southern Pacific's San Francisco-bound Coaster, was scheduled to board.

As I have come to expect since we entered the war, the terminal was teaming with men in Navy white and Army khaki. Of course, I got the usual disapproving stares from the departing men in uniform and the loved ones who came to see them off to war. These days any able-bodied guy like me in civilian clothes made people think "draft dodger." I couldn't really blame them, so I ignored the looks and went about my country's business in the manner chosen for me.

When the Japs attacked Pearl Harbor last December I was a brand new, wet-behind-the-ears FBI agent pushing papers around in the San Francisco Field Office while I waited for my first real assignment. Even though my position as a Federal law enforcement agent earned me a draft deferment, my paper-pushing was contributing nothing to the war effort, so I decided to enlist in the Army.

With a degree in European languages from Stanford University, I stood a good chance of getting into Officer Candidate School and ultimately doing something positive toward winning the war. After visiting the Army recruitment office to get the lowdown, I was ready to sign up when a guy from the Office of Strategic Services showed up at the FBI Field Office.

FDR created the Office of Strategic Services, now more

commonly known as the OSS, by executive order because he felt the need for a central agency to handle the country's war-time intelligence needs. It wasn't that we didn't have any intelligence agencies back then; the problem was we had too many of them.

The State Department, The Treasury Department, and the War Department, including the Army and the Navy, all had their own intelligence and code-breaking services. The rub was all those agencies were competing with each other for budgets, and they weren't sharing the information they gathered. So Roosevelt decided to establish the OSS as sort of a super spy outfit to serve as a central clearing house for all wartime intelligence. He appointed General William Donovan to build the organization and run it.

To avoid reinventing the wheel, Donovan decided to recruit some of his agents from the existing intelligence services. When J. Edgar Hoover, Director of the FBI, was asked to recommend some of his agents for transfer to the OSS, Hoover did what any self-respecting bureaucrat would do and made a minimally cooperative gesture by offering up a few brand new agents with little or no field experience. And that's how I became OSS Intelligence Agent, Daniel Colley.

Despite that snazzy title, I am by no stretch of imagination a spy. The OSS has much more qualified folks off in far corners of the world doing the spying. No, my job is research. I spend my time in dark, musty library basements searching old newspapers, maps, and other documents for tidbits of information that, when compiled with other bits and pieces of information, might make the tough jobs our GIs are doing a little easier. It certainly isn't glamorous, but I'm told the intelligence I gather from such unlikely sources is useful, so I guess I'm making a contribution.

Occasionally, I even get an interesting assignment. For example, I was sent on this trip to Los Angeles for the purpose of interviewing a German immigrant named Klaus Kraus. Herr Kraus was a construction engineer back in Germany. What made him worthy of OSS attention was his work on the designs for Germany's new super highways—the highly propagandized Autobahns that supposedly made possible the high-speed transportation of military equipment and personnel throughout Germany.

What I learned from two days of interviewing Kraus, however, is that the Autobahns' capability for moving men and matèriel is a lot of baloney because the grades over many key sections of the highway are too steep for heavily loaded trucks. The "super highways" apparently aren't as super as the Nazi propagandists would have us believe. Now, with my interviews complete and a valise full of notes, I was heading back to San Francisco to make my report.

After standing in line for what seemed an eternity, I got up to the ticket counter and told the woman I had a chair car reservation through to San Francisco on Coast Route train number 69. She looked through her reservation lists and found my name. Then she said, "I don't understand how this reservation was made, but I don't think we can honor it. Military personnel have top priority, and we have a long list of soldiers and sailors who need to be on that train tonight. Perhaps you can go over to the Greyhound bus terminal and . . . ."

Without saying anything to attract attention, I flashed the very official-looking identification card the OSS issued me. The sight of it stopped her in mid-sentence. She looked closely at my picture and the words OFFICE OF STRATEGIC SERVICES on the card. After consulting another piece of paper she said, "Yes, sir, Mister Colley, I have your ticket right here. You are in car number 2942. The train will be boarding in thirty minutes on track number four. Have a pleasant trip."

UNION STATION INTERIOR

I thanked the ticket agent and headed for a newsstand to buy a SAN FRANCISCO CHRONICLE. The newsstand didn't have any CHRONICLES left, so I settled for an LA TIMES, a pack of Lucky Strikes in their new white wrapper, and a Hershey bar.

Car number 2942 turned out to be the first coach behind the baggage car. I climbed aboard through the front vestibule and located my assigned seat at the back of the car. I stashed my valise under the seat in front of me and settled in for the eleven hour ride to San Francisco.

By the time the train pulled into Oxnard an hour-and-a-half later, I was already into the local news section of THE TIMES. That was where I found an article that got my attention and then some. The headline said, "German immigrant murdered in burglary." The story told how Anaheim Police were summoned to the home of Klaus Kraus early this morning and found the owner dead of a gunshot wound. Kraus apparently returned to his home the previous evening and interrupted a burglar in the process of robbing his home.

The police call was made by a housekeeper who arrived to find the front door ajar and Kraus' body in the middle of his living room floor. THE TIMES described the dead man as a recent immigrant to the United States and a widower with no immediate family in the area. The basic facts of the story were followed by the usual malarkey about how the police had not yet found the victim's assailant but were following all available leads in an effort to solve the case.

While I couldn't be sure of the exact timing, it looked very much as if Klaus Kraus left my hotel in Los Angeles last night and drove home to his death. We conducted the interviews in my hotel room because Kraus was nervous about German agents he thought were watching him. I went along with his request more to humor the old man than out of any faith I had in his concerns about German spies.

Now his sudden death left me wondering if there might have been some basis for his fears. But why would German agents waste their time on Klaus Kraus? He'd been a construction engineer, not some high-ranking Nazi who was privy to secret war plans and such. Then a question of greater personal importance finally elbowed its way to the front of my mind. If Nazis killed Kraus because they suspected him of giving away their secrets, would they next come looking for the guy they thought he gave them to, namely me?

I took inventory of my fellow travelers aboard coach 2942. Naively deciding it was unlikely Nazi agents would risk masquerading as soldiers or sailors, I concentrated on civilian passengers. There appeared to be only two other civilians—a pair of young women seated at the front of the car. I also noticed a fellow in a dark blue uniform with the upside-down wings of a British or Canadian pilot who was probably in the US for advanced training. All of the other passengers were sailors, soldiers or Marines.

Knowing full well I probably wouldn't recognize a Nazi spy if he came up and asked for a light, it still seemed prudent to at least take a stroll through the other cars. I grabbed my valise, and excusing myself as I slid past the Marine gunnery sergeant seated next to me, I headed into the vestibule at the rear of car 2942.

The northbound Coaster was carrying a total of five chair cars in front of the dining car, which was followed by a tavern car and three tourist sleeping cars. These economy class sleepers consist of eight rows of seats on each side of the car. At night, porters convert the seats into sixteen small sleeping compartments accommodating up to thirty-two passengers. In addition, there are bathroom facilities at each end of the coach.

I patiently threaded my way through the dining car, which was filled to overflowing with hungry GIs, and entered the tavern car. The "bar car," as it is more often called, was nearly as crowded as the dining car, so it took a while to make my way to the first tourist sleeper car.

S. P. COASTER

It was still early enough that only a few of the seats were already converted to sleeping compartments, so I was able to complete my scouting mission without missing many passengers. By the time I turned around at the end of the last sleeper, I had counted a total of thirteen travelers who appeared to be civilians, and the only signs of weapons I saw were the sidearms worn by three Army MPs in the car directly behind 2942.

I returned to the bar car, ordered a Rye Old Fashioned from the Negro bartender, and latched onto a center-facing seat in the middle of the car when the marine who'd been sitting in it wandered off toward the dining car. From there I could keep an eye on my fellow passengers while I pondered my situation.

Was I really in danger of being rubbed out by vicious Nazi spies? I honestly couldn't say. The Kraus murder might be exactly what the cops suspected—a burglary gone wrong when the homeowner showed up unexpectedly. It might have been that, but burglars don't usually carry guns; they rely on timing and stealth to ply their trade.

Okay, if it wasn't a burglary gone bad, did anyone else besides Nazi spies have a reason to kill Herr Kraus? Again, I didn't know. He seemed to be comfortably fixed; not rich by any means, but wealthy enough that he could retire in his newly adopted country without any apparent concern for money. And I saw no evidence that Kraus was involved in activities that would create political enemies. From all indications he led a quiet life that generated little interest from those around him, which given the country's current disdain for Germans and Japanese, made good sense.

Did Klaus Kraus actually give me any secret information the Nazis would consider valuable to their enemies? That was a question I could answer, and the answer was emphatically no. He told me some general Autobahn engineering details about the highways' inadequacies to facilitate large movements of war materials and troops, but that simply confirmed what we learned from other sources.

Did that preclude the possibility that Herr Kraus was privy to sensitive information he didn't tell me? Again, the answer was no. Nor did the actual content of our interview preclude the possibility the Nazis might think he possessed such information, whether he actually had it or not. If either of those possibilities were a reality, and since Kraus and I were the only ones who knew what he really told me, it wouldn't be unreasonable for the Nazis to think he was a security liability. That, in turn, made me a liability also, so I had to assume I was in danger.

What could I do about that? I managed to complete the FBI small arms training course without distinguishing myself as a crackerjack marksman, but at least I know how to shoot a pistol. Unfortunately, that particular skill was of little practical value unless one had a pistol to shoot. No one at the OSS, including myself, had any reason to think a guy who spent his time in libraries and newspaper morgues needed to carry a gun.

Would evil Nazi agents actually try to kill someone on a train filled with American soldiers and sailors? That seemed unlikely, so I was probably safe until the train arrived in San Francisco. What then? The Coaster was scheduled to arrive in San Francisco at 6:45 a.m. There would be no one in the San Francisco OSS field office at that hour of the morning, so I couldn't just call in and ask for help.

TAVERN CAR

Could I simply hang around public areas of the SP depot until later in the morning when there would be people in the office? Yes, that would be the thing to do. The field office was usually alive and buzzing by eight, so I would call my boss from the depot and explain my plight. My boss, Alex Johnson, came to the OSS as an experienced agent from the War Department, so he would know how to handle this situation.

Having a plan improved my morale. I lit a Lucky Strike and took a swig of my Rye Old Fashioned. Yes, indeed, all would be right with the world again once Alex Johnson was on the case.

I finished my drink and was thinking about getting another when a commotion swept through the crowd of GIs around me. Still a little on edge, I anxiously looked toward the front of the car for the cause and immediately spotted what aroused the soldiers' and sailors' interest. The two young women from car 2942 were paying a visit to the Tavern Car. It quickly became clear that was all these two gals would be paying, as practically every GI in the car joined the competition to buy drinks for the new arrivals.

VERONICA LAKE

A couple of seats near where I was sitting were cleared for the gals, which gave me an opportunity for a better look at the brave young women who dared to enter a bar-car filled with soldiers and sailors. Through a forest of white and khaki uniforms I saw that the woman facing me was a rather stunning blonde in her twenties who wore her long hair in the peek-a-boo style made popular by actress Veronica Lake. The second gal sat with her back to me, so all I could really tell about her was that she was a redhead in a dark green dress with the sort of padded shoulders that were all the rage among fashion conscious women.

As things settled down to a mild roar, I was able to tune into the conversation going around their table. That's when the four years I spent at Stanford University learning to read, write, and speak European languages proved useful in a way I never anticipated.

Even though her colloquial American English was nearly flawless, I began picking out subtle hints of an accent in the blonde's speech patterns. I wasn't sure at first because she hid it well, but the more I heard, the more certain I became that she spoke with a slight accent—a German accent. I guessed she grew up speaking German and at some point learned English as a second language. Given the current state of world affairs, it was hardly surprising she worked hard at hiding all traces of her first language. Just as anyone who looked Asian was immediately suspected of being Japanese, anyone with a recognizably German accent was quickly tagged as a Nazi.

As the train rolled along toward its next stop in Santa Barbara, I found myself listening with no small amount of amusement at the competition among the servicemen to impress the young women. Each soldier and sailor had his own approach, but the underlying theme was the same; they had a few days' leave before boarding troop transports that would carry them off to war in some far-flung corner of the world, and wouldn't the young women like to spend those last few days sightseeing in San Francisco with them?

It occurred to me that the enemies of our country couldn't do better than pick pretty young women as spies to learn the movements of our Army and Navy. To be fair, though, I have to give the guys credit for not actually divulging any specific information about when they were leaving or where they were going, but it was clear that they were all headed off to war somewhere.

Eventually it became evident that, while flattered by all the attention, the women had no intention of being talked into any liaisons in San Francisco. Our soldiers and sailors were a game bunch, though, and many of them kept on pitching even as the failure of their mission became increasingly apparent.

As amused as I was by the impromptu floor show, I was also feeling the effects of a long day. Thinking I might get a little shut-eye, I picked up my valise and headed back to car number 2942. The chair cars between the dining car and my coach were quiet, with most of the GIs snoozing. Four marines and a sailor were deeply involved in a penny-ante poker game two cars behind mine. The sailor, who was sitting on his sea bag in the aisle, seemed to be having all the luck, which wasn't improving the morale of the marines.

Approaching the last vestibule before I came to car 2942, I heard a low wolf whistle somewhere behind me. Looking back over my shoulder, I saw what inspired the admiration. Apparently the young blonde had grown weary of the bar car games and was heading back to her seat.

She was only a few steps behind me, so I held the sliding vestibule door open for her. Then, ever the gentleman, I turned quickly to open the opposite door and just about poked my eye out running into the barrel of a small black pistol that suddenly appeared in the blonde's dainty hand.

There is no denying this turn of events caught me completely by surprise. Her carefully concealed accent had rung a few alarm bells, but my earlier conclusion that I was safe aboard the train left me with my guard down. As a result, I was now alone in a noisy vestibule with a Nazi agent who was armed and dangerous.

I took an involuntary step backwards and looked at the face behind the pistol. Her eyes were as cold as steel—well, the eye that wasn't hidden by her hair was as cold as steel—and she was wearing a no nonsense expression that said I was in big trouble. Her stare never wavered behind the sights of her pistol as she said, "Step back into the corner of the vestibule and have no doubt that I will shoot you dead at the slightest provocation."

I harbored no such doubt as I took a step backward to comply with her instructions. At the same instant I knew what I had to do next. My valise was in my left hand and she held the pistol in her right hand. Without taking my eyes off her face or changing my expression to telegraph the move, I swung the valise up in an arc toward her gun. She caught the movement out of her peripheral vision and began a step backwards, but she was a fraction of a second too late, and the valise smacked into her hand.

The pistol went flying, and the impact of my valise combined with the swaying movement of the train and the stylish heels she wore left her off balance. As the pistol clattered to the steel floor, the blonde's body flew backwards. Her head hit the metal wall behind her with an audible "thunk," and she slumped to the floor like a rag doll.

As all this happened, I was experiencing some balance problems of my own. The weight and centrifugal force of the valise were pulling me forward. My feet got tangled up with her outstretched legs and I followed her down to the vestibule floor. Fortunately, I hit the wall with my shoulder instead of my head and still had the presence of mind to scramble after the pistol. I grabbed it and got myself vertical again, keeping one eye on the blonde the whole time. I needn't have been in such a hurry to get my hands on the pistol because she was out cold.

I dropped the little gun into my jacket pocket and checked her for a pulse. Relieved to feel a strong, steady beat in her right wrist, I quickly checked her purse for additional weapons and found none. My relief that I hadn't killed her was short-lived, though, as the circumstances of my situation sank in. I had a very attractive unconscious blonde at my feet on a train full of soldiers and sailors. It would be easier to convince those GIs that Adolph Hitler was Santa Claus than persuade them this woman was a dangerous Nazi spy.

Then there was her redheaded companion who was undoubtedly also armed and dangerous. While frantically trying to think of a way to handle the situation, I sensed a change in the motion of the train. It was slowing, and glancing through the window in the rear vestibule door, I saw a conductor moving through the car in my direction. He was announcing something to the passengers. I couldn't hear his words, but I guessed we were arriving in Santa Barbara where the train was scheduled to stop long enough to unload a few passengers and take on some new ones.

The stop offered at least a temporary solution to my dilemma. If I could get the blonde off the train without her redheaded accomplice knowing about it, my odds of survival would improve dramatically. The trick would be getting her off the train. I could hardly throw an unconscious woman over my shoulder and stroll onto the platform without attracting attention. I was going to need some help, preferably from the blonde, herself.

The conductor stopped to talk with a passenger about halfway through the car, so I still had a little time, but not much. I knelt next to the blonde and shook her shoulders. There was no response, so I slapped her cheek lightly. That got me a flutter of her eyelids. I smacked her a little harder and her eyes popped open.

Holding her pistol where she could see it and trying to sound like a Humphrey Bogart tough guy, I said, "Okay, Blondie, you've got one chance of getting out of this alive, and that's to do exactly what I say." She glared at me and I added, "I'd just as soon shoot you right here and now, but my boss wouldn't like that, so I'll give you one chance at doing this the easy way."

Her glare softened a little, and she said, "What do you want me to do?"

"That's a good girl. First, get on your feet."

As she started gathering herself together, I put my right hand, still holding the pistol, into my jacket pocket. Then I set the valise down and offered her my left hand. She took it, and together we managed to get her back on her feet.

She stood there a little shakily while I picked up my valise and her purse. I was stepping behind her when the conductor appeared in the rear vestibule doorway. From my vantage point, I could see a dark, matted spot on the back of her head. It looked serious, but she was functional, so the visible damage was probably superficial. At worst she might have a mild concussion.

The conductor couldn't see the wound from his vantage point, but it was still clear to him that the woman wasn't feeling well. He said, "Are you all right, Miss?"

She said nothing for a moment, and I was about to answer for her when I heard her say softly, "Yes. It's just a little motion sickness. I will be okay."

The conductor nodded and moved on through the vestibule and into car 2942. I tried not to breathe a big sigh of relief. Instead I said, "Good work, Blondie. Now, when we pull into Santa Barbara in a few minutes, you and I are leaving this train. In the meantime, we'll stay right here."

She nodded almost imperceptibly and swayed unsteadily. I moved closer behind her, and she leaned into me for support.

I was thinking I should be relieved that the blonde was being so cooperative, but I wasn't. This was almost too easy. Was she cooperating because of the concussion or did she know something I didn't?

SANTA BARBARA DEPOT

During the ten or so minutes it took the train to finally pull into the Santa Barbara station I expected the redhead to walk through the vestibule door at any moment, but the only person we saw was the conductor who showed up again to open the outside vestibule door. He unfolded the steps and offered the blonde his hand as we stepped down to the platform.

There were a few soldiers and sailors waiting to board the train, and of course, an attractive blonde who was obviously unsteady on her feet didn't escape their notice, but they were more interested in boarding the train than in blondes at that moment. Once through the terminal doors, I turned the blonde to our right and walked down to a window where I could see who else got off the train.

Luck was still with me. There was no sign of the redhead among the half-dozen sailors who climbed down from the train. A few seconds later they were followed by the British flying officer. I wondered why he was leaving the train in Santa Barbara, and then I remembered Camp Cook Army Air Corp base was just up the coast.

I looked around the depot, trying to decide on my next step. I had successfully captured a Nazi spy, but I had no idea what to do with her. All I had in the way of a plan was to call Alex Johnson for instructions, but I couldn't make that call for nearly twelve hours. I considered turning the blonde over to the local police, but that could get complicated, and I ran the risk of losing her. No, the best thing to do was to hole up someplace safe until I could call my boss.

I was considering spending the night right there in the terminal before I realized it was the first place her Nazi pals would look if they showed up in search of their missing agent. Then I noticed a bright red neon hotel sign through the street-side windows of the terminal and decided that would be as good a place as any to spend the next twelve hours.

Reprising my tough guy routine, I said, "Okay, Blondie, we're going to stroll out of the terminal and check into that hotel across the street. Behave like a good little girl, and you might just get through this alive."

Outside the terminal, we jaywalked across Montecito Street and entered the Chief Hotel. From the architecture, the place looked like it dated back to the 1920s. Still, its hacienda décor was well maintained, and more importantly, the VACANCY sign was lit.

My blonde Nazi companion remained on her very best behavior throughout the check-in process.

When we got to our assigned room on the second floor, she sat on the bed while I locked the door. After taking a look out the window at the street below and seeing no one—redheaded or otherwise—lurking about, I turned to my captive and asked, "How are you feeling?"

I thought I saw a puzzled expression cross her face, but it only lasted a split second before she said, "What's it to you, you Nazi bastard?"

It was my turn to look puzzled. Why was a German spy calling ME a Nazi bastard? In that brief moment I had my first inkling that the situation might not be exactly as I had it figured. Still, she pulled a gun on me aboard the train, and whatever she was up to now wasn't going to erase that fact. I said, "That blow on the head must have scrambled your brains, lady. You're the Nazi, not me."

"Okay, Buster, if you want to play it that way, fine. But you're wasting your act on me. We've been watching you, and I know exactly what you are."

I sat at the small writing desk on the other side of the room and studied her. Finally, I said, "All right, if you aren't a Nazi agent, who are you?"

She turned slightly on the edge of the bed to face me, an effort that was obviously painful, and said, "As if you didn't know, the name I'm using is Marjorie Moore, and I'm with British intelligence, MI-6 to be specific."

Either she was a damned good actress or something was out whack here. I said, "Can you prove that?"

"You know damned well MI-6 agents don't walk around with credentials in their pockets."

"Lady, the only thing I know is that you stuck a gun in my face back there on the train, and now you claim to be one of the good guys. That doesn't add up."

"I stuck a gun in your face because you kept wandering off where I couldn't keep an eye on you. I concluded you had somehow figured out that I was a British agent, so I decided to take you into custody. That way I could make you stay put until we got to San Francisco where my people were waiting for us."

Talking to the woman was getting me nowhere. She had a convenient answer for every question. Thinking her purse might contain a clue as to her real identity, I walked over and dumped its contents onto the bed. In amongst the expected female accoutrements, I found a one-way Southern Pacific ticket to San Francisco and a wallet with no identification documents, but a little over three-hundred dollars inside. Her purse also contained a passport identifying her as a British citizen named Marjorie Moore. The passport photo looked like the woman sitting on the bed, but none of that meant anything because one would expect a Nazi agent to have authentic-looking credentials.

Being fresh out of ideas, there was nothing more to do until morning when I could call Alex Johnson. In the meantime, I would just have to stay awake and on my toes. That didn't mean, however, I couldn't at least be civil about things. The woman was clearly in pain, so I said, "Miss Moore, I have a bottle of aspirin in my valise. Would you like a couple of them?"

She looked at me for a moment as if deciding whether or not I was going to poison her or slip her a Mickey, and then said, "Yes, Mister Colley, I would."

After swallowing two of the white pills, she lay back on the pillow and closed her eyes. She stayed in that position so long I thought she might be asleep, but she wasn't. Without opening her eyes, Marjorie Moore said, "Mister Colley, I have two questions. Will you answer them?"

"If I can. What are your questions?"

"First, what cover are you using here, and second, what did you hope to gain a while ago when you accused me of being a Nazi spy?"

Her questions compounded my confusion, but I answered them. "First, I don't have a cover, as you call it. I work for the Office of Strategic Services, and I accused you of being a Nazi spy because that's what you are."

"I see. Mister Colley, an OSS agent working in the U.S. would carry credentials. Do you have credentials?"

"Sure."

"May I see them?"

I couldn't see any reason not to show her my OSS identification, so I pulled the little black case out of my inside coat pocket and flipped it onto the bed. She picked it up and stared at my identification card for a while. Finally she closed the case and handed it back to me, saying, "Mister Colley, you are quite convincing, and that worries me."

"Worries you?"

"Yes, because if you really are who you say you are, my people have made a serious mistake, which means you and I are in big trouble."

"Then I guess we're in big trouble because I am exactly who I told you I am." After a second's pause I asked, "What sort of big trouble do you think we're in?"

"Do you remember seeing a fellow in a British flying officer's uniform on the train?"

"Yes, I saw him. He got off here in Santa Barbara."

"That's right. He is our big trouble, because he really is a German agent, and his current assignment is to kill both of us."

"If what you say is true, I can understand why he might want to kill me, but why would he want to kill you, a fellow Nazi?"

Glaring at me, she said, "I swear, you are dumber than dirt! For the last time, I am not a Nazi agent! Will you please get that through your thick skull!"

Glaring back at her, I said, "You'll have to forgive me and my thick skull, but I have difficulty believing you when less than an hour ago you were pointing a gun at me!"

"That was because MI-6 thought you were a German agent

and that you killed Klaus Kraus."

"Why would a German agent kill Herr Kraus? And why would MI-6 care about that one way or another?"

Marjorie Moore shook her head slowly in obvious exasperation. "I cannot for the life of me understand why Winston Churchill was so anxious to involve you Yanks in our war. If you are any example, the Americans will surely muck things up even worse than they already are."

When I didn't respond to her insult, she said, "Listen very carefully, and I will try to explain the situation so even you can understand it. Klaus Kraus was working for us—MI-6. Before the war, Germany sent him to the States as a spy to report on highways, airports, harbors, and so on because the Germans knew America would become their enemy before long.

"Then we broke Kraus's cover and offered him an opportunity to stay out of prison by working for us. We gave him false information to feed to the Germans, and he identified his contacts for us. After he met you in your hotel room, we concluded you were one of his contacts. When he was killed last night under mysterious circumstances, we figured you somehow tumbled to the fact that he was a double agent and killed him."

"Hell, I didn't kill Kraus! I didn't even know he was dead until I saw the article about him in the Los Angeles Times I bought to read on the train."

She cocked her head to one side and said, "You know, I believe you."

"Well, thank you very much! Now kindly explain to me why the guy in the British uniform wants to kill us."

"Like I said, he is a Nazi agent, and the Germans still believe Kraus was working for them. They no doubt concluded that you are a British or American agent and you killed Kraus because you discovered he was a spy. They would also conclude that Kraus told you who his contacts were. An American or British agent would not have killed Kraus if there was anything further to be learned from him. That makes you a risk to their intelligence network here in the States, so you need to be eliminated. Seeing you get off the train with me would have confirmed all that because he knows who I am. Now he's in a position to kill two birds with one stone."

I was having trouble following all the twists and turns in her story. I said, "Let's see if I have this straight. You're telling me the British think I'm a German spy and the Germans think I'm a British or American spy, so you both set out to kill me. Is that right?"

"Yes, that is correct, except I do not want to kill you, I simply want to put you in jail. The fellow in the British uniform, however, definitely wants to kill you. He goes by the name of Willie Watson, and he is very good at killing people. By taking us off the train, you have made it much easier for him to complete his assignment."

"What about your partner, the redhead who was on train with you? Won't she notice you and I are missing and send some help?"

"Partner? The redheaded woman? Heavens, no.! She is a nurse on her way to work at a military hospital in San Francisco. I never set eyes on her before we met in the Los Angeles station. I chatted her up so I would have a companion to make me less conspicuous on the train."

Marjorie Moore was very convincing. Everything she said made sense, but in a way I was better off when I firmly believed she was a German agent. Now I had to make a decision. If the guy in the British uniform was really out to kill us, I needed some help, and Marjorie seemed much more at home in the cloak and dagger world than me. The question was, could I trust her? Then another question occurred to me. I said, "Miss Moore, where did you learn to speak English so well?"

She paused only a second before saying, "Oh, that. You have a very good ear. Few people notice my German accent. My parents moved from Austria to England a few years before the Great War. I was born in London, but my mother and father spoke German at home, so that is what I learned to speak. When I got older, I was taught English so I could go to school. That, however, was British English. When MI-6 recruited me, I studied American English so I would fit in here. It was almost like learning an entirely different language."

I nodded and made one more attempt at making sense of my predicament. I was fairly certain of only two things. One, somebody was out to get me, and two, staying alive would require some help. What I didn't know was who wanted me dead. Was it this woman who stuck a gun in my face or was it, as she claimed, the guy in the British uniform?

Marjorie Moore's explanation of the situation was convincing because everything she told me seemed to fit, and until something more concrete turned up, her word was really all I had to go on. I said, "Okay, Miss Moore, you've convinced me. How do we get out of this mess alive?"

She looked me straight in the eye and said, "I was hoping you had a plan. After all, this is your country and you are an OSS agent."

"I only do research for the OSS. I don't know beans about this secret agent stuff."

Her expression was clear. Marjorie Moore was exasperated with me again. "Oh, swell! We're up against an experienced German agent and I've got a librarian for a partner. I will take a guess and say the only weapon you're carrying is mine. Am I right?"

I was smarting a little at being called a librarian, but now wasn't the time to indulge in hurt feelings. I nodded.

Still looking exasperated, she said, "Do you know how to use a Beretta?"

"A what?"

"A Beretta. My pistol is an Italian Beretta."

"Well, I've taken an FBI small arms course. . . ."

"And they taught you how to use a Smith & Wesson revolver, right?"

"Yes."

"That isn't going to help. My Beretta is a thirty-two caliber, semi-automatic pistol. It fires nothing at all like a revolver, and it doesn't have nearly the stopping power of the thirty-eights you learned to shoot."

I took her pistol from my coat pocket and examined it. She was right. Other than the fact that it had a trigger and a barrel, I could see very little resemblance between the pistol in my hand and any gun I ever shot before. I didn't even know where the safety was, assuming it had one. I said, "Okay, I'll admit I have no idea how this thing works, but before we go any further on that train of thought, I want to know what we can expect from this guy you say is going to kill us."

"How long have we been here?"

I glanced at my watch and said, "We got off the train a little over an hour ago."

She nodded. "Then we are already on borrowed time. He will want to get his job done and leave this small town as quickly as possible. So the first thing we must do is find out where he is. May I use the telephone?"

"Maybe. Who do you plan to call?"

"The front desk." With that, she picked up the handset from the telephone on the nightstand. It was a house phone with no dial, so she clicked the cradle a couple of times. Finally she said, "Front desk?"

After a pause, she continued, "I'm expecting a friend of mine to check in to your hotel tonight and I am wondering if he has arrived. His name is Willard Watson. He's a British flying officer and he'll be in uniform."

This was followed by a longer pause during which she looked at me and nodded. Then she said, "Oh, no, thank you. He's probably resting after his long trip. I will try calling him in the morning. Thank you very much."

Marjorie Moore hung up the telephone and said, "He's here in the hotel. I figured he wouldn't be far away."

"What do you suggest we do about that?"

She thought for a moment, and then said, "One thing is for sure; we cannot stay in this room. Willie can jimmy that old door lock faster than you can open it with a key. If we stay here, he can pick us off like sitting ducks any time he chooses."

"So where do you suggest we go?"

"Ultimately we have to get out of this town, which means we have to go back to the train station or to the bus depot, wherever that might be. He is probably watching the train station, so I vote for the bus depot. Either way, we will be a lot safer in a public place."

"How do we get out of the hotel without him seeing us?"

"This place probably has a back stairway in addition to the stairs in the lobby, and there is certain to be a rear door to the hotel. He cannot watch both exits, so he is most likely watching the train depot and the street in front of the hotel from his room. I would go down the back stairs and head for the bus depot. Once we are out of the hotel we can ask someone for directions."

"Are you feeling well enough for all that?"

"I think so. The aspirin helped. Besides, how I feel does not matter. We need to go and we need to do it now."

I nodded. "Okay, let's go."

A minute later we were peeking out the room door to be sure the hallway was clear. It seemed to be, but she pushed the door closed again and said, "Now you have to decide whether or not you trust me. My pistol is our only weapon, and I am the one who knows how to use it. Will you give it back to me?"

I expected that question sooner or later, and under the circumstances it was not an unreasonable request. I handed her the small black pistol and said, "I hope I don't regret this."

She smiled and said, "You won't. We are on the same side."

With that, I picked up my valise, and we walked quickly and quietly down the hall toward the rear of the hotel. She was right about the place having a back stairway. We took it down to the first floor and went through a heavy door marked with an exit sign. Outside, we were in a dark alley with no illumination beyond a small bulb over the hotel door.

I figured Santa Barbara's main downtown area—the most likely place to find the bus station—was to our left, so I turned in that direction and immediately felt something hard poke into my back. Marjorie Moore said, "Okay, Mister Colley, this is as far as you go. Drop your valise and face the wall."

In that instant I knew I made a fatal mistake trusting the woman. I had all the evidence I needed to prove she was a German spy, but I let her talk me into ignoring the facts. Even though I was about to pay the ultimate price for my stupidity, all I could think of to say was, "You lied to me."

She laughed at my absurdity and said, "Yes, Mister Colley, I lied to you. That is what spies do. Now drop the valise and move to the wall or I will most certainly blow your spine to bits right here and now."

The last time she held a gun on me I managed to overpower her, and she wasn't about to let that happen again. I released my grip on the valise and turned toward the rear wall of the hotel. She moved the pistol to the back of my head and said, "You Americans are so gullible! We will win this war for the Fatherland in a matter of months. Now say goodbye, Mister Colley. It has been a pleasure knowing you."

I could think of nothing else to say, so I was standing there waiting for my life to be over when a voice with a thick British accent came out of the shadows somewhere behind me. It said, "That's quite enough, Marjorie. Lay your pistol down."

The pressure of the gun barrel left the back of my neck almost immediately, and I dove for the ground. The cracks of two pistol shots sounded almost simultaneously, followed by a moment of deathly silence. Then I heard a groan and felt Marjorie Moore's body land across my legs. I started scrambling away, but the British voice said, "Relax, Mister Colley. The danger is passed."

Slowly, I got back to my feet and turned to look at Marjorie Moore. She was in a heap at my feet with her blonde hair fanned out around her head. The fellow in the British flying officer's uniform came out of the shadows across the alley and scooped up the woman's Beretta from where it had fallen a foot or so from her outstretched hand.

The Brit said, "You really ought to exercise greater care in selecting the company you keep. Marjorie here was hardly the sort of woman with whom a gentleman ought to be seen.

I looked up from the growing red stain on the front of Marjorie Moore's dress and said, "Thanks for the rescue, but I'm still a bit confused. Who are you?"

He slipped his pistol into the side pocket of his uniform jacket and offered his hand. "Willie Watson, British Intelligence, at your service, Mister Colley."

Shaking the hand he offered, I said, "Miss Moore also claimed to be with British Intelligence and told me you were a Nazi agent. Forgive my reticence, but how do I know you're who you claim to be?"

The fellow grinned and said, "Well, sir, that is an excellent question. Perhaps the best answer is to take note of the fact that you are still alive and free to go on about your business."

"I am? I mean, free to go?"

"Of course you are. In fact, the sooner we both go on about our business the better. I have an automobile at my disposal here, and I plan to resume my trip to San Francisco in it. If you fancy a lift, you are welcome to join me, but that is entirely up to you."

I looked down at Marjorie Moore and said, "What about her?"

"The chaps who provided my automobile also perform . . . ah, shall we say, clean up chores. They will take care of Miss Moore."

Roughly eight hours later Willie Watson pulled to the curb in front of the federal building that housed San Francisco's branch of the OSS and said, "Here you go, old fellow. Do try to stay out of the clutches of alluring German spies from here on out, won't you?"

I said I would and thanked Willie again for saving my life. As he drove off up Seventh Street, I looked at my watch. It was a few minutes past eight and the office was open, so I went up to the small cubicle assigned to my use and rolled a sheet of paper into my typewriter in preparation for writing my report to Alex Johnson.

It would be a two-part report containing both the information I learned from Klaus Kraus and the account of my misadventures on the way back to San Francisco. I wasn't looking forward to writing the second part, so I tackled it first to get the humiliation over with. Leaning back in my chair, I reviewed Willie Watson's answers to the myriad of questions I asked during the trip up U.S. 101 from Santa Barbara.

According to Watson, Klaus Kraus was exactly who he claimed to be, a construction engineer who retired and moved to the US. There was, however, one item on his resume that escaped the notice of both the OSS and the German bureaucrat who approved Kraus's emigration papers. It seems that in addition to working on Autobahn designs, Herr Kraus also helped develop structural improvements to the runways of top secret heavy bomber bases.

By the time the Nazis discovered the oversight, there was little they could do about it except to keep an eye on Kraus to be sure he didn't spill what he knew to American or British intelligence. They assigned that job to one of their top agents who was already over here posing as a British citizen. That agent was, of course, Marjorie Moore. So when Miss Moore discovered Klaus having clandestine meetings in a hotel with an unknown person, she assumed—correctly, as it turned out—that I was a U.S. intelligence agent.

Willie Watson explained his MI-6 assignment in the U.S. only to the extent that it included keeping a close eye on known Nazi agents working here, including Marjorie Moore. In that role, he observed Miss Moore following Klaus Kraus to our second interview meeting. Since Watson is in this country with the approval of our government and because my assignment was hardly a state secret, he was able to make some phone calls and determine that the OSS did indeed send an agent to interview Kraus. That made Watson the only one in the game who knew all the players and put him in a position to anticipate what was about to happen.

Watson figured Marjorie Moore assumed Kraus told me the locations of the secret bomber bases he worked on, and since she was known to be a ruthless agent who sometimes made decisions in the field beyond her authority, Watson wasn't surprised when he followed Moore that night and witnessed her cold-blooded murder of Kraus.

Figuring I and my valise full of interview notes would be Marjorie Moore's next targets, the MI-6 agent booked a seat to San Francisco on the same train I was taking. Kraus's death was of no concern to Watson, but he had an obligation to do what he could about preventing the murder of an OSS agent.

From my point of view, the sad thing was that, knowing nothing of Kraus's involvement with the bomber bases, I only discussed Autobahn designs with him. Had Marjorie Moore known that, she would have had no reason to kill either Kraus or me.

Watson described the rest of the previous night's adventures as a comedy of errors. When he saw me take Marjorie Moore off the train at Santa Barbara he knew she'd made her move and I'd somehow turned the tables on her.

Figuring that was only a temporary situation, however, Watson followed us off the train and made some educated guesses about what the blonde agent would try next. I don't know how he knew I was gullible enough to buy whatever story she might tell me, but he was right, and I'm damned glad he was.

That afternoon I sat in Alex Johnson's office as he read my report. I was braced for a thorough dressing down over my ineptness, but Alex surprised me. When he finished reading, he held my report up and said, "This mess is a perfect example of why the OSS was created. I found out just this morning that the FBI has a complete dossier on Klaus Kraus, including his involvement with the bomber bases. Unfortunately, that file is one of many Hoover chose not to share with us. If I'd known Kraus's full story, I never would have sent an inexperienced agent to interview him.

"All I can say at this point is thank God MI-6 was on the ball. If their agent hadn't been watching this Moore woman, the OSS would have lost a valuable employee. Even so, we missed an opportunity to learn the details of some Nazi heavy bomber bases, and that's inexcusable."

I said, "I'm sorry about that, sir."

"I am, too, but none of the blame for this fiasco falls on your shoulders. I hold J. Edgar Hoover personally responsible, and I intend to see that Mister Hoover is held accountable." Alex leaned back in his chair and stared at my report on his desk for a moment. Then more to himself than to me, he said, "One day that conniving bastard will go too far, and somebody higher up is going to have the nerve to toss him out on his ear. I only hope I'm around to see it happen."

## THE END

# Night Flight

## 19 November, 1943—Boeing Field, Seattle

Jack Collins, United States Army Air Corps, Captain, 019894041. According to the Geneva Convention of 1929, that's all I'm required to say about who I am and what I'm up to. Those few details, however, make for a pretty short story and this is a tale that deserves telling in full. Assuming, that is, anybody will believe it. Frankly, I'm not sure I would believe it if I hadn't seen it with my own eyes. So, here's the whole story, minus the parts Uncle Sam classifies as secrets.

It was 19 November, 1943—a stormy Friday, if it matters—and I was trying to stay dry in the doorway of an assembly building at the Boeing plant a few miles south of Seattle. What they assemble in the building and why I happened to be there are a couple of those secrets I mentioned. About all I can say regarding my job in this man's Army is I test airplanes—a chore I usually perform a thousand miles to the south at North American Aviation's plant at Mines Field, otherwise known as Los Angeles Municipal Airport.

B-25 ON TOKYO RAID

North American is a pretty big outfit, and their most recent claim to fame happened about a year-and-a-half ago when 16 modified versions of NAA's B-25 "Mitchell" bomber took off from a secret location in the Pacific and bombed Tokyo. This daring raid was led by Lieutenant Colonel Jimmy Doolittle and, as bombing missions go, it didn't do much physical damage, but it was the first US raid on Japan since the Japs bombed Pearl Harbor, and the morale value was terrific.

I didn't get in on any of that, though. My specialty is pursuit ships, like the P-51B parked about a hundred feet from where I was sheltering from a downpour of soggy Seattle sunshine. My "Mustang," as the British dubbed the plane, was less than a month old, and letting it sit out in the rain seemed like a shabby way to treat a new airplane, but the ship didn't seem to mind. It just sat there looking sleek and mean, even with sheets of water running off its sleek skin. The Army doesn't believe in pampering its airplanes.

P-51 "G FOR GEORGE"

What makes the B variant of the P-51 special is the engine behind its big four-bladed prop. Previous Mustangs were equipped with an Allison aircraft engine, and while they performed okay at low altitude, they weren't worth much at high altitudes where P-51s were expected to protect bombers from enemy fighters.

New Mustangs beginning with the B variant have a Packard-built version of the British Rolls-Royce Merlin V-12 engine that did such a swell job in Hurricanes and Spitfires during the Battle of Britain. With a top speed well over 400 miles-per-hour—how much over is another of Uncle Sam's secrets—P-51s could easily match the performance of German and Japanese fighters. Yup, the P-51B was fast, maneuverable and spoiling for a fight.

So was I—spoiling for a fight, that is. Unfortunately, the Army Air Forces in their infinite wisdom decided a guy who could fly the wings off of any pursuit ship they had was of more value finding out how much punishment the ships could take than he would be flying them in combat. I disagreed with that idea, but until they start letting captains make command level decisions, I was stuck with test piloting.

Anyway, there I stood staring gloomily at my trusty steed—call sign G for George—and waiting for the storm to pass so I could climb aboard and point her nose south. It wasn't that I couldn't fly in the rain, but there were some pretty tall mountains between Seattle and LA, and if they were obscured by clouds, there was a good chance of flying smack dab into a chunk of cumulous granite without more sophisticated navigation instrumentation than my ship carried. So I waited. Hell of a way to fight a war!

It was nearly 1800—six o'clock in the evening by civilian time—when the dark clouds began breaking up and letting some clear sky through. I checked in with the meteorological gurus in operations. The consensus was that, though the storm was headed the same way I was headed, the front was dissipating and wouldn't present much of a problem.

"CUMULOUS GRANITE"

That settled, I filed a standard military flight plan and went out to make a thorough preflight inspection of G for George. With a long-range fuel tank hanging on each of her wings, she has a range of . . . well, that's another secret. Let's just say I had plenty of fuel to make LA without a stop. Cruising at an easy-going speed of 325 mph the trip would take about three hours and twenty minutes, putting me into Inglewood about 2200 hours—ten p.m., if you haven't figured the military time thing out by now. That meant I'd be flying most of the trip after the sun set, but I was heading for familiar territory and Mines field had lights . . . a piece of cake.

My landing gear came up at precisely 1842 hours and I pointed G for George's nose up and south. Actually, it turned out to be a great evening for flying. Less than two hours in the air put me south of the highest mountains I would encounter, which meant I could drop down to 5,000 feet so I could see my landmarks on the ground more clearly. Blackouts were in force all along the west coast and even spotting a city the size of San Francisco when all its lights are off is as difficult for me as it would be for a Jap bomber pilot.

I saw San Francisco, though, mostly because of a full moon reflecting off the waters of San Francisco Bay to my right. From then on it was just a matter of moseying on down California's central valley until I got to the mountains just north of Los Angeles. At least that's what I was expecting.

Further down the valley, around Fresno, the moon disappeared behind some high cloud cover and I was back to trusting in my compass, commonly called "dead reckoning," to keep myself on track. That's when I saw IT.

Off toward the mountains on my left I noticed the lights of another aircraft. After watching those lights for a few minutes, several things became very apparent. For one thing the other ship was traveling about the same speed as I was. For another thing, we were on converging courses. In other words if one of us didn't turn, we would soon end up trying to occupy the same piece of sky simultaneously. Then I noticed something really odd. The mystery ship's lights were screwy.

Since we were heading more or less in the same direction and he was on my left, I should have been able to see a green navigation light on the wingtip closest to me, a white running light near the rear of the ship, and if it was a military aircraft, red, green and amber identification lights along the centerline of the fuselage. The closer we got, the more it became apparent this ship had an entirely different set of lights.

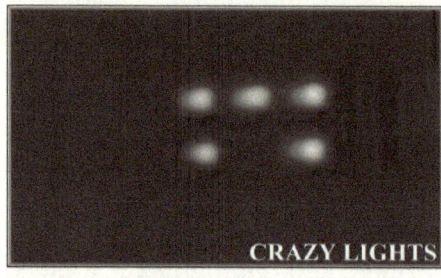

CRAZY LIGHTS

About where the wings should have been, there was a row of three bright blue lights. Below those was another row of lights that seemed to blink back and forth between pink and orange. While I was sitting there trying to figure out the lighting pattern and waiting to see if the other pilot was going to change course, the damned thing went straight up, made a ninety degree turn to the right and sailed right over my canopy at a high rate of speed. He cut it so close, G for George was jarred by his prop wash, assuming he had a propeller which I would not have bet on. That, my friends, was an impossible maneuver for any aircraft. I blinked my eyes a couple of times, wondering if I was seeing things.

Apparently he'd really done what I thought I saw because he now fell in behind me and slightly to my right. Looking back over my shoulder at what I presumed to be the ship's nose, I now saw a fairly bright white light surrounded by half a dozen flashing red lights. What the hell was this thing?

Grabbing my flight chart, I looked up the radio frequency for Hammer joint Army-Navy airfield near Fresno. I was easily within range of their radar, assuming they were so equipped. After taking another look over my shoulder to be sure the other ship was still there, I dialed in the frequency and transmitted, "Hammer Field Radio from Army Flight Two-Four-One-Niner. Over."

Twenty-four-nineteen was G for George's squadron call sign and Hammer radio's response came in loud and clear. "Army Two-Four-One-Niner from Hammer Radio. We have you five-by-five. Over."

"Hammer Radio, are you radar-equipped? Over."

"Army two-four-one-niner, affirmative. What is your current estimated position? Over."

"Hammer Radio, I should be approximately ten miles south of the field at five thousand feet on a heading of one-six-zero. Over."

Apparently they thought I was asking for a position check because they came back about five seconds later. "Army Two-Four-One-Niner, we have you on our scope. You are exactly where you think you are. Over."

"Hammer Radio, there's another aircraft up here less than a mile behind me and he's making some strange maneuvers. Do you have it on your scope and can you identify it? Over."

It took nearly thirty seconds for Hammer to come back with, "Army Two-Four-One-Niner, the only other aircraft we have in the area is a Navy transport eight miles north of us at twenty-thousand feet on a westerly heading. Over."

That reply certainly wasn't what I expected. "Hammer Radio, are you absolutely sure about that? Over."

"Army Two-Four-One-Niner, absolutely positive. Whatever you think you are seeing must be an optical illusion. There are no other aircraft in your immediate vicinity. Hammer Radio, OUT."

From the exasperated emphasis he placed on the word "out" I knew that was the end of our conversation. I mumbled, "Thanks, Hammer Radio. Army Two-Four-One-Niner out."

I took another look over my shoulder. The mystery ship was still back there, holding position like it was glued to my tail. Either Hammer Field didn't know how to read their damned scope or there was something going on out here I wasn't supposed to know about—maybe some kind of classified experimental ship on a test flight. If that was the case, though, they ought to send fleets of those ships to Europe and the Pacific immediately because whatever that was back there could fly circles around anything else in the air that I knew about.

Or could it? If the ship's pilot was game, it might be fun to find out.

I gradually opened the throttle to gain a little altitude. I was rapidly approaching the mountain ranges north of the Los Angeles basin and I wanted some maneuvering room. As I approached 10,000 feet, I checked behind me again. The mystery ship was still there. I thought, "Good! Now let's see what you guys can really do."

I went to full military power by shoving the throttle to the stop. G for George jumped forward like it was shot from a cannon. We were soon in the 400 mile per hour-plus range and I started to turn back for another look at the mystery ship. I didn't have to turn very far. The ship had moved up alongside me and seemed to be pulling ahead.

Then they hit me with a bright spotlight and proceeded to fly circles around me. I was moving at more than 400 miles per hour and that damned ship was literally circling me like I was standing still. Worse, I couldn't see a damned thing because their light killed my night vision.

I turned the instrument post lights up to full bright and tried to concentrate on what I saw there. The rate of climb indicator caught my eye first. It was dropping into the negative . . . way into the negative. I was descending at a rate of more than three thousand feet per minute! I pulled back on the stick hard and absolutely nothing happened. I wasn't positive about my exact position, but I was pretty sure there were mountains below and coming up fast. That thought had me seriously considering leaving G for George to her own devices and bailing out.

Then just as quickly as the descent began, it reversed itself and we were going straight up so fast the vertical climb indicator was off the scale. It felt like twice the ship's maximum rate of climb . . . that would make it something like seven thousand feet per minute! I'd encountered mountain up and down drafts before plenty of times, but they were nothing like this! If whatever was going on didn't stop soon, it would rip my wings off! I yanked the throttle closed, but it had no effect whatsoever.

I was as close to a state of panic as I'd ever been in the cockpit of an airplane when the mystery ship's spotlight went out and my climb gradually came to a stop like an elevator reaching the top floor. The altimeter was pointing to 17,500 feet. G for George had climbed at least 12,000 feet in less time than it takes me to tell it!

Lowering the nose I began a slow descent and looked around for the mystery ship. I spotted it directly in front of my nose. I could see the white light surrounded by the flashing red lights again, just as I had when the ship was following me. Either that ship looked the same from both ends or it was flying backwards, which at this point would not have surprised me in the least. I was wondering what the pilot was planning next when the ship bobbed at me—almost like a nod of recognition—and shot away to the east. In a matter of seconds it was completely out of sight.

I descended into Los Angeles and landed at Mines Field without further incident, which almost disappointed me. After parking G for George in one of the North American hangars, I gave her an affectionate pat on the wing. I was pretty sure she and I had just witnessed something few pilots would ever see.

Outside, I leaned against the hanger wall, lit a smoke, and stared up at the twinkling stars. Somewhere up there on a planet orbiting around one of those little stars I figured a pilot was telling his buddies about the grand time he had scaring the living daylights out of some Earthman who'd been flying around in an ancient aircraft with wings and a propeller. I tossed him a salute and said, "Thanks for stoppin' by, pal. Drop in again sometime when you're out this way."

## THE END

# E A

*The Hoax*

*In 1937 the United States launched a daring spy mission to learn what the Japanese were up to in the South Pacific. The secrecy of that mission depended on the perpetration of an audacious hoax with international implications. Ultimately the mission was a complete success, but the hoax contained at its heart a single human flaw. That flaw exposed the cover up just long enough for one man to learn the truth. E A is that man's story.*

## San Francisco Municipal Airport (Mills Field)
## 18 June, 1947

At three a.m. Mills Field was quiet as a graveyard. A soggy wool blanket of San Francisco fog hanging over the runways swallowed up the rasp of my shoes on wet concrete and drizzled its silent silver mist through the glare from hangar floodlights. A shiny new United DC-4 Mainliner stood quietly dripping next to the terminal building while half a dozen DC-3s poked their blunt noses out of the shadows surrounding the parking ramp. From where I stood, the only signs of life on the field were the throbbing in my head and a lingering ache inside the plaster cast encasing my right arm.

The pain killer they gave me at the hospital wasn't putting up much of a fight, but the doctor expected me to stay in bed where anyone with a concussion and a lick of sense should be. Apparently I didn't have a lick of sense. What I did have was an intense need to solve a mystery, and to do that I had to be at the airfield.

Our old C-47 war horse was the last ship on the ramp. It stood out from its DC-3 twin sisters because of the leaping cat silhouette on its broad tail fin. The cat seemed an appropriate insignia for an outfit calling itself Coastal Air Transport, or C-A-T for short. If things really happened the way my scrambled brains remembered them, the solution to my mystery was in the cockpit of that ship. What I found there would either make sense out of my confusion or prove beyond a doubt that I was due for a Section Eight.

During the taxi ride from the hospital I thought it all through for the umpteenth time, methodically examining the past two-and-a-half years of my life beginning with the day everything changed. That was 12 November, 1945—the day I came home to Los Angeles after three years of touring Europe from the driver's seat of a B-17. I survived thirty-four bombing missions over Germany, so I figured returning to the minor trials and tribulations of civilian life would be a piece of cake. Brother, was I off the beam!

## Los Angeles - November, 1945

My best friend, Nate Parsons, was already home from island-hopping around the Pacific. Before the war we were both loyal employees of Trans-National Airways. I flew their DC-3s on cross-country passenger routes and Nate was TNA's Operations Manager. Then, while we were busy saving the world from Nazis and Japs, Trans-National was bought out by another line. So when we showed up expecting to get our jobs back like the government said we would, the airline simply said our jobs didn't exist anymore. That left Nate and me out pounding the pavement with a zillion other unemployed GIs.

B-24 "LIBERATOR"

It was a bad time to be an out-of-work pilot. What was an elite profession before the war was suddenly loaded with die-cast throttle jockeys cranked out by Uncle Sam's instant pilot factories.

Now don't read me wrong on this. I've got a lot of respect for guys who logged their two hundredth hour trying to keep a B-24 in the air while a bunch of Krauts in Messerschmitt 109s turned the bomber into Swiss cheese. But the war was over and it seemed like the civilian airline jobs should go to guys like Nate and me—guys who helped build commercial aviation into a thriving industry before the war.

Unfortunately, the airlines didn't see it that way. They could hire less experienced pilots for less money, so while I was holding out for a fair wage, the demand for commercial pilots evaporated. And if my prospects were poor, Nate's were downright lousy. He left most of his left arm on some obscure atoll out in the Pacific, and hero or not, there weren't a lot of openings for one-armed airline executives.

We both saved a few bucks before the war, so we weren't starving, but concern over the rapidly dwindling balance in my retirement fund had me scraping close to the bottom of the employment barrel. Then one morning when I was about to leave for a job interview with an auto insurance company, Nate called and asked me to meet him for coffee.

He said he had a proposition to discuss with me. He wouldn't say what his idea was, just that it had something to do with our employment prospects or the lack thereof. In my frame of mind, the simple fact that Nate had an idea was justification for canceling my interview with the insurance company. We met at our old hangout, a doughnut shop in Inglewood near Mines Field.

Nate is one of those freckle-faced redheads who will still look twenty when he's fifty, and on those occasions when he's particularly pleased with himself, Nate gets a twinkle in his eyes you can see fifty yards away. The twinkle was turned up to full power that morning. Nate greeted me with enthusiasm and got right down to brass tacks. "Chip, I've been thinking about our situation, and I have the answer."

"Great, I'm all ears!"

He dunked his glazed old fashioned and said, "It's so damned simple I can't think why we didn't figure it out before. If we can't find jobs doing what we do best, we make our own jobs."

"Brilliant, Einstein! And while we're at it, let's hire ourselves on at about fifty-thousand per."

Nate concentrated on his dunking. "Okay, if you don't want to hear the best idea I ever had . . . ."

I sighed. "Sorry, Nate. Tell me your idea."

He began by reminding me of some things I already knew. The air cargo business was booming. In fact, there was so much business, the big carriers could afford to be choosey about the freight they flew. Since there was more money to be made on big loads and long hauls, large cross-country shippers got the good rates. The little guys who needed short-haul service either paid through the nose or sent their freight by truck.

Nate said he looked into things and figured there was enough cargo business for a few small enterprising companies flying the San Francisco-Los Angeles route at a reasonable rate to make a profit. In a nutshell, Nate's plan was that he and I should start such a company.

I was dubious, to say the least. "That's all fine and dandy, Amigo, but where do we get the moolah to buy airplanes and hire pilots?"

"That's the beauty of it! We don't need a whole fleet of ships to start with. We can do it with one plane. And you'll do the flying, so the only employees we'll need are a copilot, a reliable mechanic and an agent in San Francisco. Alice and I can handle the operations from this end. Then, after we get established, we can add a ship or two and expand our route up the coast to Portland and Seattle."

Alice is Nate's wife and she's a real go-getter. I had no doubt that between them Nate and Alice could easily run a small cargo airline, but that was the only part of his plan in which I had any faith. "Nate, we'd have to have a big, economical twin, like a DC-3, and unless Don Douglas is givin' 'em away, I don't know how the hell we can afford one."

DC-3 (C-47/R4D)

"Douglas isn't givin' ships away, but our good old Uncle Sam is. At least, he's selling them so cheap that even we can afford one. Hell, between us we've collected enough overseas points the War Assets Administration will probably pay us for taking a surplus R4D off their hands.

"Plus we both have a little cash stashed. If we put our savings together, we've got enough to convince a bank that we're serious about this thing. Add our combined experience to all that, and I think we've got a damned good chance of getting a loan to make this thing work."

The airplanes Uncle Sam was selling so cheaply were surplus R4Ds and C-47s, the Navy and Army transport versions of the DC-3. Most of them were beat to hell during the war, but I heard that if you picked the right ship, there were a few good deals to be made.

Even if we found a good ship to buy cheap, there would still be fuel, maintenance, and a hundred other operating costs I couldn't even begin to think of. Nate had it all figured out, though, right down to the last detail, and his arguments were pretty convincing. In the end I agreed to part with what was left of my savings in exchange for becoming Coastal Air Transport's Chief Pilot. Nate was right about one thing for sure. Landing a job is a lot easier when you own the company. It turned out he was right about everything else, too.

We celebrated C-A-T's first anniversary by extending our route to Seattle with a stop in Portland. At the end of our second year we were in the black with two ships and ten employees.

I give Nate and Alice full credit for our success. They did the hard part. Aside from a lot of monotony during long hours in the cockpit, the only real problems I had to contend with were occasional bad weather and a copilot with a taste for booze. I couldn't do anything about the weather, but I sure as hell did something about the copilot.

Don wasn't drinking that much at first. Sure, he'd be out late once in a while and show up with a hangover the next morning, but he still did his job. Then his nights on the town and his hangovers grew more frequent to the point he was all but worthless in the air, to say nothing of the Civil Aeronautics Board rules he was violating. It was a bum deal because sober, Don was a pretty conscientious guy.

The last straw came about an hour out of Portland on a bumpy southbound flight. Don said he was going back to check the cargo tie-downs, and when he was gone longer than he should have been, I leaned over and looked back through the cockpit door to see if he was having trouble with the load. I could see him back there all right, but the only load he was concerned with was the one he was taking on from a pint of Old Forester.

C-47 CARGO AREA

When we landed in Los Angeles I told Don I had no use for a drunk in the cockpit and to get his last check from Alice because he was through flying for C-A-T. Surprisingly, he didn't put up an argument. He just accepted the situation like he'd been expecting it and walked off.

Nate didn't take it nearly as well. "Geez, Chip! Couldn't you have waited a little before canning the guy so we'd have time to find a replacement? How we gonna keep the schedule?"

"I don't think you heard what I said, Nate. The guy was tying one on right there in the cargo bay at ten-thousand feet! I've got enough to do up there without nurse-maiding a damned drunk! I'd sooner fly the ship all by myself."

As it turned out, I didn't have to fly by myself. An old Trans-National buddy, Jack Titus, had two weeks' vacation coming from Pan American. For old time's sake and a few bucks under the table, he agreed to fly the right seat while Nate looked for a new copilot.

Truthfully, I felt a little guilty about sticking Nate with the problem. Two years earlier we could have tacked a note to the nearest telephone pole and there would have been out of work fliers lined up around the block within an hour. But things had changed.

Most ex-G.I. pilots had either found flying jobs or they were selling shoes and insurance. The glut was over and qualified pilots were getting hard to find again. Also, I hadn't made Nate's job any easier by telling him in no uncertain terms that I wanted a right-seat jockey with absolutely no vices . . . no womanizing, no boozing, no nothing!

Nate mumbled something about finding a saint with wings and set off on his quest. Two weeks later, after my last trip with Jack, I went to see what sort of whiz-kid Nate had hired—assuming he'd found a whiz-kid to hire.

I should have been suspicious the minute I walked into his office. Nate's twinkle flashed to high beam and he greeted me with a good deal more enthusiasm than usual. I said, "From the way you're grinnin' like the Cheshire cat, I gather you've got good news."

"I have indeed, Chip, old boy. After a meticulous and exhaustive search, I have found you the perfect copilot."

Figuring there had to be catch, I asked, "Has he got multi-engine time?"

"Tons of it—a fat logbook with scads of time in Threes, 247s and Electras."

"What about the other stuff? Is he reliable?"

"This pilot is just exactly what you ordered. There's no problem with booze, and I guarantee there will be no womanizing."

By this time I was skeptical as hell. "Okay, what's the catch? If this guy's so wonderful, how come he's available?"

"Been flying out on the east coast and got tired of the lousy weather. Came into LA a few days ago and heard about our opening."

I relaxed a little. Maybe Nate really had found a saint with wings. "Okay. I'd like to check this guy out before our first trip together on Monday. When do I meet him?"

"I told her to stop by this afternoon. She should be here any minute."

I came out of my chair like a V-2 rocket! "SHE? Geez, Nate! You didn't hire a woman? Tell me you didn't do that to me!"

"Calm down, partner. You'll like her. She's got great qualifications, and she's straight as an arrow. This gal's just what the doctor ordered."

"Not this doctor, buddy boy!"

"Aw, come on, Chip. What's so wrong with havin' a woman in the right seat?"

"What's wrong? I'll tell you what's wrong. There isn't a woman born who can think about anything besides her looks long enough to drive an automobile safely, let alone fly an airplane."

I was just getting warmed up, and Nate looked like he was having the time of his life. If this was his way of getting even with me for firing Don at the last minute, he wasn't gonna get away with it. "Hell, Nate, we'll spend all our time mushin' around the pattern waitin' for her to get her face out of a mirror long enough to lower the gear!"

Unfortunately, I was so busy fussing and fuming I didn't hear the office door open behind me. So when someone behind me responded to my tirade, it took me by surprise. "I assure you, Captain Williams, the gear will be down just as soon as you ask for it."

The female voice was rich and low-pitched. It carried no hint of irritation. She was just stating fact, and that was that. I felt my face redden as I turned around. Nate put his hand on my shoulder and said, "Chip, Old Pal, meet your new copilot, Emily Aarons. Miss Aarons, as you've already concluded, this is Coastal Air Transport's Chief Pilot, Chip Williams."

Emily Aarons was tall and slender in baggy white slacks and a dark blue sweater under a well-worn leather flight jacket with a blue and white scarf tied cowboy-style around her neck. She had high cheekbones and narrow features that were softened a little by auburn hair that hung almost to her shoulders. She wasn't bad looking, but dressed that way, you'd be hard pressed to tell at a distance whether Emily Aarons was a he or a she.

I shook the hand she offered and stammered what I hoped

sounded like a sincere apology. "I'm sorry you had to hear that outburst, Miss Aarons. Please understand, I have nothing against you personally. I just don't feel . . . I mean . . . ."

"I didn't take your comments personally, Captain Williams, but I think you ought to give me a chance before putting me in the same category with an old girlfriend or whoever it was that gave you such a low opinion of women."

I felt my face heating up all over again, and I was about to tell Miss Emily Aarons where to get off in no uncertain terms when Nate stepped between us. "Now, children, let's play nice. Chip, why don't you show Emily around? I'm sure she'd appreciate a personal tour."

Nate didn't leave me a whole lot of choice in the matter, so I showed her around, all the while vowing that this matter was by no means settled. As we walked through the hangar, you could have carried the silence between us in buckets. I was somewhat relieved to discover, however, that Miss Aarons really did know her way around a C-47. While I wasn't looking forward to Monday's flight, I was heartened by the knowledge that there certainly wouldn't be a lot of unnecessary chitchat in the cockpit.

The way things went, the following week turned out to be a big lesson in humility for yours truly. Emily Aarons was all business. She carried out my orders efficiently with an uncanny knack for anticipating what needed to be done. Copilots don't come with that kind of smarts built in so I began to wonder where she learned her stuff. Wherever it was, she obviously knew what she was doing, and in an effort to give credit where due, I told her so. Emily thanked me for the compliment, but there was something in her smile and tone of voice that made me feel like I just told Joe DiMaggio he was a pretty fair ball player.

The ice was broken, though, and during the next few weeks we even began to develop a little of the camaraderie I experienced with flight crews during the war. The biggest difference was that the favorite topics of conversation then were mostly friends and family back home. Emily talked about neither, except once. We were northbound out of San Francisco and the subject of booze came up. I was telling Emily how I caught her predecessor drinking on the job, and quickly found out we'd hit a subject about which she had strong feelings.

When I finished the story she said, "You really have to wonder about a flier like that. They say alcoholics drink to escape reality, but with all this freedom," she gestured toward the brilliant blue sky beyond our windshield, "Why would anybody need to drink?

"I knew a fellow once who was probably the best navigator in the business. But he started drinking, and after that, the only fliers who would touch him with a ten-foot pole were the ones who knew him before and felt sorry for him. He navigated for me a few times, and the last time, when the pressure was really on us to hit our spot, he let me down and very nearly got us both killed."

It was the only time Emily ever talked about her past or people she knew. Maybe that aura of mystery was one of the reasons I found myself more and more attracted to her. Whatever the attraction, I enjoyed flying with Emily and we even began spending time together on the ground.

We would meet on our Sundays off for a steamer trip to Catalina or an afternoon on the pier at Santa Monica. Emily didn't care for crowds, though, so more often we took a picnic up to the less populated beaches near Ventura.

On those occasions she was perfectly content to sit on a rock and watch the breakers. Or she got out her notebook and wrote. Emily never showed me what was in the notebook, but I could tell she was writing something serious because her mood became contemplative and she would stare out at the ocean for long moments between writing lines on the page.

Then her mood would suddenly change to giddiness and I would find myself challenged to a sprint through the surf or a footrace out to the point and back. As the day cooled, we would build a driftwood fire and huddle close to it while we enjoyed spectacular Pacific sunsets.

I can't recall ever being happier than I was during those lazy days off at the beach, and on our last Sunday together, Emily let me know she felt the same way. As we watched the red sun-disk turn our ocean from deep blue to fiery orange, she kissed my cheek.

"Mmm, what was that for?"

She said quietly, "That was for being the way you are and for letting me be the way I am."

"Oh? And how are you?"

"Content . . . free . . . far from people who want to hold me down."

I put my arm around her, and she leaned against my shoulder.

Then, as the Pacific's orange glow faded to black velvet, a friendship that grew out of animosity turned into love.

## San Francisco Municipal Airport (Mills Field)
## 18 June, 1947

Since that night, Emily and I had flown more than a thousand miles, from Los Angeles to Seattle and back here to San Francisco. Now I would be making the last leg of our trip without her.

My bum arm turned the simple job of opening the small passenger door set in the C-47's cargo hatch into a task of monumental proportions. When I finally mastered it and scrambled inside, the hangar lights cast distorted shadows against the curved interior walls and gave the empty cargo bay a gloomy feeling that was a perfect match for my mood.

To my right, the toilet compartment hatch and the smaller tail access hatch beyond it were still open, just the way I left them twenty-thousand feet above Eureka, California. Under the circumstances, though, I was pretty sure the Gods of Aviation would forgive me for not battening down all the hatches.

We climbed out of Seattle yesterday morning into a glorious sunrise. The sun always seems brighter after a storm cleans the air, and old Sol was in all his glory. A fierce weather front had moved down from the north during the night, and we caught up with the tail end of it just as we entered the pattern at Portland-Columbia. The field was thoroughly drenched, and we heard the spray kicked up by our main gear as we splashed through puddles the size of small lakes.

While C-A-T's Portland agent directed the loading and unloading of our cargo, Emily and I headed into the terminal for coffee and a weather briefing. The Java was bad and the briefing was worse.

We were chasing a wide front that extended nearly two hundred miles inland from the coast. The only good news was that the front was moving southeast. If we jogged west and followed the coastline rather than taking a straight-line route to San Francisco, we could slip through the trailing edge of the storm. We would still get wet, but we'd miss the worst of it. The plan looked okay on paper, but half an hour out of Portland we were in the soup up to our necks.

The C-47 is a tough old bird, and every pilot who's ever logged time in one has a hair-raising tale or two about how the Gooney

Bird managed to get him out of some impossible predicament he should have had sense enough to avoid in the first place. In spite of the plane's tough reputation, however, even experienced pilots have some doubts when flying into a storm like the one we were facing.

The rain pounding against our thin aluminum skin sounded like someone was out there slinging handfuls of gravel at us. The airframe creaked and groaned loudly as we rode out the endless turbulence, and water leaked in around the windshield panels like they weren't even there.

Emily and I had flown through weather before, and though our pulses were probably up a beat or two, neither of us felt any panic. In fact, I was even feeling a bit of exhilaration . . . until the first brilliant flash of lightning lit up the cockpit.

While it would take one hell of a storm to tear a C-47 apart, it only takes one lightning strike to knock out the ship's electrical system. Even then, the old bird will keep on flying. It's the risk of fire you worry about. When wires designed to carry twenty-four volts are suddenly charged with ten thousand times that amount, insulation melts instantly and sparks fly.

The greatest danger we faced, however, was icing. Flying through cold air loaded with moisture causes thin layers of ice buildup along the leading edges of the wings and tail surfaces. The shapes of those surfaces were carefully designed to provide the lift that keeps a ship in the air, so when ice layers change those shapes enough to affect the flow of air over them, flight characteristics change drastically for the worse.

The designers of the C-47 anticipated the possibility that some fool might fly their airplane into icing conditions, though, and provided pneumatic deicing boots along the leading edges of the wings and tail. The idea is, after a little ice builds up, you press a button that inflates black rubber boots enough to break the ice free. It's a simple system that usually works.

Since leaving Portland we inflated the deicing boots three times. We could see the ice forming along the leading edges of the wings, and when I began feeling sluggishness in the controls, Emily pushed the button and the ice broke away. The last time, however, I still felt stiffness in the rudder pedals after deicing.

My first guess was the deicing boot on the tail fin had failed to operate. Since we couldn't see the tail from the cockpit, I asked Emily to slip back into the radio compartment and take a look through the astral dome—a small Plexiglas bubble in the roof designed for use by those intrepid navigators who still knew how to operate a sextant. At least it's handy for looking at the tail.

Emily reported she couldn't see any ice on the tail fin or around the rudder. I tried the pedals again, and it took a lot of pressure to induce the slightest yawing motion. Something was definitely out of whack back there. Then I remembered the puddles on Portland's runway and came up with a pretty fair guess as to what was wrong. I told Emily to take over while I grabbed the flashlight and headed aft.

Douglas engineers built a lot of range into the C-47, and knowing pilots tend to consume considerable quantities of coffee, the engineers thoughtfully provided a toilet behind the cargo bay. In the aft bulkhead of the toilet compartment, there is a small hatch which gives access to the tail section of the fuselage. A quick inspection of this tiny compartment with the flashlight confirmed my suspicions. Everything was covered with a thick coating of ice, including the rudder control cables. The ice was making it difficult for the cables to do their job. I even had a pretty good idea how all that ice got there.

TAIL GEAR STRUT

The C-47's tail wheel strut extends down through a hole in the fuselage. Originally, there was a rubber boot around the strut to seal the opening, but over time the boots disintegrate and no one bothers to replace them. As a result, a lot of water splashed up through the hole during our landing and takeoff at Portland. It wasn't something that happened very often, and even when it did, water in the tail section wasn't a serious problem—unless you happened to be flying through extremely cold air, which was exactly what we happened to be doing.

I shook my head at the ice coating the braided-wire rudder control cables and their pulleys. At least the problem was correctable. I fished out my pocket knife to scrape the ice away and squeezed my shoulders through the small hatch so I could reach each entire cable. It was colder than Greenland back there and my fingers quickly went numb. I thought about going forward to warm up, but the ice was chipping away fairly easily, so I stayed with it to finish the job.

Next to the cold, the toughest part of the job was the turbulence. Back there, as far from the supporting wings as I could be, it was like riding a bucking bronco. To reach the rearmost sections of cable, I braced my hand against the tail wheel strut, which tilts forward at about a thirty degree angle. Just as I reached past the strut and leaned aft, the ship gave one hell of a lurch. I felt my hand slipping down the strut's frosty surface and I remember seeing the tail plane cross-member flying up at my face.

"Chip! Chip, wake up!"

I wished she wouldn't yell like that. My head was already pounding like a bass drum and . . . . A sharp movement of the ship sent a lightning bolt of pain through my right arm and jolted me wide awake.

Emily yelled in my ear again. "Chip, I can't stay back here. The autopilot won't hold it for long. Can you make it forward?"

I nodded with more confidence than I felt, and she hurried back to the cockpit. Besides the pain in my head and arm, there also seemed to be a little problem with my vision. I wasn't exactly seeing two of everything, but what I did see was fuzzy and a little dim around the edges.

Recovering the flashlight from the compartment floor, I worked my way forward past our cargo, but it was slow going. My head kept spinning, and I had to stop several times to regain my balance and fight down nausea. Eventually, I made it and even had the presence of mind to grab the first-aid kit from its brackets on the cargo bay forward bulkhead before stepping into the cockpit.

Emily had moved to the left seat. It's easier for a right-handed pilot to fly the ship from there, and it was obvious she was going to be doing the flying for a while. I fell into the right seat and managed to get the belt across my lap so I'd stay there. My next concern was doing something about the pounding in my head and the pain in my right arm. It would be a hell of a lot easier to think clearly without those distractions.

I found some aspirin in the first-aid kit and forced a few of the little white pills down. I was sort of sitting there in a daze, waiting for the aspirin to do something, when Emily nudged my arm. I turned and she yelled to be heard over the combined racket of our engines and the storm. "Chip, put something on that head wound to stop the bleeding."

Dimly wondering what head wound she was talking about, I reached up and wiped at my forehead. Even in the dark cockpit, I saw the blood on my hand. There was an alarming amount of it.

Doing everything one-handed was awkward as hell, but I finally got a roll of gauze wrapped and taped around my head. Then I used the rag we kept in the cockpit for mopping up windshield leaks to wipe away some of the blood from my face and jacket. If nothing else, I was determined to be tidy.

I looked at Emily again and she nodded approval of my first aid technique. I felt rather pleased with myself and decided to tackle the next challenge, which was to find some way of keeping my right arm pinned in place. The arm was obviously broken, and every time the ship was jarred by turbulence, I got a jolt of pain like an electric shock.

Emily saw me grappling with the problem and came to the rescue again. She hollered, "There's a long scarf in my flight bag. Use it for a sling."

Her bag was jammed down along the right side of my seat and getting into it with my left hand took some doing. When I finally found the scarf, tying it into a sling became a whole new challenge which I managed to meet with the help of my teeth. But once I had it around my neck, the makeshift sling worked pretty well. "Wow," I thought, "a white silk sling-monogrammed, no less. I'm really traveling in style!"

The first-aid chores completed, I turned what attention I could muster to our situation. Even with something less than twenty-twenty vision I could see it was considerably darker outside than it was before I went aft. That meant the clouds above us were getting denser and every turn of the props was pulling us deeper into the heart of the storm.

About that time I remembered why I'd gone aft in the first place. I yelled across the cockpit, "How are the rudder pedals?"

She yelled back, "They're freer now. Whatever you did solved the problem."

"It was ice on the cables."

Emily nodded and returned her attention to the job at hand. She was doing just fine on her own, but it seemed like I ought to be contributing something to the task of getting us back in one piece. I stared at the jiggling instruments in front of me and tried to make some sense out of their gyrating needles.

The magnetic compass ball bounced around between one-sixty and one-ninety. That meant we'd passed Eureka, a coastal community just south of the California-Oregon border, and Emily had already made the course change that was taking us down along the coast to San Francisco. The airspeed indicator was swinging back and forth over the two-ten mark. Since Eureka is about two hundred and fifty miles from San Francisco, we had less than an hour to go—that is, if the heavy winds hadn't blown us off course or altered our ground speed too much.

As I studied the instruments, lightning lit the cockpit like a flashbulb. For a second Emily's face was captured in its harsh blue-white light, like a Kodak snapshot. There was no hint of panic in her expression, only calm determination. If I hadn't already known it, I knew it then for sure; Emily had been here before.

Seconds later another brilliant flash lit up the cockpit and the ship lurched with a bang. We'd been hit! Sparks flew from under the instrument panel and clouds of acrid fumes burned my nose and throat. Almost immediately there was a loud snap and the instrument panel lights winked out.

I was still struggling with my seat belt buckle so I could reach the fire extinguisher on the bulkhead behind me when I realized the smoke was clearing. The snap we heard was the circuit breakers kicking in. They popped under the high voltage load, which prevented a fire, but the acrid smoke told us the breakers and a fair amount of wiring had been fried in the process. That meant we would be making the rest of the trip without radios, instrument lights, or anything else that ran on electricity.

I dug the flashlight out and pointed it toward the panel in front of Emily. I held the beam of light as steady as I could, but the turbulence made it dance over the instrument faces like a drunken firefly.

"There," Emily yelled. "Point it over there!"

She was gesturing to the engine instruments at the center of the panel. It took a moment, but I finally spotted the problem. The needle on the starboard engine oil temperature gauge was over in the red and the corresponding oil pressure gauge was pointing at zero. Since neither of these gauges was electrical, there was no reason to doubt what they were telling us. They were stating the undeniable fact that the big fourteen-cylinder Pratt and Whitney radial just beyond my cockpit window was about to pack it in.

After the lightning strike, the engine failure didn't surprise me, even though the two problems were probably unrelated. It stood to reason something else was bound to break because, on an airplane, things never go wrong one at a time.

The engine might have run a while longer if Emily hadn't cut its magneto switch and feathered the prop, but shutting the engine down reduced the risk of fire and probably saved us the considerable difference in cost between a rebuild job and a new engine. As the starboard prop spun to a stop, the reliable old C-47 did exactly what she was supposed to do; she yawed hard to starboard, turning toward the dead engine.

Emily shoved the port throttle forward to compensate for the loss of power and stomped hard on the left rudder peddle to keep us headed in the right direction. With the engine failure Emily's job got twice as hard. She had to adjust the rudder trim to avoid flying with constant pressure on the left rudder pedal.

Also, altitude was now a serious concern. Under normal circumstances the ship could hold its altitude on one engine, but bouncing around in the storm with a full cargo hold left our faithful craft clawing at the air for dear life and gradually losing her grip.

I renewed my efforts to keep the flashlight aimed at her side of the panel. I also stared into the massive black clouds beyond our windshield and forced my fuzzy brain to think about how the hell we were going to get out of this mess.

Essentially, we were the pastrami in a cloud sandwich. There was a thick layer about two thousand feet over our heads and another about a thousand feet below us. The storm obviously wasn't behaving the way the Portland weather guys predicted. My guess was the front hadn't moved as far east as expected and we'd stumbled right into the heart of it. On the plus side, we had fuel to spare, and Emily was doing a good job of hanging on to as much of our altitude as possible. So unless we lost the other engine or something equally disastrous happened, we would make it to San Francisco. The question was, what would we find when we got there?

Mills Field is a busy airport right on the edge of San Francisco Bay, which is surrounded by hills and countless manmade obstacles, like radio antennas and bridge towers. In other words, it's a lousy place to be when you can't see what's in front of you during a landing approach.

If the cloud deck below us wasn't too thick, the visibility under it might not be bad, but without a radio, the only way to find out was to go down and take a look for ourselves. That wasn't a good idea for two reasons. First, there was a range of mountains along the coast below us. Without knowing our exact position the odds of flying into a chunk of cumulus granite were pretty good. And even if we avoided a collision with terra firma, we didn't have the power to climb back up through the clouds on one engine. We'd be stuck down on the deck whether we found better visibility or not.

Suddenly a down draft dropped us thirty or forty feet and we hit bottom with a jar that sent needles through my broken arm. I must have winced because Emily looked over and yelled, "How are you doing, Chip? You gonna make it?"

"Hell, yes! I feel great! I'm just featherbedding over here so you can get some stick time."

She smiled briefly at my attempted humor and said, "I think we're about thirty minutes out now. What do you want to do?"

Obviously Emily had also been considering our situation and hadn't come up with any brilliant solutions either, but it was decision time, so I took my best guess. "We should have more than ninety minutes of fuel left. How 'bout dropping down on top of those clouds so we can hunt around for a hole and maybe see what's under this mess?"

"You think we'll find one?"

"Do we have any choice?"

With a grim nod, Emily gently pushed the ship's nose over. The turbulence got noticeably more violent with every foot of altitude we lost, and by the time Emily leveled off a hundred feet above the clouds, we were bouncing around like a ping pong ball.

I leaned close to the cockpit window on my side and searched the thick swirling mass below us for a hole or a spot thin enough to give me some idea how far down the cloud deck extended. It didn't look promising.

Most of the turbulence we were experiencing was vertical-sharp up and down jolts-and I had braced myself accordingly. That's why I wasn't prepared for what happened next. Suddenly the ship rolled right, then back to the left with a violent jerk. My forehead smacked the window with a resounding thud and the clouds in my brain turned as black as the ones outside. I went out like a cheap light bulb.

The next thing I remember was wondering where the guys in the white coats came from. I was pretty sure we didn't have any passengers aboard when we left Portland. I looked around, and I could see rain still beating against the windshield. I was rather surprised, however, to see that the Mills Field terminal building was also out there. Somehow, I astutely observed, Emily had managed to get us down in one piece without any assistance from me.

Therefore, I concluded, the fellows fussing over me were much more likely to be ambulance attendants than stowaways. One of them was splinting my right arm. He tossed my makeshift sling on the cockpit floor, and then the other guy helped manhandle me onto a stretcher in the radio compartment.

The next solid piece of reality I grabbed hold of came in the shape of a hospital room. Along with my clothes, my watch was missing, so I had no idea how much time had passed since my last peek at the real world.

A large nurse, who bore a striking resemblance to my bootcamp drill sergeant, marched in while I was trying to sort things out. She informed me it was eight p.m. and I was being treated for a concussion and a broken arm. After some poking and prodding, she also let me in on the news that I was feeling much better and wanted something to eat.

I told her I wasn't hungry, but Sergeant Nurse returned a few minutes later with a dinner tray. If I wanted to get well, she explained, I was to eat every yummy bite. In passing, she mentioned that the adorable little lady who came in with me had left with her friends, but would no doubt be back in the morning. In the meantime, I could read the note she left me.

> Freedom was the reward offered for
> Courageous deed,
> But when the battle's won, the payment
> They won't concede.
> They say the bill's too high. They can't
> Afford the cost.
> So the reward for freedom's flight is only
> Freedom lost.
>
> CHIP,
> MAYBE YOU UNDERSTAND WHY I HAVE TO LEAVE. IF NOT,
> AT LEAST UNDERSTAND THAT I DO NOT LEAVE BY CHOICE.
> THOUGH THIS WAS BOUND TO HAPPEN, I PRAYED IT WOULD
> NOT. TREASURE THE MEMORIES OF OUR TIME TOGETHER
> AS DO I AND KNOW I WILL LOVE YOU ALWAYS.
> EMILY

The envelope on my dinner tray was addressed to "Chip" in the same precise printing I'd seen in Emily's logbook. I expected the note to include some explanation of how we got down through the storm or at least some word about when she'd be back to see me. Instead, what I found was a poem. The paper was a little worn, as if she'd been carrying it around for some time. The words were curious.

I read the note addressed to me at the bottom over and over, but its meaning eluded me. Why did she have to leave? What was bound to happen? And what in blazes was the poem supposed to mean?

When the nurse showed up again, she was quite upset with me for not touching my dinner. I tried to cheer her up by obediently swallowing the pill she brought me. Then I asked, "You said the lady who came with me left with some friends. Did you see them?"

"Oh, yes. Two gentlemen came in a little after she got here. They talked for a while out in the corridor, and then they all left together."

"Did she seem happy to see them?"

"I wouldn't know about that, but they seemed very friendly when they stopped at the desk to ask which room you were in." She thought for a moment and added, "One of the gentlemen was a naval officer—a captain, I believe. Now get some sleep. She'll be back to see you in the morning."

Given the finality of Emily's note, that seemed highly unlikely. There was something very wrong about all of this, but I couldn't seem to focus on the details. Finally it dawned on me that the pill I obediently swallowed was a Mickey. I floated away on a heaving sea of nightmares.

## Mills Hospital, Burlingame, California
### 18 June, 1947

Emily and I were on the beach at Ventura when the sky suddenly turned dark and a fierce storm blew in. I gathered up our blanket and picnic basket so we could run to the car, but when I looked up again, Emily was gone. I started searching for her. Suddenly I had help—lots of help. Hundreds of sailors were running all over the beach, and they were looking for her, too.

The newspaper reported Emily's disappearance on the front page. They printed her picture and the headline, "A. E.

Disappears! Navy Searches South Pacific for Lost Aviatrix."

I tried to tell them they had it all wrong. Emily hadn't disappeared in the South Pacific, and the newspapers printed her initials backwards. They were E. A., not A. E. I kept waving her monogrammed scarf at them to prove it, but the headlines kept screaming, "A. E.! A. E.! A. E.!"

I woke up slowly and the nightmare images gradually dissolved into those of the real world, my darkened hospital room, the heavy plaster cast on my arm, and the empty feeling you get when someone you love leaves your life. The pictures from my dream were still there, too. And as I reexamined those images, I realized they weren't all products of my imagination. Some of them were as real as the stiffly starched pillow case under my head.

In an instant of what seemed like very clear thinking, I put it all together. But what I'd figured out couldn't be. There had to be another explanation. Or did there? How could I find out?

The monogram on Emily's scarf! If she didn't pick it up when we left the ship, the scarf would still be on the cockpit floor where the ambulance attendant dropped it.

Trying gamely to ignore the pounding in my head, I climbed out of bed and found my clothes in a small closet near the door. I put them on, and with my leather flight jacket half on and half draped over my right shoulder, I walked out.

Sergeant Nurse stopped me in the corridor and ordered me back to bed. When I finally convinced her that I was really leaving, she grudgingly gave me my watch and wallet in exchange for a promise to come back and settle my bill when the administration office opened later. It was a few minutes after two a.m. when I called Yellow Cab from a public telephone in the hospital lobby.

Now the moment of truth—or what I hoped would be a moment of truth—was here. I stepped through the radio compartment and into the cockpit. My heart pounded and my head kept time with it as I leaned over to look for the scarf.

It wasn't there. Cursing myself for running off on a fool's errand, I halfheartedly groped further back under the right seat. Then my fingers touched silk. I grabbed the scarf and turned quickly to read the monogram in the light coming through the windshield. They were an "A" and an "E" in that order.

# EPILOGUE

I never saw Emily Aarons again. I have a picture of her,

though; one I carefully clipped out of a decade-old Life Magazine. I keep it and Emily's note wrapped up in her silk scarf.

MISSING AVIATRIX
AMELIA EARHART

Every so often, usually when I'm feeling a little lonely, I get the small bundle out of my top dresser drawer and reread the note she left for me at the hospital. Then I look at the photo. She's a little younger in the picture and her hair was much shorter when the photo was made, but the eyes are the same. They look back at me from the magazine photo with a hint of amusement, as though the world was a joke and she was the only one who knew the punch line.

No, that isn't quite right. She chose to share the joke with me. And sometimes I even appreciate the humor in it.

## THE END

# A Song For Ally

Saturday, May 5, 2018
Sunset Cabaret, Hollywood

We were finishing up the first week of a guaranteed one month booking at the Sunset Cabaret and we all agreed it was just about the best gig we've ever had. The money was good and the crowds were great.

A decade of playing clubs from one end of LA to the other taught us that crowds out on the west side could be downright brutal if they didn't like the band, but we'd found ourselves a gem this time. In case you're wondering, "we" are Jimmy Bishop, that's me, and the Temescal Canyon Band, the five guys who make me sound good. We play a little bit of everything—blues, rock, jazz, and even disco if the audience wants to hear it.

Besides landing the Sunset Cabaret gig, we had even more good fortune to keep us smiling. A month or so ago we released a single, and after bouncing around just below the charts for what seemed like forever, SHOW ME YOUR HEART suddenly took off. We were about half-way to the top of the Billboard Top 100 and still climbing. That made us six of the happiest guys on the west coast.

The next fortune we encountered came directly at me and it took a while to find out if it was good fortune or bad. I noticed her at the club the first Saturday night we played there. She was sitting at the back of the room with some girlfriends and she didn't look like she was having a good time. In appearance, she was a strikingly attractive tall blonde who would stand out in any crowd, but she was doing her best to make herself invisible—kind of looking down at the table except when we were actually playing.

For example, we did SHOW ME YOUR HEART next, and when I sang, "*Show me your heart, that's a good start,*" she looked me straight in the eye with intense concentration on her face, as if she was trying to fathom some deep meaning behind every word I sang. We stayed like that, looking into each other's eyes off and on for almost the entire two minutes and twenty seconds of the song. When the last chord faded away and the applause began, my new friend returned her blank gaze to the table and slowly swirled the ice cubes in her drink.

Since that was the last song of the set, I decided to go meet this enchantress. Into the microphone I said, "Thank you folks. We're gonna take ten minutes to recharge our batteries, and then we'll be back to keep the party rolling."

I stepped away from the microphone, and as I turned to jump down from the stage, I saw my blonde and her friends leaving the room. I elbowed my way through the audience fast as I could and caught up just as the last of the five girls, a short brunette, got to the exit. I tried to step around her, but we crashed. She turned, looked surprised, and said, "You're him! You're Jimmy Bishop."

"Yeah, but please excuse me. I'm in kind of a hurry."

Leaving the girl standing there with her mouth open, I flew through the exit and looked up and down the sidewalk. There were lots of folks on the Strip, but there was no sign of the blonde. It was as if she vanished into thin air. Her friend, the girl I'd bumped into at the door, arrived at my side and stood there staring at me with an expression on her face that said she was trying to decide whether or not I was a raving lunatic.

I looked back at her and said, "I'm sorry for running into you back there, but I'm trying to catch up with someone. Actually, she was with your group—the blonde girl in the black outfit. Can you tell me her name?"

The short brunette continued staring at me for a long moment, and then shook her head slightly. "I can tell you her name, but it won't do you any good."

"Why not?"

"Because Ally—that's her name—is kind of . . . different. She keeps to herself and doesn't go out much. It took us all week to convince her she should come with us tonight. Just so you know, the argument that finally persuaded her was she would get see you in person. She is a fan—a big fan—of yours."

Noticing the girl didn't mention that she was also a big fan, I smiled, and said, "Well, maybe she would like to meet me."

JOANIE

"Mister Bishop, the thought of meeting you in person would absolutely terrify Ally. We would never get her out the door again." After a momentary pause, she asked, "Tell me something. Are you playing here again next weekend?"

"Yes, we're here for three more weeks."

"Okay, I'll make you a deal. I will try to convince Ally to come back with us next week in exchange for your autograph."

"Hell, you get her back here and I'll autograph anything you want."

She grinned at me for a moment, probably considering possible comebacks to my rash promise. Finally, she said, "Just a photograph would be adequate. By the way, even though you couldn't care less, my name is Joanie. I'll see you in a week, Mister Bishop."

I watched her walk into the crowd on the sidewalk in hope Joanie might meet up with her friends, including Ally, but I was interrupted by Josh, our bass guy. He came out to find me so we could start the next set. It seemed my only hope of seeing Ally again now rested with Joanie and how badly she wanted my autograph.

During the next six days my mind kept returning to the back row of tables at the Sunset Cabaret. Ally came walking into my thoughts first thing in the morning and stayed long after I turned out the lights at night.

That she so completely dominated my thoughts was a strange and unique experience. No woman ever had that effect on me before. It was particularly weird because I knew absolutely nothing about her except her first name and she was beautiful. No, I also knew something else. I knew I was going to meet her . . . somehow.

When Saturday finally arrived, Joanie proved to be as good as her word. She and her four friends, including Ally, joined the audience around nine. We were just about to do Be Who You Are, and I got an idea. The microphone I use is wireless, which means it works pretty much all over the room without a cord.

Kevin and Donny kicked the intro off on keyboard and drums.

When the rest of us jumped in, I watched Ally. She did the same thing as the week before, she looked up and watched me intently. This time I did more than look back.

Stepping down from the stage, I sang my way through the audience until I arrived at Ally's table, where I sang the song directly to her. I could see Joanie grinning from the corner of my eye. Ally, on the other hand looked horrified and her eyes got so full of tears they began rolling down both cheeks. Despite her emotional state, Ally was still absolutely gorgeous.

By the time we ended the song, she was covering her face with her hands, except for her eyes. They were still locked to mine. The crowd applauded and I bowed slightly to Ally, whereupon she jumped up and ran out of the room. I thought, "Good work, Jimmy. Keep it up and she won't let you within ten miles of her."

Acknowledging the crowd and feeling a very dark shade of miserable, I walked back to the stage. When I turned around, Ally's friends were gone. About halfway through the last set of the night, though, Joanie returned by herself. By the time we loaded our gear in the van, the club was empty . . . except for Joanie.

I walked over to her table and flopped into a chair. "I guess I pretty much blew that one all to hell."

Joanie smiled at me. She seemed to smile a lot. "Well, yes, but it wasn't entirely your fault. There are some things about Ally you don't know. I suppose I should have told you more when I realized you were interested in her, but some of it is kind of personal and I don't like to tell other people's secrets unless there is an important reason."

I nodded. "I understand. She's your friend and her secrets are none of my business."

She touched my arm. "Mister Bishop, . . . ."

"Call me Jimmy."

"Okay, Jimmy. I think maybe some of Ally's secrets are kind of your business. You would never know it by her behavior, but Ally thinks you are a very special guy."

I almost laughed. "No way. That's just fan stuff. She loves our music and the idea of me being kind of a rock star, although I'm really not."

Joanie looked me straight in the eye. "You're wrong, Jimmy, very wrong."

"She ran out of the room in tears, for crying out loud!"

"Yes, she did, but you don't know why. I do. Will you listen to me for a few minutes?"

I slouched back in my chair and nodded. "Sure."

Joanie took a deep breath and sighed, apparently in preparation for what she was about to tell me. "Jimmy, Ally was orphaned when she was only three years old. Her folks just dumped her off at the county child welfare center and disappeared. So you could say Ally learned about rejection early in her life."

Shaking my head, I said, "Oh, swell."

"But that's not the worst of it. While the county tried to find her folks, they placed Ally in foster homes. Because of some technicality, the County never put her up for adoption, and she ended up spending most of her life until she was eighteen being bounced from one foster home to another.

"That was bad enough, but on top of it all, the mother in the last home she was in abused Ally terribly. It wasn't physical abuse, it was mental. I'm guessing she was jealous of Ally's looks or something and for eight years the woman told Ally over and over she was ugly and worthless and stupid."

"Why on earth didn't the family send her back to the County if they didn't like her?"

"I sometimes think the foster mother actually enjoyed mistreating Ally, but there is another reason they kept her. There can be good money in foster parenting these days, especially if you have more than one kid in the house. In Ally's case there was an older foster sister, and when that sister finally got out of the house for good, she went straight to the County and told them how Ally was being treated. The county looked into it, decided the story was true, and removed Ally from the home."

By this time I was in a state of amazement. "Good! Thank God for the older sister!"

"Yes, and I guess it won't hurt anything at this point for you to know I am Ally's older foster sister."

"Wow."

"Yeah, and to make a long and awful story shorter, Ally stayed on at the County until she was eighteen, and then they tossed her out. Ally came to live with me then and we found her this terrific job as a commercial artist's assistant. Ally has super artistic talents. Back in the bad days, she used to make herself feel better by drawing pretty pictures in sketchbooks. They are really beautiful.

"Anyway, the bottom line to all of this is Ally's sense of self-worth—her self-esteem—is practically nonexistent. She honestly believes she's ugly and worthless. She is finally getting some help from a therapist, but she still has a very hard time accepting that she might be pretty and smart and that a good man would want to be around her."

I shook my head again. "Well, this is one man who definitely wants to be around her."

Joanie stared at me for a moment. "Even after hearing about her life?"

"Especially after hearing about her life."

Joanie smiled. "Jimmy Bishop, I think I like you. Now all you have to do is find a way to make Ally believe you think she's special and you want to know her."

"I don't know how to do that yet, but I will find a way."

That challenge was still on my mind the next day. I was supposed to be working on a new song. I intended it to be an "up" tune with a bouncy little melody. I had a melody that bounced, but the lyrics just were not coming to me.

I was sitting at my composing keyboard and about to throw my pencil across the room for the tenth time, when a thought hit me. Why not turn the melody into a musical letter to Ally? Then the lyrics came at me almost faster than I could write them down.

I spent some time smoothing out the rough edges by adjusting here and there, but before it was time to leave for the club, I had what I thought was a darn good little song. I gave it a title, THE WAY THAT GOD MADE YOU, and set off to the club.

I spent a couple of days working out an arrangement and writing parts for the guys. We went through it a few times at our rehearsal Tuesday evening and the band seemed to like what they were playing. I incorporated a few of their suggestions, and presto, I had a brand new song for Ally.

The only problem remaining was getting her to the club so she could hear it. I called the cell phone number Joanie gave me and we talked about it. She warned me not to get my hopes up because she wasn't sure she could get Ally back to the Sunset Cabaret again after the last fiasco.

After a lot of begging and pleading on my part, Joanie finally agreed to try one more time. She cautioned me sternly, though, not to try the same stunt I pulled the last time Ally was there. I pledged a solemn oath to behave myself and kept my fingers crossed for the rest of the week. Did you ever try to play guitar with crossed fingers? I can tell you it isn't easy.

Come Saturday night I'd just about worried myself into a nervous wreck. We went out on the stand, I took a deep breath and we kicked the set off with SHOW ME YOUR HEART, which was practically the band's theme song now, and we went on from there. I'm not sure exactly why, but we played a lot of blues that night.

By ten I'd nearly given up on Joanie getting Ally back to the Sunset Cabaret, and then they walked in, just the two of them. We had a packed house, so they had to settle for a tiny table off to the side about halfway back from the bandstand. Ally's hair was down for a change, but except for a white blouse, she was dressed in black as usual. Joanie was wearing a smile, also as usual.

I'd made a few special plans for the moment when I would sing Ally's song for her, if that moment ever came. I told Josh, who usually stood to my left, I wanted to do THE WAY THAT GOD MADE YOU, and then gestured to the Sunset Cabaret's stage hand. He understood my gesture and walked out onto the stage with a wooden stool and placed it on a spotlight mark.

I put the microphone stand where it needed to be and hopped up on the stool. Then the stage lights went down and a single spot lit me up on the stool. I said, "Ladies and gentlemen, tonight we are going to do a brand new song for you. We expect to be releasing it soon as a single, but we'd like to preview it for you and see what you think. It's called THE WAY THAT GOD MADE YOU, and it goes like this."

I raised my right hand and counted off four to give Josh and Kevin the tempo I wanted. They kicked the song off with a two-bar intro, and then everybody joined in and it was my turn.

*"Your smile lights up a room.*
*There's not a single thing that I would change about you*
*'Cause you're perfect the way that God made you.*
*The way that God made you."*

With the spotlight in my face, I couldn't see Ally or anyone else in the audience, but I felt her. I knew she was watching me with her intense stare. Mostly, I just closed my eyes and pictured

Ally in my mind. I felt very peaceful and relaxed despite the fact there were at least a hundred pairs of eyes watching me.

I was so relaxed, that when the last strains of the keyboard and the bass faded from the room, I just sat there a few seconds with my eyes closed. Then the applause darn near knocked me off the stool. It smashed the mood all to hell and the house lights came up.

Now I could see Ally. She was looking at me with an odd expression that slowly turned into a smile. It wasn't a big smile, but it was a smile, and it was meant for me. I smiled back and in that moment a love was born big enough to last two lifetimes, Ally's and mine.

THE END

# Bluesy

Thursday, June 7, 2018—Burbank, California

The dramatic/comedy cable series, THE STREETS OF WINSLOW, on which I am the lead writer, made it through two seasons and ABC picked up their option for 2018/19, so everybody at PWP—Pacific West Productions—was on the gravy train for another year. That was the good news. The bad news was our well-deserved respite between seasons was over and it was time to get back to work.

Toward that end, I was struggling to pry a banker's box of scripts from the passenger seat of my '63 Split Window in the Warner Bros. parking lot. The Acura MDX next to my reserved spot was crooked in its parking place and taking up room I needed to get the Vette's door open far enough to remove the cardboard box.

1963 CORVETTE STINGRAY

That's when Lauren Campbell walked up, took a look at my predicament, and said, "That's a beautiful car, Ben, but not too practical for hauling boxes. Can I help?"

"Yeah, go show the owner of this glorified Honda, here, how to park straight."

Lauren laughed. "Sorry, Ben, but as my grandfather used to say, 'That's above my pay grade.'"

Actually, what Lauren's grandfather used to say still carries a good deal of weight around here. Her grandfather was Jeffrey S. Campbell, the most successful writer/producer of network TV from the 1970s into the 1990s.

In fairness, I must add Lauren has made it a point to base her career on her own accomplishments, not her grandfather's name. That, and the strong impression she has no interest in her fellow toilers in the vineyard, romantic or otherwise, is the sum total of my knowledge about the aloof Ms Lauren Campbell. That was all about to change.

Anyway, with Lauren making sure my passenger door didn't bang into the badly parked SUV, I finally got the box of scripts out of the Vette. Then, with her running ahead to get the doors, we successfully transported our cargo to my office on the top floor of WB's TV office building.

Once there, I dumped the box of scripts on the sofa and thanked Lauren for her help. With a big smile, she said, "You're welcome, Ben. Now I want to ask you a favor."

Figuring she needed some help with the production schedule or some such thing, I said, "Sure, whatcha need?"

Reaching into her tote bag, Lauren threw me a curve. "You're into old cars, so I hope you can tell me about this." She handed me an owners' manual for, of all things, a 1937 Cord.

The booklet looked almost too pristine to be an original from 1937, but on close examination, I could see the manual was the real McCoy. "Say, you've got yourself quite a treasure here. Too bad you don't have the car to go with it."

"I do."

I looked up from the manual. "You do what?"

"Have the car to go with that manual."

"You're kidding!"

"No. I found it under a cover while I was cleaning accumulated junk out of the garage at my great-great-grandmother's home. The house was left to me in my grandfather's will and I decided to clean it out so I can figure out what to do with it. Strangely, I'm finding I like the old place so much, I might even move into it."

"Well, I hope the garage has a good sturdy lock on the door."

Lauren tilted her head and gave me a look of curiosity. "Not really. Why?"

"Because, depending on condition, that Cord you found is worth a hundred grand, maybe even two hundred."

Her jaw dropped. "That much?"

"That much, but for if to bring that kind of money, all the parts would have to be there and restorable."

"Ben, this car looks like it just rolled out the dealer's

showroom. The mileage thing only shows three thousand one hundred and fifty miles. I haven't tried starting it, but . . . ."

LAUREN CAMPBELL

"Good! It's possible your Cord will run like new, but there are procedures for starting an engine that hasn't been run in a long time. If they aren't followed, trying to start the engine could destroy it."

She gave me a sly look. "I suspected something like that. Ben, are you doing anything this weekend?"

I knew what her next question would be, so I gave her a two-for-one answer. "What am I doing this weekend? Probably trying to start a 1937 Cord 812 Roadster."

## Saturday, June 9, 2018—Simi Valley, California

Lauren's Great-Great-Grandmother Emma Baker must have really been into privacy. Her large hacienda-style house sits on a rocky hillside at the east end of the Simi Valley near the old Corriganville movie ranch. For those who don't know southern California, Simi Valley is now a rapidly growing suburb about forty miles northwest of Los Angeles, but it was the middle of nowhere when the house was built.

1957 CHEVROLET PICK-UP

I drove up a steep driveway and parked my bright red '57 Chevy stepside in front of an old three-car garage with wooden overlapping sliding doors. My truck was loaded with tools, a battery, a variety of lubricants, and other stuff— hopefully, everything I would need to coax Lauren's Cord back to life.

Lauren, in jeans and a black top, was waiting for me in front of the garage and proved herself an excellent hostess by handing me a mug of black coffee as she greeted me. "Good morning, Ben.

Do you always work on cars at this ungodly hour?"

I couldn't help laughing. "Ungodly hour? Heck, all the early birds caught their worms and left hours ago."

With a smile that was anything but aloof. "Sure they did. Come on, I'll show you my hundred-grand treasure."

The garage wasn't just three cars wide, it was also two cars deep. Despite the roominess, though, we had to run an obstacle course through a variety of junk—old lawnmowers, a rusted out water heater, and other items that were beyond description.

Then I got my first look at the Cord. Its axles were up on blocks, but otherwise the car looked as if we could jump in and drive away. Admiring the car's modern styling, I said, "Geneva Blue."

"Is that what they called this color?"

"Yup, I looked at a Cord color chart for 1937 on the Internet last night. The interior color is Burgundy."

Lauren said, "This reminds me of cars in the old Buck Rogers comic books my granddad collected. It's nothing like other 1930s cars I've seen."

"That's what led to the Cord's success . . . and its demise. People were attracted to the futuristic design, but the car had to be built on a budget that wasn't quite big enough to work out all the bugs in its innovations, and the thirty-seven Cord had a bunch of innovations.

"It was the first car to have practical front-engine/front wheel drive. The Cord also had an electric transmission shifter, hidden headlights, a horn ring on the steering wheel, and the list goes on and on."

Judging by her expression, Lauren was developing an appreciation for her newfound treasure. "Gosh, Bluesy was quite a gal in her day."

"Bluesy?"

"Yeah. That's the name Grandmother Emma gave the car."

"Oh? How do you know that?"

"It's in the owner's manual. Inside the front cover she printed, 'Bluesy's Book.'"

To make a long and sweaty story short, we spent the morning getting things moved around so we could work on the car without tripping over stuff. By noon we had the Cord off the blocks, rolling on four original, but questionable tires. Next, we pushed it to a space we cleared just inside one of the three sliding garage doors.

Having gotten that far, we took a brief break, lunching on homemade tuna sandwiches and corn chips. While enjoying a tasty sandwich made from Great-Great-Grandmother Emma's own tuna salad recipe, I raised the Cord's hood for a look.

Fine craftsmanship was evident throughout the engine compartment. Everything on the Lycoming 170 horsepower supercharged V8 engine was in its proper place and there were factory brackets, straps, and bolts to keep it there. E. L. Cord ran a tight ship.

After lunch, Lauren handed me tools and kept track of loose parts while I removed the engine's oil sump drain plug and its eight sparkplugs. When the sump was empty, I refilled it with light detergent oil and squirted a little more oil into each of the sparkplug holes.

The next step was using a breaker bar to turn the crankshaft one full turn, thus distributing the oil in the cylinders more thoroughly. After that, I siphoned the fuel tank dry and left the cap off to let the lingering fumes from the prehistoric gasoline evaporate. Finally, I drained the radiator into a bucket and refilled it with hundred percent Prestone Dex-Cool Antifreeze.

By the time I completed those chores and chased a few spiders out of the carburetor, the shadows were getting long. I stood back, and gave Lauren's treasure a long look. "Well, I think we're almost ready for phase two of the starting process, but we need to let Bluesy sit like he is overnight so the fluids we put in can do their jobs."

Lauren nodded her understanding. "Ben, I hate for you to drive all the way back to civilization and then turn around and drive all the way back in the morning. Grandmother Emma had a couple of comfortable guest rooms for visitors. You're welcome to use one of them tonight."

In truth, I never had any intention of driving thirty-some miles home just to retrace my steps in the morning. The intention I did have was to spend the night at a Holiday Inn Express up on Highway One-Eighteen. That was why I had a bag with me, which made accepting Lauren's offer of a guest room an easy decision.

Taking advantage of each other's company Lauren and I had a great evening. We started out with dinner at a classy steak and seafood place called Barton's, where the food was as good as it gets in this part of the world.

After dinner, Lauren climbed into the driver's seat of my pickup and had fun cruising it around town while showing me the sights. Once we got the seat adjusted so Lauren could reach the pedals, she handled the four-speed and Blue-Flame six like a pro.

Finally, we went back to Grandmother Emma's to study some procedures in the Cord manual. I told her I was pretty sure we could get the engine running, and that meant she needed to know how to drive the car, which was trickier than it sounds.

Bluesy had an entire owner's manual full of idiosyncrasies. We covered them all, from the little hand cranks on the dashboard that opened the headlight covers to the operation of the nifty gearshift pre-selector.

By the time we trotted off to our separate bedrooms, I was certain Lauren could drive the Cord with the best of them. Not too surprisingly, Lauren wandered in and out of my dreams Saturday night.

## Sunday, June 10, 2018—Simi Valley, California

I thought I was getting up with the sun Sunday morning, but Lauren beat me. She already had the coffee made and handed me a mug as she asked, "How did you sleep, Ben?"

Accepting the coffee, I said, "Great, thank you. It's very quiet and restful up here."

"That's one of the reasons I've been thinking about moving in rather than selling the house."

"If it wasn't for the commute, I'd do it in a heartbeat."

Lauren's eyes studied me for a long moment over the top of her coffee mug before she said, "That's what I've been thinking. It might even be worth the commute."

On that note we went out and got back to work. After replacing the cleaning oil in the sump with oil of the recommended driving viscosity, I poured two gallons of fresh gasoline from my jerry can into the tank, gapped and screwed eight fresh sparkplugs into the heads, and dragged a six-volt battery with jumper cables out of my truck and set them near the Cord's engine compartment.

"Well, Ms Campbell, I believe the moment of truth has arrived. Do you remember the starting procedure we read in the book last night?"

TRANSMISSION PRE-SELECTOR

Lauren nodded with enthusiasm. "We move that cute little transmission pre-selector to the neutral position, set the throttle and choke to their start positions, turn the ignition key on, and step on the clutch pedal, which activates the starter. Right?"

"Perfect, except we're going to do it just a little differently the first time."

With a mock frown on her face, Lauren said, "Don't you confuse me!"

I grinned at her. "This isn't too tricky. We'll leave the throttle and choke closed to begin with. That's because it takes the fuel pump a few cranks to get gas up into the carburetor. If we open the throttle too soon, we could get a backfire that would make us both jump a foot. Okay?"

"Got it."

Grinning like Lewis Carroll's Cheshire Cat, Lauren climbed in behind the wheel and looked at me for the go-ahead to crank the starter. I connected the battery and gave her a nod. The

Lycoming's starter motor began cranking for all it was worth. I gestured for Lauren to keep going. After about a minute, I said, "Okay. That's good."

"Are we ready to really start it?"

"We're going to give it a try. If it . . . . No, WHEN, it starts adjust the hand-throttle in small increments so the tach stays just under one thousand RPM. As the engine warms up, we can open the choke gradually until the carburetor is breathing all the air it wants. Ready?"

"Yes!"

"Give it a go."

Again the starter motor cranked, and after a few seconds the Lycoming gave a healthy cough. That was a good sign and I wasn't smelling strong gas fumes, so the fuel system was doing its job.

"Crank it again."

This time the Lycoming coughed three times and sprang to life. Over the engine noise, I heard Lauren scream, "It's running, it's running!"

I moved to the open driver side door. "Okay, foot off the clutch and watch the tachometer."

 As I looked on, Lauren gradually adjusted the throttle. "Good. The revs are just right." I pointed to the water temperature gauge. "Keep an eye on this one, too. The red liquid should begin moving up the scale as the engine coolant warms up just like a regular thermometer. The concern is that it doesn't go up into the red numbers."

At first the Lycoming's idle was a little rough, surging and falling off. As the engine continued to run, though, the idle gradually smoothed out. After ten minutes or so, the Lycoming was fully warmed up and humming along like a fine watch.

I said, "Okay, let's shut it off and check a few things."

Lauren reached for the ignition key and looked back at me, almost as if she was afraid to shut the engine off. I smiled at her. "Don't worry, it will start again. Oh, and be sure the pre-selector is in the neutral position. That's important every time you shut the engine off."

In a leap of faith, Lauren turned the ignition key to the OFF position and the Lycoming stopped without any dieseling or backfires. Lauren sat there for a minute with her hands on the steering wheel and I got the idea she was imagining what it would be like to actually drive Bluesy.

Suddenly, she jumped to the ground and threw her arms around my neck. "You did it, Ben! You're a genius! You got Bluesy working again after seventy years!" Lauren followed the hug with a kiss right on the lips.

After that, though, she backed away a little as if afraid she'd crossed a boundary into forbidden territory. To show her it wasn't forbidden territory by my rules, I reached out and gave her a hug around her slim waist. "You know, Lauren, you're wrong about that."

She looked confused. "Wrong about what?"

"I didn't get Bluesy working again, WE did. In fact, I think he kind of likes you. I bet if it had been my foot on the clutch he wouldn't have been so anxious to run.

Eyes sparkling, Lauren shook her head. "I think it's you SHE likes. Bluesy is a girl car and I think she's fallen in love with you!"

I had the strong sensation there was more to Lauren's comment about falling in love than kidding. With a silly grin that matched hers, I said, "Could be. Come on, we need to button some things up here so we can take HER out for a ride."

Fortunately, the new Optima Yellow Top six-volt battery I brought fit into the Cord's battery box. I tightened the hold-down bracket, and then attached the battery cables.

Next, I examined the tires. They held air overnight, but I wasn't counting on that condition lasting much longer. Closing the hood, I said, "Okay, next step: Are you ready to drive Bluesy to a gas station?"

Lauren was sitting sideways in the driver's seat with her legs dangling through the open door. She sat up straight. "Can we?"

"I hope so, 'cuz Dominoes doesn't deliver gasoline, but we'll have to make it a short trip. I don't have much faith in these tires and we don't have a spare."

"Okay, maybe you'd better drive."

"Hell, no. This is your eighty-one-year-old car. I'm just here as a consultant."

I didn't have to twist her arm. Lauren swiveled around to face the wheel and I closed the driver-side door. When I climbed in the passenger seat I discovered the Cord's size was deceiving. As big as it seemed from the outside, the front seat was a snug fit for two average size adults.

Resting my arm on the seatback behind Lauren's head, I said, "You'll have to reserve rides in Bluesy for your closest friends. It's kind of cozy in here."

"I'M ALREADY DOING THAT."

She gave me another grin. "I'm already doing that. Shall I start her up?"

"Have at it."

Thankfully for Lauren's opinion of my mechanic skills, the Lycoming sprang to life again. She looked at me again. "I guess I should ask where we're going."

"To the nearest gas station. Just go easy on the corners. Those tires aren't going to last much longer."

It turned out to be quite a ways to the nearest gas station, which was a Union 76 station in the little town of Santa Susanna to the south. Of course, the Cord got everybody's attention when we pulled into the station. While I filled the seventeen-gallon tank with ninety-one octane fuel, several people came over to question us about Bluesy.

When we finally got headed back, I said, "Get used to that, Lauren. The lookie-lous will drive you nuts."

Lauren grinned her engaging grin again. "Hey, those aren't lookie-lous. They're Bluesy fans. She's a natural-born celebrity."

A little later, as we passed a large park with three baseball fields, Lauren looked at the place and said, "That's new. I wonder when they built that?"

Now, that isn't a particularly unusual thing for someone to say . . . except during our drive the previous night Lauren spent several minutes telling me all about the very same park.

I looked over at her and said, "I thought you me told about that park last night."

Lauren had sort of a far-away expression on her face and looked at me as if I was the one who was saying strange stuff. Then she blinked and said, "I'm sorry, Ben, what did you say?"

Her mind had obviously been somewhere else. Seeing no reason to make an issue of it, I changed the subject. "You know, we need to talk about finishing Bluesy's resurrection. Aside from a little spit and polish, the major things she still needs are some fresh tires and a new roadster top."

Back with me now, Lauren said, "I think there's an America's Tire Store on First Street. Should I take her in there for tires?"

I smiled. "Nope. Bluesy needs original equipment tires to keep her historically correct. I'll order the right ones from Coker Tires and have them rush the delivery."

"Coker? I never heard of them."

"Coker is an outfit in Tennessee specializing in original equipment tires for vintage cars. I'll call 'em tomorrow, and they should be able to get what we need shipped here by next weekend.

"Also, I know an upholstery shop in Burbank that does first class work. I'll talk to them tomorrow, too. They do a lot of restoration jobs, so maybe they can track down a pattern so all we have to do is bring Bluesy in to have it installed."

When we made it back to Grandmother Emma's, Lauren carefully pulled Bluesy into the garage spot we cleared for her and shut the engine off. She turned in the seat to look at me and said, "Ben, you're being awfully generous with your time. I had no idea there was so much involved, but you know what?"

"What?"

Her big smile was back. "A few minutes ago you said WE would do something. Hearing that made me feel kind of. . . different."

"Did I say that? I didn't realize it. I'm sorry if I . . . ."

"Ben, I meant I felt different in a good way. All my life I've been on my own. Now, for the first time in a long while, I feel part of something important because you make me feel like I'm really contributing to Bluesy's restoration. I like it . . . a lot."

"Well, I hope I wasn't taking too much for granted."

She looked into my eyes. "Sometimes I think you don't take enough for granted." Lauren looked at me a few more seconds as if she was waiting for me to say something. When I didn't, she said, "Look, darn it, I really want to kiss you right now, but I can't tell how you feel about that. Will you PLEASE give me a hint?"

I pulled her closer and gave her a hint. It was the second time we'd kissed, only this time it had nothing to do with celebrating the restarting of an 81 year old automobile.

Back at WB on Monday, Lauren and I didn't have much time for chatting. We had our hands full with our shares of the chores we needed to accomplish before The Streets Of Winslow could begin shooting. Instead, we talked via telephone every night. We did, that is, until Thursday night.

## Thursday, June 14, 2018
## Stone Canyon, Los Angeles County, California

I sat in my home office and stared at the cell phone on my desk. Lauren left the office at lunch time to run a personal errand and I couldn't find anyone who'd seen her since. Now, after calling her condo in Toluca Lake three times without getting an answer or a call back, I was becoming concerned. Disappearing wasn't a normal behavior for Lauren.

Just sitting there waiting for the phone to ring, however, was not making me any less worried, so I decided on a long shot. I pointed the Vette toward Simi Valley. I had no reason to think Lauren was there, but it was the only place other than her condo I knew of to look for her. I also thought about how silly I was going to feel if she returned my call when I was all the way out in Simi.

I felt immediate relief when I saw Lauren's Subaru Outback parked at the top of the driveway by the garage, but that relief only lasted about ten seconds, until I realized the garage door where we'd parked the Cord was open and there was no sign of the Cord.

Surely she hadn't driven up here just to take a ride in the Cord, especially after I'd warned her about the tires. She wouldn't do that, would she? A moment later I knew she would.

Trying to cover all the bases, I knocked on the front door. While I was standing there waiting for no one to answer my knock, I read the note that explained how I knew no one was going to answer my knock. Stuck to the door with an old green metal thumbtack was a piece of paper with six words and a signature on it. In a flowery script I couldn't imagine Lauren using, the note said:

### *I AM GONE TO THE MARKET, EMMA*

It would have been perfectly natural for a note from Emma Baker to be tacked to the front door of her own home, except Emma had been dead for six or seven decades. That was when my mind flashed back to the park we passed returning from the gas station last Sunday and Lauren's reaction to it.

## Thursday, June 21, 2018
## Warner Bros., Burbank, California

Lauren has now been missing for a week and I'm resigning

myself to never seeing her again. The Ventura County Sheriff's deputies have put their hearts and souls into finding Lauren, but the only clues they came up with are clothes. They found the clothes she wore to work last Thursday on the bed in the room Lauren used the night I stayed with her.

The deputies' second clothing clue came from a neighbor a few houses down Clear Springs Road from Emma Baker's house. The neighbor said she saw Lauren drive by in an old fashioned blue convertible car. The neighbor thought Lauren might be going to a costume event of some kind because she was wearing a fancy hat and a fur stole like wealthy women wore in the 1930s.

Those clues meant little to the deputies, but to me they explained why I was certain I would never see Lauren again. It was an incredible story from the paranormal world I didn't want to believe, but had to because, despite its improbability, it was the only explanation that fit all the pieces of the puzzle.

In a nutshell that story involved the spirit of Emma Baker, for whom I unknowingly created a time machine she used to take herself back to her own heyday. Apparently her scheme also required Lauren's participation, but probably not her permission.

I was making myself miserable looking at cellphone photos I made of Lauren and the Cord while we were restoring the car. Thinking I might want to look at them again one day, I decided to print a couple of the images. I sent one of the Cord images to the laser printer in my office.

When I looked at the print, I was shocked by the realization Lauren, or at least her spirit, was still with me. To the air around me, I quietly said, "Thanks, Kiddo. I miss you more than I can say. Please take good care of yourself and give my regards to Bluesy."

## THE END

# Burlington Betty

Thursday, July 12, 2018—Port Costa, California
(A True Story . . . More or Less)

By craft, I am a writer of fiction. In simple terms, I write novels. Simplified even further, I am a storyteller. I write because I enjoy the work and occasionally people buy my books, which puts food on the table and a roof overhead.

One of the things about writing I like most is the research that goes into a story. I write historic fiction, so my research takes me to some interesting periods and places. I especially love visiting historic locations that still exist—not necessarily museums or historic landmarks, but old places that have managed to remain standing despite "progress."

Sometimes, however, visiting old places can be more than just interesting. Take, for example, a place I visited when writing the Johnny Spicer Caper, PACIFICA. The story is set at the 1939 Golden Gate Exposition, which was held on Treasure Island in San Francisco. The story also visits other locales in the Bay Area, including a tiny burg called Port Costa.

PORT COSTA

Post Costa is located in Contra Costa County east of Oakland on the west bank of the Carquinez Strait. The town—an exaggeration of its size—was founded in 1879 and owes its existence to the Central Pacific Railroad. When planning its transcontinental route, CP ran into a small problem when it got to the Bay Area; namely, the bay and its related bodies of water. The railroad was supposed to end in San Francisco, but the Carquinez

Strait was smack-dab in their way.

The Central Pacific's options were to build a bridge or operate a railroad ferry across the strait. The latter option appealed to them for some reason, so they created Port Costa as the western terminus for their railroad ferryboat, the SOLANO.

Thus, Port Costa consisted mostly of a switching yard, a large warehouse, a hotel for passengers, and a few shops providing goods for the employees who lived and worked in the town. Many of these buildings still exist and date back to the 1880s. Incidentally, the Central Pacific was gobbled up in 1959 by the Southern Pacific Railroad, so for the latter part of its life, Port Costa was owned by the SP.

Today, the switching yard is gone, and the town's main and only drag, Canyon Lake Drive, ends at a gravel and dirt tourist parking lot where a network of tracks once stood next to the water. Lest my reference to a "tourist parking lot" mislead you, I hasten to add that very few actual tourists actually park in that lot. Mostly, Port Costa's visitors are members of Bay Area motorcycle clubs who show up on weekends to drink beer and behave badly, which seems to be just fine with the locals because the proceeds from the aforementioned beer help a decaying town survive a little longer.

My main interests in Port Costa were the old railroad warehouse, containing a small café, saloon, and antique emporium, and the hotel across the street. The hotel is being restored, but is still more or less in the same dilapidated condition it had been in since the 1930s.

While arranging for my research visit I was told the Burlington Hotel was not yet operational and to get the keys from the bartender in the warehouse bar across the street. He had no qualms about giving me the keys so I could look around and get a feeling for what the hotel was like in the 1930s. Actually, the bartender was quite impressed with meeting an author. I think he might have actually read a book once.

In addition to the front door keys, the bartender also gave me a couple of suggestions for my tour, including a visit to Betty, a room that was fully restored. A room named Betty? Yup. Local rumor has it that the Burlington was once a bordello and the rooms were named for the ladies who entertained in them. Sure, why not?

SECOND FLOOR HALLWAY

Despite its rundown condition, there was enough left of the Burlington to appreciate its Victorian heritage, complete with half-hexagonal bay windows jutting out over the sidewalk from the rooms on the second and third floors. Inside, wainscoting and chair rails decorated the lower halves of the hallway walls above a carpet with an elaborate geometric pattern that might have been maroon at one time, but was so threadbare it would take chemical analysis to be sure.

Several of the room doors I passed were hanging by one hinge, or were missing entirely. In the gloom beyond these openings, I could make out bedframes with broken and rusting springs and the remains of small three-light chandeliers dangling from the ceilings at odd angles on brass chains. Despite the hotel's condition, I was getting a firsthand look at the aging relics of a long-gone era.

I found Betty on the second floor after negotiating a stairway that creaked and groaned with every step I took. A glance at the stair railing, apparently held in place by two loose screws and a wad of chewing gum, told me the quickest way back down to the first floor would be to lean on it.

Betty was a grand old lady from her elaborately carved closet door frame to the ornate corbels—L-shaped brackets—used to strengthen the wall opening created to make Betty into a two-room suite. Her furnishings were genuine antiques lovingly restored, but from many different periods and in a variety of styles. She had a little of everything from classical to traditional.

Standing at the bay window next to the closet door, I looked down at a street on which nothing stirred on a lazy spring afternoon in Port Costa. The wall of the warehouse across the street wore a few vines of ivy for character; utility poles leaned, but no two in the same direction; and large trees created a foliage canopy over Canyon Lake Drive.

I could also see the water off to my left. It lapped against a couple of rotting pilings that might once have been part of the ferry dock. Except for a few modern cars parked along the street, the scenes outside were the decaying remnants of a once bustling company town where men worked hard and, judging by the hotel's reputation and the number of shuttered bars along the street, also played hard.

Gradually, I was roused from my window musings by a sound—a rustling coming from somewhere close. I turned to my right, the direction from which the sound seemed to be emanating, and found myself face to face with the closet door and its elaborately carved frame. From the volume of the rustling, I concluded they had some dang big mice in these parts.

I took a step toward the door and the rustling stopped. I reached out and turned the doorknob. The already quiet room seemed to get even quieter, as if holding its breath for what was about to happen. The thought that I might be reading too many Stephen King stories passed through my mind as I pulled the door open, and . . . absolutely nothing happened, at least not right away.

After a few seconds, though, the room temperature began to drop. I mean it was getting cold in a big hurry. I stepped forward and leaned into the closet. Yup, that was where the frosty air came from. It was like a refrigerator in there, which made me think the old hotel needed some new insulation. Then it dawned on me that the cold air in the closet couldn't be coming from outside the building. The air outside was much, much warmer than what I felt in the closet.

By then I realized something else was happening, and it was happening to me. An anxious feeling was spreading through me. The hairs on the back of my neck were actually standing up. Resisting a strong urge to get the hell out of there, I studied the interior of the closet. So far as I could see it held nothing more sinister than a discarded paint rag. There had to be something in there I wasn't seeing, and was probably better off not seeing.

I reached for the closet door to close it and something directly behind me said, "Yeowp!"

I jumped a foot straight up and spun around. There sitting on the bed calmly washing a paw was the thing that said "Yeowp." I knew that because the big orange-stripped cat on the bed said it again. She looked me in the eye and clearly said, "Yeowp."

As my pulse slowly returned to the near normal range, I said, "Hello there. Where did you come from?"

The cat gave me a look that clearly said, "Now, that's a dumb question."

I looked at the hallway doors. There were two, one at each end of the suite, and both were closed. Since Betty shared a bathroom down the hall, the closet had the only other door in the room. I looked back at the closet. It had changed. The air inside was almost room temperature now. How could air that cold instantly warm up to seventy degrees? The goings-on in Betty's room weren't just mysterious, they were downright weird.

Closing the closet door, I asked the cat, "You know anything about this?"

The cat stretched lazily, said "Yeowp" again, which seemed to be her answer to most questions in life. Then she hopped down from the bed and strolled to the hall door, where she waited until I opened it. She beat me out the door and shot around the corner like an orange streak. To the empty hallway I said, "Thanks for stopping by for a visit."

A few minutes later I was back in the warehouse bar returning the bartender's hotel keys. He asked, "See everything you wanted to see?"

I nodded. "Yes, I did. Thank you for the loan of your keys."

He grinned slyly. "Sure. Anything strange happen while you were in Betty?"

I got the picture. The refrigerated closet gag was a common occurrence and he'd set me up for the spooks by sending me to Betty. Determined not to give him the satisfaction of a laugh on me, I looked innocent and said, "No, why?"

He looked disappointed. "Oh, nothing. People say that room is haunted or some silly thing. It seems Betty, the hooker the room was named for, committed suicide in there—hung herself from a rafter in the closet.

"Some visitors say the air in the closet is freezing cold and they feel uneasy, just nonsense like that. One of those paranormal TV shows even sent a crew out to film ghosts last year. They didn't see any, but it was fun to watch those guys and their ghost-busting gadgets at work."

I smiled. "I'm sure it was." Glancing at my watch, I said, "I guess I'd best get a move on if I want to beat the traffic back to San Francisco. Thanks again for your help."

"Sure. I hope your story comes out okay."

"I think it will. In fact, thanks to you, I may have gotten another story idea about the hotel."

He put on a big grin. "Did ya? Hey, that's great. Glad to help!"

Walking back to my car, I passed the hotel, and ran into a friend. There, on the entrance steps, sat the orange-striped cat I met in Betty. Seeing her gave me an idea. I stopped walking and the cat stopped washing the paw she was working on. For cats, cleanliness truly is next to Godliness.

I said, "Hi, again. Say, by any chance would your name be Betty?"

She looked up at me and said an emphatic, "Yeowp!"

"I thought so. Nice to meet you. I have to go now, but I'll come back and visit you another time, if that's okay with you."

The cat got up, hopped down the two steps and rubbed briefly against my leg. I said, "The same to you, Betty. Take good care."

## THE END

# Miss Josephine

June 15, 2018—Palm Springs

I write novels. More specifically, I write historical novels, most of which are set in the 1920s, '30s, and '40s.

It might surprise some to know that writing believable fictional history requires knowing a good deal of factual history. For that reason I spend a lot of time in libraries and museums. Research is one of my favorite parts of the craft, especially time spent in museums. For example, my current book project is about a group of World War Two pilots so I was on my way to bone up on some WWII warbird details.

Now, depending on the type of aircraft in which you are interested, there are two excellent air museums not far from my home in Santa Monica, California. One is the Planes of Fame Museum in Chino, and the other is the Palm Springs Air Museum. It was to the latter of those two I was headed.

Even though most museums offer research docent services, I prefer to do museums on my own. If I tell a docent what I think I want to see, I will generally walk right past what I really needed to see while following my guide to what I thought I needed to see. I think it has something to do with serendipity.

AT-6 TRAINER

Unfortunately, this is one of those times when a docent is a necessary evil. Despite being a licensed pilot and having restored a warbird of my own, owners of aircraft in museums who don't know me tend to be very protective of their million-dollar babies, insisting that a docent accompany anyone who wants to go beyond the ropes and get close enough to take in the details. I can't really blame them. I'm the same way about my vintage AT-6 trainer, and it represents little more than a drop in the bucket compared to the high-dollar restorations I knew awaited me at my destination.

The Palm Springs Air Museum is housed in a small cluster of modern buildings on the east side of the runway at Palm Springs International Airport. Yes, Palm Springs actually has an "international airport." At least that's what they call it.

I found a shady parking spot near the administration building, although heat was not a big issue by the time I arrived. That was another condition on which the museum insisted; my visit had to be after closing time. My guess was they didn't want paying guests to see someone receiving preferential treatment.

Walking into the museum lobby was like strolling into a refrigerator. I'm not sure what they thought would melt if they turned the A/C up to a reasonable setting, but I would not have been surprised to see icicles hanging from the display cases. Maybe they rent a back room out to the county morgue.

A fellow in a snappy uniform behind the reception counter put on a sad face as I approached. "I'm sorry, Sir, but we're just closing. Can you come back tomorrow?"

I smiled. "I don't think I'll need to do that. I have an appointment for some after-hours research with . . . ." I checked the name I scribbled in my notebook when I made the original arrangements. "With Moira O'Brien."

He returned my smile and said, "Oh, yes." Glancing to his left, he said, "Moira's on the telephone, but I'm sure she'll be right with you."

I looked where he looked and saw a shock of very red hair above a big smile and a smart phone. The rest of Moira O'Brien was in a gray T-shirt, blue jeans, and well-worn athletic shoes. She was leaning against a wall and in the midst of an animated conversation with whomever was on the other end of her cell connection. From my vantage point, Moira O'Brien appeared to be about fifteen. Swell.

It was about then that Miss O'Brien looked toward the counter and the fellow behind it pointed to me and then at her. She glanced at me and nodded to him. It took her less than a minute to finish her conversation and begin walking in my direction.

MOIRA O'BRIAN

I was glad to see her put on a year or two of age with every step she took in my direction. I don't mean she turned into an old hag or anything, but face to face, I figured her age to be about the same as mine—late twenties, give or take, but I bet she still shows her ID to a lot of bartenders.

Offering her hand, she said, "Good afternoon, Mister Coleman. I'm Moira O'Brien. Sorry to keep you waiting."

I shook the hand she offered. The girl had a firm grip. "You didn't keep me waiting, Ms O'Brien. I might have even been a little early."

She beamed a bright smile at me. "Oh, good! Let's grab some coffee in the café while you tell me what it is you specifically want to see."

According to the sign, the Freedom Fighters Café was closed for the day, but a few folks were dawdling. Moira stepped behind the counter and filled two mugs of coffee from a glass pot. The coffee was strong, but drinkable.

"Now, Mister Coleman, what are you here to see?"

The jury was still out, but I was beginning to think Ms O'Brien might be okay. "Well, how 'bout we get on a first name basis and eliminate some syllables? I'm Matt."

She gave me another of her bright smiles. She seemed to have a never-ending supply. "All right, Matt. I'm Moira."

"Irish, right?"

Moira was still smiling when she said, "Yes. It means rebellious woman, so watch out."

"I will heed your advice on that matter. To answer your question about why I'm here, I'm particularly interested in the American Volunteer Group P-40B in your collection."

She nodded. "Miss Josephine. The restorers did a beautiful

144

job on her. She looks like she just rolled off the assembly line. Now she has the paint scheme of the 14th Air Force after it took over from the China Air Task Force and the AVG. I can assure you from the ship's records, though, she definitely served with the AVG. I assume you know some of the P-40's history in China?"

"I'm familiar with the basic story. I understand the American Volunteer Group ships were P-40Bs, sort of a cross between the P-40 Tomahawk Curtiss-Wright was building for the Brits and earlier versions of the US Warhawk."

Moira nodded and picked up the story where I left off. "A hundred P-40Bs were crated up at the Curtiss plant in Buffalo, New York and shipped to Rangoon, where the ships received what they called the 'government-furnished equipment'—things like gunsights, radios, and guns. Then, the hundred P-40s were delivered to the AVG at Toungoo, Burma."

We were playing a game historians play to show off, and I had one up on her. Either that or she thought she had me.

Doing a little smiling of my own, I said, "Except the AVG only got ninety-nine P-40s."

Moira gave me a puzzled look, and then the light dawned. "Oh, yes. One of the crates fell overboard during shipping and a wing assembly was destroyed so the hundredth ship couldn't be assembled." She looked me in the eye, gave me a slightly downgraded version of her smile, and said, "I stand corrected, Mister Coleman."

"It's Matt, remember?"

Moira looked down, avoiding my eyes. I also noticed her signature smile was missing. "Yes. I seem to be forgetting a lot of stuff today . . . Matt."

Nice going, Coleman, now you've embarrassed her. That surprised me a little. Most historians have thicker skins. Oh well, this wasn't a date, it was work.

By this time we were the only ones left in the café, so I said, "Okay if we take a look at Miss Josephine now?"

She nodded. "Sure. It's this way."

I followed her down a hallway and beyond a pair of double doors opening into a dark hangar interior. My footsteps echoed eerily between the metal walls and high ceiling. The dark shapes of aircraft were a bit ominous in the dim light coming through the open hall door.

Then, Moira switched on the lights and everything changed. Suddenly I was as close as anyone can come to going back in time. As if I'd been transported to the 1940s, I was surrounded by many of the warbirds that helped win World War Two for the Allies. These were not recreations—they were the very ships in which brave young American pilots faced our Nazi and Jap enemies.

Even with eight or ten aircraft crowded into the large hangar, my eye was immediately drawn to Miss Josephine. She stood proudly between a North American B-25 Mitchell Bomber and a Navy Chance-Vought F4U Corsair. Moira understated the case when she said the restorers had done a beautiful job on the P-40.

CURTISS P-40B "WARHAWK"

Miss Josephine's green and tan camouflage paint literally sparkled and her shark's mouth nose art looked like it wouldn't hesitate to take a bite out of anything that got too close. Of course when these ships were flying daily missions they didn't stay so pretty for long, but it was a thrill to see what they might have looked like to a combat pilot the day his new ship arrived.

I ducked under the yellow wing of an AT-6 similar to mine and walked up to Miss Josephine. I was about to step over the rope intended to keep visitors from getting too familiar with her, but I stopped and looked at Moira.

She nodded her approval and a moment later we were standing side by side near the blue and white US star-and-bar insignia on the ship's fuselage between the port wing and tail. As I appreciated Miss Josephine's sleek lines from nose to tail, I had the feeling I was being watched.

I looked at Moira. She was, indeed, watching me. I was happy to see her smile was back.

"You know, Matt, I've seen a lot of men look at these planes, but never the way you're looking at Miss Josephine now. If I didn't know better, I'd say I was watching a man looking his best girl."

Returning her smile, I said, "I don't know, maybe you are, or at least as close to a best girl as I've got at the moment."

From there we worked our way around the P-40 while I snapped detail photos here and there. Moira took note of what I was photographing and occasionally asked what function the part served. She knew the history of the ships in the museum, but not much about how they worked.

For example, I made a close up photo of the three 30-cal barrels poking out of the port wing, and she asked, "Those are guns, right?"

.30 CAL WING GUNS

"They are. You're looking at the business ends of three point-30 caliber machineguns. The P-40B has a total of six. It also has a pair of point-50-cal guns synchronized to fire through the prop from that cowling above the engine. Of course, unless the owner is a real stickler for authenticity, these are mock guns. or even just pipes made to look like barrels."

"I bet they made a . . . what's that sound?"

I heard it, too—a low-pitched whine gradually increasing in pitch and volume. I knew the sound, but it took me a moment to convince myself I was really hearing what I thought I was hearing. I looked toward the canopy. It was closed tight and there was nobody in the cockpit, which confused me even more.

Explaining what seemed to be going on to Moira, I said, "That sound is an instrument gyro winding up. Somebody or something just turned on Miss Josephine's master electrical switch."

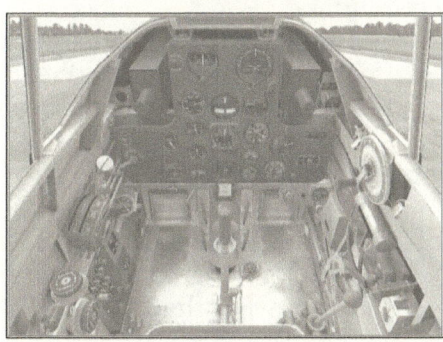

Moira looked as confused as I felt. "Aren't all the electrical switches in the cockpit? There's nobody up there!"

Putting a hand on her shoulder, I gently directed Moira along the wing further from the propeller. "The switches most certainly are in the cockpit. I don't know what's going on, but we might be wise to keep away from that prop until we find out."

Now she looked a little panicky. "Is someone is trying to start the engine? That's not allowed in the hangar."

I was about to say she needed to explain the rules to whoever flipped the master switch when I heard something else—three distinct metallic clicks. They came from the wing about three feet away from my right arm. There was only one thing in that wing that could click.

I threw my arm around Moira's waist and dove for the concrete floor. Just as we got there, all hell broke loose over our heads.

Thirty caliber machineguns are relatively small as aircraft guns go, but six of them firing simultaneously inside a metal hangar sounded like the arrival of Armageddon. Throw in the added racket made by twenty rounds per second slamming into the metal hangar door thirty feet in front of the P-40, and you have a din loud enough to wake the dead. And just to make it all even more exciting, the guns were showering us with hot metal shell casings from the gun ejector slots under the wing.

SHELL EJECTOR SLOTS

Yelling to be heard over the racket, I said, "Come on, let's scoot out from under this wing!"

Moira and I took off on our hands and knees like scalded dogs, which, now that I think about it, is a rather apt description. We were just clear of the wing when the shooting abruptly ended with the sound of the last few brass shell casings bouncing on the concrete floor.

Now I know what they mean when they say "the silence was deafening." I also now know how it feels to have a cute redhead hanging on to me as if her life depended on it, which it had a few seconds earlier.

"It's okay now, Moira. I think it's safe for us to get out of here."

We got back to our feet and she kissed my cheek. "Until I think of a better way to repay you, thanks for saving my life, Matt. If you hadn't heard those sounds and known what they meant, I'd be Swiss cheese."

I chuckled. "Hell, girl, I was saving my own hide. I just sort of brought you along for company."

In the lobby and Moira leaned wearily against the reception counter and pulled her trusty cell phone out of the right hip pocket of her jeans. She stood there looking at the screen for several seconds, and then looked at me. "I know I should call someone, but I have no idea who."

"I don't know either. Surely someone heard the racket those 30-cals were making, even out here in the boondocks."

Moira shook her head. "Not if a commercial jet was taking off from the airport beyond the museum property."

"Damn, I forgot all about the airport! I sure hope none of their jets were taking off. Miss Josephine could easily have shot one of them right out of the sky. I think my suggestion about who to call would be to hold off a minute more and take another look at things in that hangar."

Moira frowned. "Do you think it's safe to go back in there?"

"As long as we don't stand in front of Miss Josephine."

"Matt, in case you didn't notice, there are nine other aircraft in that hangar and most of them have guns too."

"True, but I have a feeling Miss Josephine is unique in the behavior we just witnessed."

Still looking at me as I was nuts for wanting to go back to the hangar, Moira said, "Well, let's not piss her off again!"

We peeked through the hangar doorway. Inside everything had changed.

For one thing, there was a strong smell of burned cordite in the hangar when we ran out earlier. There was no trace of it now. In fact everything looked just as it had before Miss Josephine threw her temper tantrum.

The two gaping holes in the big hangar door made by her thirty-cal machinegun slugs were gone. The piles of brass shell casings under her wings were also gone. Well, almost gone. Something glinted at me from behind the port main gear tire. I picked up the warm brass shell casing and dropped it into my pocket.

Moira was standing behind Miss Josephine shaking her head. "Matt, what the hell just happened to us?"

I shook my head and said, "Well, at least we know who to call now."

That comment puzzled Moira. "Who?"

"Ghost Busters."

That got a laugh out of Moira. Her smile returned. "You nut!"

Then her concerned expression returned. "What in heaven's name should we do? We'll feel pretty silly telling anyone that preposterous story if there's no proof it happened. They'd think we imagined the whole thing. Hell, maybe we did!"

"Maybe we did. Since no permanent damage seems to have been done, I suggest we get the heck out of here and have some dinner while we consider our next step. I don't think well on an empty stomach."

Moira nodded. "Okay, but I need to go home first. I ripped the knee in my jeans when we landed on the floor." In a put-on upper crust voice she added, "One simply does not go out to dine in Palm

Springs with a hole in one's jeans. It's so last year."

"I see. Okay. Do you want to meet somewhere or should I just follow you?"

"Well, it's a little more complicated than that. I rode my bike today, but my legs are still shaking so much, I'm not sure I could ride it home right now. Matt, If I asked real nice, would you give me a ride home."

"Sure, let's go."

CALLENGER HELLCAT WIDE-BODY

Moira locked the lobby entrance doors and we walked into the parking lot. I clicked a button on my remote key fob. Fifty feet away a dark red Dodge Challenger SRT Hellcat woke up and blinked its lights at us. Pointing to it, I said, "That's mine."

Moira looked where I pointed and laughed out loud. "That's funny!"

Faking an irritated tone, I said, "You can still ride your bicycle home, you know."

"No, no. It's not funny that you have a Hellcat wide-body. What's funny is my brother is an engineer at Dodge performance vehicles. He helped design that car and he's been promising to borrow one so I can have a ride in it, but he hasn't been able to get one. Now I can tell him not to bother."

"Oh. Well, it might be better not to say anything about it. I don't want your brother mad at me."

Moira looked at me. "He wouldn't be, but what difference does it make if he's mad at you? You don't even know him."

"True, but I have a hard and fast rule not to make people mad at me who design fast cars and have cute sisters."

Cocking her head to the side, she said, "I see, and how long have you had this hard and fast rule?"

I glanced at my watch for effect. "Oh, about sixty seconds."

Donning an expression of coyness, Moira said, "And you think I'm cute?"

"I'll reserve judgment on that until I see how you look in the Hellcat."

A few minutes later we were parked in front of a golf course home near the intersection of Frank Sinatra Drive and Bob Hope

Drive. I said, "Wow, classy digs."

"Oh, this place isn't mine. It's my folks' winter place. They don't use it much anymore, so I moved in to save some rent while I do my internship at the museum. Matt?"

"Yes?"

"Would it be all right with you if we sent out for a pizza and had dinner here?"

"I guess so. Are you all right?"

"I think so. What happened in the hangar a while ago gave me what my grandpa used to call the heebie-jeebies. I just need some quiet time to settle down."

"Sure. I can take off and we can meet up again in the morning to talk."

She almost shouted, "No!" Moira got an embarrassed look on her face and added in a calmer tone, "I mean I think we need to discuss what happened and we need a quiet place and . . . ."

Her voice trailed off. "That's fine with me, Moira."

My hand was on the console. She squeezed it gently and said, "Thanks for understanding, Matt."

The interior of her folks' place was first class all the way—hardwood floors, built-in cabinetry, and large windows overlooking a small lake on the golf course. Moira poured herself a glass of Ravenswood Old Vine Zinfandel that, according to the bottle, came from Lodi, California. I asked if she had any beer, and she handed me a bottle of Fat Tire Belgian ale made in Denver, Colorado. Next she asked me what I like on my pizza.

"Salami and black olives—green olives if they have 'em."

"Okay, I'll call Giuseppe's. They are like Palm Springs' gourmet pizza joint, and they actually do make the best pizza in town. They might even have green olives."

Moira ordered a large deep-dish pie with half salami and olives and half pepperoni and artichoke hearts. Then she set her cell phone on the coffee table and said, "I'm going to take a quick shower. That okay?"

I chuckled. "Not that you need my permission to take a shower in your own home, but, sure. You can even take slow shower. I'll be here."

Her expression turned soft and she looked me in the eye for a long moment. "I'm counting on that."

I didn't say so, but there was no way I was leaving now. I was getting a completely different vibe from Moira than I did at first. Not only that, but I was experiencing some pretty warm feelings in response.

As things turned out, Giuseppe was faster at making a pizza than Moira was at taking a shower. I was just paying the delivery girl when my hostess reappeared.

Moira had swapped her gray T-shirt for a maroon one, her holey jeans for a well-worn but unholey pair, and her athletic shoes for bare feet. As she came closer, I detected the warm fresh scent some women bring with them when they step out of the shower. Her skin glowed with a soft radiance that matched her scent.

Noting the pizza box in my hands, she said, "Oh, I didn't mean for you to pay for dinner. I'm not very good at this hostess stuff. I don't get much company."

I set the pizza box on the kitchen counter and said, "Don't worry about it. I'd planned on taking you out to the classiest joint in town, so I got off cheap."

She stood close to me and leaned over to sniff the pizza. "Mmmm, smells wonderful! Come on, let's eat. Is it okay with you if we eat in the kitchen?"

Kidding, I said, "Well, I was hoping for romantic candlelight on the terrace, but . . . ."

Quickly turning toward a cabinet, she said, "Oh, I have some candles!"

I reached out and grabbed her arm. Pulling her close, I said, "We don't need candles."

Moira looked into my eyes with a meaning I could not misunderstand and we kissed a very long kiss that gave me tingles from head to toe.

When we broke for air, I gently embraced her and she rested her head on my chest. Softly, she said, "Does this mean I passed the Hellcat test?"

That threw me. "What the heck are you talking about, woman?"

She put one of her big smiles on. "Back in the museum parking lot when we were talking about my brother, you said something about him having a cute sister. I asked if you thought I was cute. You said . . . ."

I interrupted her with a second kiss. It was another terrific kiss, but Moira had one track mind. "And you said you couldn't answer my question about being cute until you saw how I looked in . . . ."

I put a hand over her mouth. "Yes, Moira, you passed. You passed!"

Looking like she'd just aced a history test on the Croatian renaissance, she said, "Oh, good! I've always wanted to be cute!"

I shook my head at her feigned exuberance. "Girl, you were born cute, and you damned well know it."

After the pizza, we shared a dessert that wasn't on Giuseppe's delivery menu, and then we collapsed in the living room. Moira's laptop was open on the floor next to the cushion on which she was sitting.

Half asleep from a long and eventful day and too much pizza, I asked, "You workin' or playin'?"

She looked up from the screen. "I think I'm working. I remembered something from Miss Josephine's aircraft history file. I'm checking to find out if I'm remembering it correctly."

"Will it explain what happened earlier?"

Moira shook her head. "I'm not sure anything will entirely explain it, but it might be a clue. Here it is."

Now she had my attention and I was wide awake. "Okay, what have you got?"

"This concerns an incident at the AVG base at Toungoo, Burma. There are only a couple of paragraphs and essentially they're about volunteer pilots who never saw combat because they were killed or wounded in Japanese raids while waiting for replacement ships to arrive. One of those pilots was waiting for Miss Josephine, or at least a ship with her sequence number.

"The second paragraph mentions other pilots who flew her later claiming she had an eerie ability to get on the tails of Zeros and shoot them down. Some said she was charmed and others actually said they thought she was haunted."

By this time I was reading over her shoulder. "That sort of fits what happened tonight . . . if you believe in ghosts. Do they give the name of the pilot who died?"

"Not in this article, but I have another way of tracking it down. Hang on."

I was definitely hanging on. I was also imagining an ectoplasmic shape in Miss Josephine's cockpit blasting Jap Zeros out of the sky while shooting holes in one of the Palm Springs Air Museum's hangar doors.

"Okay. Here it is. The pilot's name was Lieutenant Don Kiefer. He was born 15 June, 1919 in . . . I don't believe this! He was born in Cathedral City, California. That's just down the road six or seven miles."

"What's more," I said, "Today is the Fifteenth of June. It would have been his ninety-ninth birthday."

Moira looked at me with amazement all over her face. "You don't suppose that . . . that . . . ."

"That Lieutenant Don Kiefer, US Army Air Force, was in Miss Josephine's cockpit tonight doing a little celebrating?"

She shook her head. "Matt, this is getting crazy. Now we've got a ghost doing something so real it scared the hell out of us, or at least me, but according to the evidence, never even happened!"

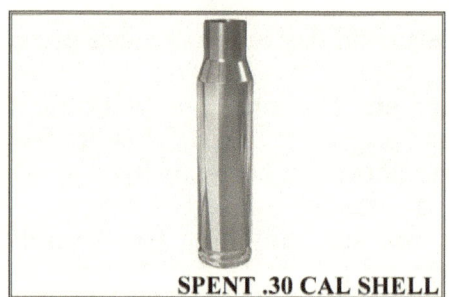
SPENT .30 CAL SHELL

Reaching into my pocket, I pulled out the thirty-caliber shell casing I found in the hangar and tossed it on the floor between the pillow Moira was sitting on and her laptop. The brass made an all too familiar ringing clatter when it hit the hardwood floor.

With a grin, I asked, "Didn't it?"

Moira's eyes went wide as she stared at the shiny brass tube. "That's a shell casing! Where did you get that?"

"From the hangar floor behind Miss Josephine's port main gear."

Looking completely flummoxed, Moira threw up her hands. "This is crazy!"

"Maybe it's not a crazy as we think. Maybe Don left us a souvenir from his 99th birthday party."

- - - - -

During the next few weeks, Moira O'Brien gradually replaced Miss Josephine as my best girl and we began seeing each other nearly every weekend. On one of those weekends, Moira lead me a display area in the hangar where Miss Josephine was parked.

There were a variety of plaques and framed certificates on one section of the wall, and she pointed to one of the plaques on which a shiny brass .30-caliber shell casing was mounted. Below the casing, the engraving said:

In Memory of
FIRST LIEUTENANT DONALD KIEFER, USAAF
June 15, 1919 – February 21, 1942
"They Also Serve Who Only Stand And Wait" ~John Milton

THE END

# Beach Girl

Friday, September 12, 2018—Avila Beach, California

I've always thought the name "Jessica" had a classy ring to it, but to me, this Jessica will always be the Beach Girl. That is partly because we met on a beach, and partly because Jessica looks exactly like she belongs on a beach from her perpetually wind-tousled hair to her always bare feet.

JESSICA

Besides her name, I knew very little about Jessica. I guessed her to be in her mid- to late-twenties. She doesn't seem to be employed, yet her home is in a gated community above Avila Beach. Ocean view home prices in that neighborhood begin around 1.5 million and run as high as five million.

On the few occasions when her travels require transportation beyond shank's mare, Jessica tools around in a screaming scarlet P-1800. If you don't recognize the name, the P-1800 was Volvo's sporty GT export of the 1960s and '70s.

VOLVO P1800

This is an odd choice for someone living in a rural location because, no matter how well built, any fifty-plus-year-old automobile requires TLC from time to time. So far as I know, however, the nearest Volvo repair service is clear over in San Luis Obispo and there are no service stations or auto repair shops of any kind in Avila Beach.

From another perspective, though, the little red Volvo is a

perfect fit for Jessica. It is a car that enjoys being driven with skillful verve and in a spritely fashion, which is exactly how she drives the little Swedish machine.

That's it. That's all I knew about Jessica, but I hasten to add my lack of knowledge about the Beach Girl was much more a matter of not wanting to scare her off by appearing too snoopy than not wanting to know her better. During our conversations I gave her many openings to talk about herself, but either I was too subtle or she figured her life was her business and none of mine.

The odd thing about our relationship back then was, despite her evasiveness on personal matters, Jessica apparently enjoyed our conversations about life and such. Also, she listened with great interest when I answered her questions about what I do and why I was in Avila Beach. Sometimes we would talk an entire afternoon away while strolling the length of beach along Front Street and on out to the sport fishing pier, a mile or so past the San Luis Bay Inn.

BEACH ALONG FRONT STREET

Oh, in case you're curious, the answer to her question about what I do is I am a screen writer. The answer to what I am doing in Avila Beach is I just completed an intense project and I needed a long vacation to recover from overexposure to the motion picture industry.

Unlike most folks I encounter, Jessica is only mildly interested in show business, which is just fine with me. Her lack of interest indicates a high degree of intelligence. It also implies an imagination quite capable of keeping its owner entertained without watching shadows of mediocre acting cavorting on a motion picture screen.

So there you have from my perspective, the story of Jessica. Her story, that is, until yesterday. Today, the world is a different place.

Jessica and I spent yesterday afternoon absorbed in our usual daily beachcombing. At one point we stopped to observe two youngsters cavorting in the surf under the watchful eyes of an older couple we guessed might be the kids' grandparents. The scene was appropriate to a conversation we were having about families and how they influence the lives of their children.

Responding to a comment I made about how caring the kids' grandparents must be to devote so much time to them, Jessica nodded less than enthusiastically and said, "Mitch, have you ever considered that too much devotion to a child can be more destructive than nurturing?"

That struck me as an odd thing to say. My writer's instinct told me the comment referred to something in Jessica's past—something significant. Even more curious about the Beach Girl now, I said, "I'm not sure I follow you. I mean, I understand parents can be overprotective and fail to prepare a child to be self-sufficient when they are faced with the real world, but . . . ."

"No, that's not what I'm talking about. I mean it is actually possible to love a child too much—to love her to death."

"I guess that could be possible, but I'm having trouble imagining such a situation. Can you give me an example?"

That question got a response I was not expecting. Jessie removed her big floppy hat and leaned her head against my shoulder. That was a big surprise. Physical contact beyond an occasional high-five when we agreed on something was not part of our relationship. "I'm sorry, Mitch. I'm just babbling now."

When she didn't step away after several seconds, I did something perfectly natural. I slid my hand around her waist and gave her a gentle squeeze. Jessie didn't seem to mind my familiarity. In fact, she put her arm around me and we continued our stroll like that. It made walking awkward, but very pleasant.

Jessica was wearing one of her bikinis and my reaction to the warmth and velvety texture of her bare skin against my hand surprised me. It was almost intoxicating. Even more surprising, just as the word "intoxicating" entered my mind, Jessie pulled herself more tightly against me. It was as if she was reading my mind and approved of the direction my thoughts were going. Impossible? The way I felt at that moment, nothing seemed impossible.

After a few minutes I felt Jessie shiver. It was time to get into some warmer clothes or leave the beach or both, but I didn't want the exciting new bridge between us to evaporate yet. I tried something else beyond our previous experience.

"Hey, Kiddo, it's getting a little chilly. How about we traipse over to Mister Rick's and warm up?"

I found myself holding my breath while I waited the few seconds it took her to answer. The last time I felt like that was when I asked the prettiest girl at our high school to the prom.

With a big grin and enthusiasm, Jessica said, "Yes. That sounds great, but I need to freshen up first. Would it be okay if I meet you at Rick's in half an hour or so?"

I watched her drive off up Front Street in her little red Volvo. My GT350 was next to where Jessie was parked, so I popped the trunk and slipped into the Topsiders and a windbreaker I keep there for just such impromptu excursions into frolicsome abandon.

And, yes, I also drive vintage sheet metal. The difference between my Hertz Shelby Mustang and Jessie's Volvo is I can disassemble and reassemble my '68 Mustang in my sleep if required, plus most of the parts or emergency make-do parts are available in auto parts stores or even at auto dismantlers.

Next, I walked across Front Street to Mister Rick's, a purveyor of spirits across from the beach. During spring breaks the seaside-themed tourist bar caters to students from Cal Poly in San Luis Obispo, or SLO as the burg is known to the cool kids. Come summer, Rick's clientele switches to folks who travel from the San Joaquin Valley to escape the heat in places like Fresno and Bakersfield.

After nursing a Carta Blanca for nearly an hour in Rick's small open air terrace next to the sidewalk, I was beginning to wonder if "meet you at Rick's in half an hour" was Jessica's polite way of telling me to buzz off. Thus, I was relieved when she walked into Mister Rick's a few minutes later, but I had to look twice to be sure it was her.

Jessie's hair was now neatly brushed to a luster that made me think of shampoo commercials and she wore just the smallest hints of eyeliner and pale lipstick. She also changed her outfit from a bikini that would easily fit in my shirt pocket to jeans, a burgundy turtleneck, a classy leather jacket, and shoes . . . well, sandals. Overall, the effect of the transformation was stunning.

Jessie's freshening up even went beyond her appearance to her personality, which needed no such enhancement. She came straight to the table and leaned over to give me a kiss on the cheek. Then, before I could stand to hold her chair for her, Jessie slid the chair so close to mine she nearly ended up sitting in my lap.

Once seated, she said, "I'm sorry I took longer than I said. One thing led to another and before I knew it I'd started from scratch with a shower and everything. Were you ready to give up on me, Baby?"

Now I was "Baby?" That called for a comment, but before I figured out what that comment ought to be, Rick's barmaid, Kellie, arrived to take Jessica's drink order. Jessie glanced at me and noticed something in my expression that caused a small frown to wrinkle her forehead. To Kellie she said, "I'll have a glass of Alapay Cabernet, please."

Kellie looked at me and I gestured to my beer stein for a refill. Kellie nodded, and as she walked away, Jessie looked at me and rested her hand on my arm. "I'm sorry, Mitch. I messed up, didn't I?"

This is a good example of why you seldom hear the same dialogue in a film as you hear among a group of friends in the real world. The intent of the conversation must be spelled out in a film because viewers seldom get enough visual cues from a film scene to understand subtle or vague dialogue. Trying to catch up, I said, "I don't know, Jessie. What did you do?"

She looked down, and then back at me. "I think I tried too hard."

I thought I had an idea of what she was getting at, but I wasn't sure. "You tried too hard? Tried what too hard? I'm sorry, I'm confused."

Jessie shook her head. "I don't think you're really confused, but you're right to make me spell it out. That's how we learn about each other. Mitch, I've wanted to get closer to you since our very first walk on the beach, but you scare the hell out of me."

Now I was really confused. "I scare you? How do I do that?"

Shaking her head, Jessie said, "It's nothing you do, really. It's who you are—a big Hollywood movie guy used to hobnobbing with other big shots and beautiful sexy actresses. That's why I've stayed at arm's length. I was afraid of making a fool of myself and scaring you off."

"Jessie . . . ."

She held her hand up to stop me. "Please let me finish. This is taking all the nerve I have left."

I shrugged and she took a deep breath. "This afternoon I decided I had to try something to make you see me as a woman instead of just a pal. To do that I thought I had to stop being a beach bunny and be more attractive and sophisticated like the women you're used to." After a short pause, Jessie added, "That's how I messed up. I overdid it and ended up doing what I was trying most to avoid; I made a fool of myself. I'm really sorry and if you want me to go away, I will understand."

Kellie delivered our drinks and I took Jessie's hand in mine. After staring at her intently for several seconds, I leaned forward and kissed her lips. It was one of the most exciting kisses I've ever experienced.

Now it was Jessie's turn to stare at me, which she also did for several seconds. Finally, she whispered, "Oh, my."

"Yes, 'oh my.' Is it my turn to talk now?"

Jessie lowered her eyes and said, "Yes, Dear." Then she quickly looked up and added, "Is 'dear' okay? I could tell you didn't like 'baby'."

"Yes, Jessie, 'dear' is okay because it sounds like a term of endearment you might really use. Am I right?"

She nodded and I said, "Good, then I like it. Now, let's get down to cases. First, I am not a big shot and I do not hobnob with movie people. I am just a writer and I avoid movie people whenever possible. Remember? That's one reason I'm up here in Avila Beach. I'm recuperating from overexposure to movie people. Did you get all that?"

Jessie nodded again, but said nothing. "Okay, about our relationship for the past few weeks. I don't know how you missed my hints. I thought I was being pretty damned obvious about doing everything BUT ignoring you. That's because I feel the same way about you as you feel about me."

Her eyes widened. "You do?"

"You bet I do. Everything about you from the way you think, to the way you look at me, to your cute butt have been driving me nuts for weeks."

Apparently feeling relieved, Jessie grinned at me and teased, "Do you really think my butt is cute?"

Feigning frustration with her, I shook my head and said, "Yes, your butt is the very definition of cute!"

A couple of gals at the table next to ours apparently overheard me and giggled. Jessie turned beet red and I glared at the girls, and said, "Well, it is!"

That just made them giggle all the more. Ignoring them I turned back to Jessie and said, "Okay, are we straight on all that now?"

"Yes, Dear. I think we're straight."

Standing, I said, "Good. Come on."

"YES, DEAR"

"Mitch! I just got here! Where are we going?"

Helping Jessie from her chair, I said, "We are going to suite 312 at the San Luis Bay Inn, where I have a heated view-balcony and room service that will bring us just about anything we could possibly want. How long you stay there is entirely up to you, but I think you'll agree we need some privacy to discuss this turn of events.

Jessie looked up with a coy smile. "Yes, Dear."

## Saturday, September 13, 2018
## San Luis Bay Inn–Avila Beach, California

By unanimous consent Jessie and I decided to spend Saturday together, starting with breakfast at the Custom House. We got there, however, by a circuitous route necessitated by a stop at Jessie's house to drop off her Volvo and change her clothes.

While she changed, I wandered around taking in the décor. Among the items I found interesting was a framed black and white photo in the family room. It showed a woman nursing a baby. I guessed it was a family photo, but it was not the sort of thing one expected to see on a family room wall.

I was still in the family room when Jessie tracked me down. "There you are. I was afraid I'd lost you."

I smiled. "That ain't gonna happen. I was just admiring your home. This is a great house and you've made it very homey."

"Thanks, Mitch, but I don't get credit for the décor. My mother did most of the decorating when she lived here."

Would that be you and her over there on the wall?"

I thought Jessie blushed a little. "Yes, that's mother and me. That was a long time ago. She's gone now."

"Oh? I'm sorry to hear that."

Jessie's expression turned to something complex I couldn't identify. Softly, she said, "Don't be."

Jessica seemed to be going from one life mystery to another. Getting a handle on the whole story was becoming a long process. I heard the first installment Friday night when she told me her father left their home while Jessie was still a child of ten.

At the Custom House, Rick's next-door neighbor, we ordered breakfast, after which Jessie got a sort of faraway look on her face. I said, "Hello? Earth to pretty lady . . . whatcha thinkin' about?"

Jessie jumped a little as if she was surprised to suddenly wake up and find herself in a place she didn't remember going. Looking at me, she said, "You must think I'm a real mess."

"For the record, I do not think that, but even if I did, I would think you're the cutest mess I ever saw."

That got me a smile. "Okay, I'm a cute mess, but you have to be curious about me and all the drama in my life."

"Of course I'm curious. That's because you've become special to me. I'm also patient. If there are things in your past you want me to know, you'll get around to telling me about them. In the meantime I'm just enjoying the view."

I earned another smile. "I think you enjoyed more than the view last night. I sure did!"

There was no doubt she was right about that. I lost track of how many times we woke up in each other's arms and succumbed to the throes of endless pent up passion. Be that as it may, however, Jessie had just skillfully redirected our conversation away from all that drama in her life. I decided to let her get away with it, but she wasn't going to let herself get away with it.

"I'm sorry, Mitch. That was rotten of me."

"It was only tricky of you, not rotten. Also, I'm getting a little tired of you apologizing for things. How 'bout we do this? When you do something I think deserves an apology, I'll let you know."

The arrival of our breakfasts—a Belgian waffle with fresh strawberries for Jessie and Eggs Benny for me—acted like one of those reset buttons on electronic devices that restore the operating system to its original state. She took a swallow of her coffee and said, "Okay, Mitch, I'm not sorry, but you deserve some answers so you know what you're getting yourself into."

"Well, unless you're an ax murderer, let's save the answers until we get to the beach. Okay?"

Jessie looked down at her plate and said, "Okay."

Across the street where I'd parked the Shelby, the sun was shining brightly on our beach and the air was warming up nicely. In celebration of all that, Jessie stripped off her pink and white striped top and white jeans, revealing another pocket-sized bikini. From there, she took my hand and we set off along the beach toward Fossil Point to the south.

After walking for only a short distance, Jessie stopped. There were some rocks along the low cliff to our left. She pointed to them and said, "Let's sit for a minute."

I knew she wasn't suggesting we sit because she was tired. Jessie could outwalk me and then some, so I got the idea I was about to get another chapter of the Jessica story. I was right.

Turning to face me, Jessie took my hand and said, "I didn't do it with an ax, but I did murder someone."

That one caught me completely off guard. All I could think of to say was, "Oh? Should I be in fear for my life?"

She shook her head as if my question was intended to be taken seriously. "You're the last person in the world I want to kill, or even hurt. That's why I'm telling you this. The person I killed was my mother."

My Beach Girl was just full of surprises. The only reply I could think of this time was: "I'm guessing that probably happened for a good reason."

Jessie nodded. "Yes, at the time there was a reason, but that doesn't make it any easier to live with the fact that I killed my own mother. The County of San Luis Obispo Grand Jury said it was 'justifiable homicide' because the coroner and the sheriff agreed the evidence supported my story that I killed her in self-defense."

"Then, that's it; end of story."

She shook her head. "No, that's not the end of the story. If you and I are going to . . . well, going to do whatever this is we're doing, you have to hear what I did and why. Otherwise you will always wonder . . . ."

I stifled a sigh. "Alright, tell me the story."

Jessie took a deep breath. "I told you my father left my mother and me when I was only ten, but there is more to it. I didn't learn the entire truth until I found his suicide note among my mother's papers after she . . . died.

"In that note father wrote words to the effect he was going to kill himself because he feared he would do something terrible to me if he continued to live." Jessie paused for several moments before taking another deep breath and continuing her story.

Now there was a sob in her voice. "He was afraid he would molest me because he couldn't help himself. Father loved me . . . so much . . . he killed himself . . . rather than . . . ."

"Jessie, your father wasn't thinking clearly. He could have gotten help . . . ."

"I know that, Mitch, but to him there was some kind of logic to what he was doing. The thing is, I never had the slightest sense of father doing anything wrong . . . like touching me inappropriately or . . . or anything. In fact, I doted on him. I always felt much closer to him than to mother. He really was a good man."

A realization finally caught up with me. That realization completely reversed the perspective of our conversation the previous day. "This is what you were talking about yesterday when you said it was possible to love a child too much, isn't it? You weren't talking about too much love hurting the child, you meant the parent."

"Yes, Darling. I didn't intend to be so mysterious about it. I guess I said that because I wanted to tell you about all this then, but I couldn't do it because I was afraid you would think I was nuts or something."

"The only nutty thing I've seen you do is fall in love with me, that is, assuming this is love."

Jessie gave me a small smile. "I'm pretty sure it's love, alright, and falling in love with you wasn't nutty. It is the only thing I've done lately that actually makes sense, but please let me finish this story. I need to find out if you . . . you still love me after . . . ."

I wasn't really enthusiastic about watching Jessie torture herself further, but it was apparently something she needed to do for herself, as well as for me. "Okay, go ahead."

"Father built a successful plastics manufacturing company in LA and he left an estate of something like fifteen million. After he died, mother sold our big house in Avila Beach and moved to the smaller place I have now. The rest of the estate is well managed and nets me something like three hundred thousand a year. Mostly, it all just sits there making more money than I can possibly spend."

I laughed. "Sounds like a terrible problem to me."

Jessie shook her head. "That has nothing to do with any of this. I only told you that part so you wouldn't think I was only interested in you as a meal ticket."

"That idea never occurred to me."

"Anyway, six or seven years after father 'disappeared,' mother began behaving strangely. Before that she was always kind of flighty, but suddenly she was angry and agitated all of the time. I got her in to see her doctor and he prescribed some pills to calm her down, but she didn't like taking them because of their side-effects. The situation got worse almost by the day.

"The problem was, no matter what I did, I couldn't please her. All I could do was stay off her radar. Then one night it all came to a head. I was just drifting off to sleep when my bedroom door slammed open and mother came in. She screamed at me . . . calling me all kinds of names and saying stuff like, 'You killed my man and made me a widow . . . you dirty slut.'"

Jessie's voice grew shrill and louder as she described the nightmare scene in her bedroom that night. "Mother kept saying It over and over, 'You dirty slut . . . you dirty slut,' and then light from the window flashed on something in her hand and I saw the knife. Dad was an amateur chef and she had dad's favorite chef's knife. It looked huge in mother's hand."

"By time time I was out of bed and trying to get out of the room, but she had me cornered. She raised that big knife over her head with both hands. The point of the blade was aimed right at my chest. All the time she was still screaming, 'You killed him . . . you dirty slut . . .you dirty slut!'"

Looking into Jessie's eyes and I saw pure terror. She was living that horrible night all over again. I started to reach for her, but she shrank away from me. We were in very different worlds at that moment.

Breathing faster, Jessie went on with her narrative. "I didn't know what to do. I couldn't get away from her. Finally, she swung the knife at me. I sidestepped far enough that the blade only grazed my arm and stuck in the wall. While mother was pulling at the knife, trying to get it loose, I moved toward the door as fast as I could.

"I squeezed past her and was nearly to the door when the knife came unstuck from the wall. She spun around and came at me again. I grabbed for the only thing I could reach, my desk lamp. It was one of those adjustable ones with a heavy base. I grabbed it by its shade end and swung it at mother. The heavy base gave the lamp a lot of centrifugal force. It was almost like swinging a baseball bat. The base hit her in the left temple.

"She staggered and began turning her head left and right as if she was looking for me, but couldn't see me. She made a hideous noise in her throat like a choked scream, and then she sort of melted onto the floor a little at a time. When she stopped moving, that horrible knife was still in her hand."

Now Jessie was literally gasping for breath, but she kept on talking between gasps. "I ran into the kitchen . . . and dialed nine-one . . . one. I told the operator . . . she sent paramedics and sheriff's . . . ."

Suddenly Jessie just went limp. She fell against me and I held her for at least a minute until she looked up at me. I doubt she could see me clearly, though. Her eyes were filled with tears.

"Jessie, just breathe slowly and relax. It's all over. You did what you believed you had to do that night and again just now, but it's over and you're okay."

She wiped some of the tears from her eyes and looked at me again. "Do . . . do you still want me after what I did? I mean, do you still . . . ."

"Do I still love you? Yes, more than ever. You went through hell that night, and the fact that you were willing to relive it for my benefit now leaves no doubt about your feelings for me. In fact, I wouldn't be at all surprised if we found ourselves standing in front of a preacher one of these days, assuming you believe in such traditional goings on."

"Oh, Mitch! I believe in them more than ever now. I love you so much. I don't know how I lived without you."

I smiled at Jessie. "You got along without me because you're one smart, brave woman . . . and . . . ."

Now she was smiling despite the tears on her cheeks. "Yes? And what?"

"And you've still got the cutest butt on the west coast."

Still wiping the tears away, Jessie frowned at me. "Only on the west coast?"

## THE END

# Spirit Grandmother

Friday, November 16, 2018—Brookings, Oregon

Brookings, Oregon is not at all what you would call a major metropolis, or for that matter, even a minor metropolis. It is simply a quiet little seaside town just north of the California border with a total of about thirteen thousand residents if you include a large surrounding area.

BROOKINGS, OREGON

The average age of Brookings' residents is "retired," although some work at California's Pelican Bay State Prison near Crescent City a few miles south of the border. Pelican Bay State Prison is a maximum security facility with most of its inmates doing time for violent crimes.

While Pelican Bay State Prison is hardly a vacation destination, it had a lot to do with why I was in Brookings. More accurately, I was in an ocean view room at the Best Western Beachfront Inn—what serves as upscale accommodations in Brookings—courtesy of Del Hamner, head honcho of Magic Productions, LLC located clear down at the opposite end of California in Burbank.

I'm writing a motion picture treatment for Hamner based on an actual event at the prison and I'm in Brookings to do background research. It seems a prisoner escaped a while back and showed up in Brookings, where he proceeded to terrify the town.

So far, I've read what the history books and period newspapers said about the escape. I also took a look at the prison—as much of it as they would let me see—and familiarized myself with the local geography. Now what I needed was a local point of view—the human experience of having a fellow who has been described as a "crazed murderer" running amuck in a small town.

According to nearly everyone with whom I've spoken, the best source for the background I needed was a young woman named Sharyne Brennan who is officially in charge of the Brookings office of the Western Oregon Visitors Association. Unofficially, she is a leading authority on coastal Oregon history.

SHARYNE BRENNAN

When I spoke with her long-distance to make an appointment, Ms. Brennan was both knowledgeable and cooperative. I looked forward to meeting her, which was the first item on my agenda for the day. By the way, I checked— Sharyne is pronounced with the emphasis on the second syllable, which has a long E sound, like Shar•reen'.

You don't have to spend more than a minute or two with Sharyne to know she's a country girl through and through from her blue jeans to her sneakers. I didn't even know they still made Keds.

In addition to being tall and slender with a contagious smile, another of Ms Brennan's notable features is a good deal of Native American ancestry. However, that quality is contradicted by bright blue eyes and auburn hair, which is short in what I believe is called a "pixie" cut. Then she throws us a big city curve in the form of a wide blonde streak from the top of her head to her bangs. I kind of hoped the do was indicative of her personality.

Her personal office removes any doubt about Sharyne's enthusiasm for history. Besides more books than had any right to be in a tiny ten-by-twelve SRO space, there are old maps on the walls with many more maps poking out of cardboard tubes. There are also banker's boxes overflowing with black and white photographs on the shelves that weren't already sagging under the weight of books. Being something of a history nut, myself, I could have spent weeks exploring Sharyne's treasures. Yeah, those treasures, too.

When a cheerful young woman who introduced herself as Susie showed me into Sharyne's office, which Susie said was being reorganized, Ms Brennan was standing in the midst of chaos with a bankers box in her arms and looking up at an empty spot on a shelf well above her head. I said, "If the that box goes in that hole up there, maybe I can help."

Just like that, she turned and handed me the box. "Hello, Mister Radcliff. You're just in time to save me the trouble of scrounging a stepladder. Please be sure the label end of the box faces out."

I slid the box into its slot, and when I turned around, she handed me a nine-by-twelve manila envelope. There were no markings on it, so I asked the obvious question. "What do I have here, Ms Brennan?"

"It's Sharyne, and what you have there is a photograph of the man you came to talk about, Eric Grover. I had it duplicated from my file copy, so you can keep that one."

"I'm Travis, or Trav if you prefer." We shook hands, and I thanked her for the photo as I opened the envelope. Removing the eight-by-ten photo, I was immediately struck by the intensity of the image. For a moment I thought I could actually feel the man's savage fury.

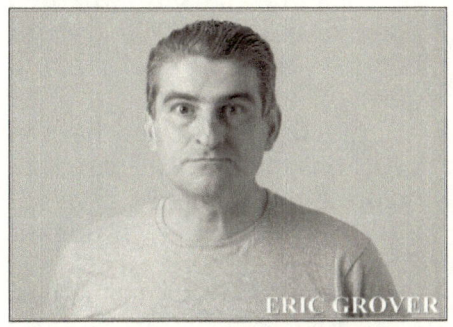

ERIC GROVER

"Damn. This guy couldn't have been as mean as he looks."

"I'm pretty certain he is."

I looked up at her. "Is? I thought Grover died during his escape attempt."

Sharyne nodded and said, "According to the official record, he did, but some folks who ought to know the score aren't so sure. For one thing, his body was never recovered."

Staring at the photo in my hand, my mind quickly filled with possibilities Sharyne's revelation brought with it. The possibility that Grover survived changed several aspects of my project, not the least of which was the ending of the screen treatment I was developing. Sherlock Holmes' creator, Arthur Conan Doyle, made considerable success out of a mysterious villain who showed a definite inclination toward immortality. Of course, to make use of those possibilities, there had to be some evidence to support the possibility Grover survived the manhunt.

"And I take it you think they might be right."

Sharyne gave her head a thoughtful tilt. "I haven't made up my mind yet, but the arguments supporting his being alive come from knowledgeable local people, some of whom were eyewitnesses and are quite convincing . . . that is if you know the people."

"And, presumably, you know the people."

That got me a smile. "You don't miss much, do you?"

I smiled back. "I try not to. How about giving me kind of a blow-by-blow summary of what happened from the time this guy escaped Pelican Bay until he . . . disappeared?"

"I can do better than that. If it will help, I can give you a guided tour with the story so you can see the locations where things happened."

"That's more than I could have hoped for."

"Then you've got it. Let's go."

She checked out with Susie, and as we left the building, Sharyne said, "I'm afraid my pickup is in the shop, so we'll have to go in the Association van. That will limit us a little if we need to visit a remote location. Off-roading in these parts is hazardous without lots of ground clearance and four-wheel-drive."

"Maybe we should take my vehicle, then."

Sharyne looked where I pointed and said, "Wow, that's not new is it? It looks brand new!"

"Well, she was new back in 1969, but she was well cared for before I got her, and I gave her a complete frame-off restoration, so let's say she's 'sort of' brand new."

"It's beautiful! We shouldn't have any trouble going where we want to go in it, but tell me something. Why do men always refer to cars as females?"

"Not all men do that. My vehicles remind me of people I know. Some are men and some are women. Now, the Scout here has always struck me as female, and since I met you, I'm sure of it."

Sharyne cocked her head and with a half-smile she asked, "Oh? Why is that?"

"Because the Scout shines up pretty, but she's not afraid to get a little mud on her fenders if the situation calls for it. I'm willing to bet money you and she have those qualities in common."

Sharyne responded with a self-conscious smile that might have said she wasn't comfortable with compliments. On the other hand, she gave as good as she got.

"All right, you smooth talkin' writer guy, let's see you put your money where your mouth is. You gonna let me drive your gal Scout?"

I tossed her the keys. "I was hoping you'd offer."

From the visitor center we headed south through town on Highway 101 and pulled into the parking lot of a Mexican food-to-go place called Cielito Lindo. It's on the east side of the road a short distance north of the highway bridge over the Chetco River that sort of marks what most people think of as the southern boundary of Brookings proper.

"WHERE IT ALL BEGAN"

Sharyne leaned back in the seat and said, "This is where it all began, at least as far as Brookings is concerned. Back then this was a Conoco station with a convenience market. After what happened here, they decided to move the station on down the highway a block or so."

"And what happened here?"

"According to surviving witnesses, Grover charged into the convenience market waving a large revolver and ordering three customers who were in the store to the floor. Grover then made the attendant open the cash register and proceeded to take the paper cash it contained—fifty-seven dollars.

"Next, he demanded to know who owned a white SUV parked outside and got their keys. While Grover was doing that, the attendant shifted position slightly behind the counter. Witnesses say it was not a threatening move, but Grover shot him twice, and then shot the customer, a woman, who owned the SUV, both victims died. After that, he took a handful of Twinkies and left."

"A gourmet on top of everything else."

Sharyne made a face, put the Scout in gear, and turned back to the north on the highway. She continued her narrative as we passed at least a dozen antique stores—Oregon is big on antique stores—interspersed with dog grooming establishments. "He took the SUV and drove up Highway One-Oh-One like this to Loring's sporting goods store, which is up here on our right."

Two blocks later my guide pulled to the curb in front of a single story green building. "Grover parked behind the store so the SUV was out of sight while he was in the store. Loring's clerk reported Grover held him at gunpoint and forced him to carry several loads of merchandise out to the SUV.

"In addition to more than a hundred dollars from the register, Grover took a down sleeping bag and other camping paraphernalia, a Remington 870 shotgun, a Marlin .357 magnum carbine, a Glock nine millimeter pistol, and enough ammunition to outfit an army."

"Geez!"

"Yeah, I imagine that's what the local cops thought when they finally got on Grover's trail. Remember, though, they were well behind him at this point because they started at the gas station convenience market with two dead bodies and very little idea how they got that way.

"When authorities finally realized who they were dealing with, practically every cop and sheriff's deputy in the county was brought in. California also sent several correctional officers from the prison up to help."

"Do they know where Grover went next?"

"Yes. An alert customer saw Grover's picture on a TV news alert about his escape and called in to say she was sure he was the same man who was in front of her in line at the Fred Meyer store half an hour later.

"The cops went to the register lane the woman was in and talked to the clerk. When they showed him a mug shot, he clearly remembered Grover, saying he paid cash for two bags of groceries that were mostly canned and other processed foods that were easy to prepare."

Sharyne pulled into the huge parking lot of the giant Fred Meyer hypermarket that was easily the largest store in Brookings. I said, "Coming here was a smart move on his part. The place is huge, so it's only a matter of bad luck that someone noticed and remembered him."

"I'm sure that's what he was thinking. Also, all of this happened on a Saturday morning, like between ten and eleven, which is when everybody around here does their weekly shopping. The long and the short of it is the Fred Meyer information trimmed Grover's lead by a bunch. Now the cops were only about thirty minutes behind Grover, but then they hit a solid brick wall."

"How did they turn him up again?"

"By helicopter. I'll show you, but this is where things start to get weird."

She pulled out of Fred Meyer's parking lot and took Highway 101 south. At the north end of the Chetco River Bridge, she turned left onto the aptly named North Bank Chetco River Road.

Sharyne continued her story. "The County Sheriff even went up in a rented helicopter looking for the SUV Grover swiped and found it in plain sight next to a residence on this road."

"I guess that proves you have to have more than a mean streak to be a successful bad guy. You need a little common sense. too. I gather he lit out before they could surround the place."

Sharyne shook her head. "He wasn't even that bright. It was almost as if Grover wanted a shootout, and he sure got one. This is where it happened."

SHOOTOUT LOCATION

She pulled off onto the unpaved shoulder, saying, "The house was where those smaller trees are now. It burned to the ground during the shootout. The foliage has already filled in the spot so all that's left is a short section of concrete curbing where the driveway was. You can't see it from here because of the trees, but the river is just on the other side of the property."

"Got it. Am I likely to be shot for trespassing if I get out and look around a little?"

Sharyne laughed. "No worry, paleface. Me heap brave Indian squaw. Me protect white eyes from evil spirits."

I made a face at her, and opening the door, I said, "Okay, Sacagawea, let's go."

Once we were past the shrubbery closest to the road, we were in a jungle. Overhead branches blocked out a lot of light, turning the remaining bits and pieces of debris on the site into trip hazards. Sharyne walked ahead of me and I was impressed with her lightness of step and nimble dodging of obstacles.

As we picked our way along, I asked, "So what makes those folks you mentioned earlier think Grover got away and is still alive?"

Over her shoulder, Sharyne replied, "One of their main arguments is the coroner's inability to identify the body or bodies the police found among this debris. The fire was super-hot and reduced the remains to pieces of bone and ashes."

"I understand, but even with nothing but bones, the coroner should have been able to estimate height, weight, and body type. Also dental records should've helped."

"True. The thing is, there should have been two bodies in the debris, Grover and the fellow who owned the house, but the remains they were able to recover were so badly destroyed, the coroner couldn't say for sure whether there were actually two sets of remains. On top of that, there are no dental records available for either man. So the question is, if one of the men didn't die in the shootout and fire, which one was it?"

"I see, and since nobody has seen the owner of the house since, those who think Grover survived figure the remains all belonged to the owner, right?"

Sharyne stopped and turned to face me. "Hey, paleface heap smart feller!"

"Yeah, and fair Injun maiden heap smart ass."

She grinned. "Okay, I had that coming. Sometimes, with strangers, I get a little defensive about my Native American heritage."

I grinned back at here. "So I see, but save that for those who don't respect your heritage. I most certainly do."

Her face turned serious. "Thank you, Travis. I appreciate that and apologize for being a brat."

I smiled. "Your apology is unnecessary, but I accept it anyway. How much further is the river bank?"

Gesturing to the trees and bush ahead, she said, "Just on the other of this foliage. Come on."

Sharyne warned me to watch my step and pushed some branches aside. Suddenly, I was on a bluff looking down at the Chetco River. The bank stretched hundred-fifty feet or so from the bottom of our bluff to thick brush at the very edge of the river. I estimated the Chetco River at 800 feet wide with a swift current flowing toward the sea to our right. The highway bridge was also to our right about 200 yards further down-river. Beyond the bridge on the other side of the water was a marina. Just beyond the marina the river emptied into the ocean.

We scooted down the bluff, and as we walked toward the river, I said, "Do you know if the river current was running this fast when Grover would have been here?"

"Probably. It was about this time of year and the snow pack was feeding it then, just like it is now."

"Well if Grover got this far, he had plenty of options for his getaway, at least on this side of the river. It would take a strong swimmer to get across without being pulled out to the marina and beyond.

Looking up the bank behind us and then at the river again, I said, "You know, I'm not sure Grover was, or is, as dumb as we think. He set up a perfect disappearance scenario here."

Sharyne grinned. "I'm getting the feeling you have joined the ranks of those who think Grover didn't die in that house fire."

Shrugging, I said, "Maybe. They're sure both men were in the house?"

"According to the reports, there was no doubt about that or who they were."

"And what explanation did the police give for the missing body?"

"The cops didn't actually have an explanation What they said was they had the property so tightly contained nobody could have slipped away. Also, they claimed the remains they found could have been from two men, even though the coroner couldn't distinguish between them. Finally, they point out that pieces of at least one of the guns Grover stole from Loring's Sporting Goods were among the house debris."

Shaking my head, I said, "I hate to say this, but I think the law enforcement community was doing a lot of wishful thinking back then. Grover picked Brookings for a reason. Maybe he knew the area already and conceived of a way everyone would think he died while he disappeared into thin air."

Sharyne said, "I have to give the cops credit, though, they brought top crime scene investigators in from Sacramento and Salem, and they spent nearly a week looking for explanations. So they tried . . . sort of."

"Yeah, I have copies of several reports and summaries, but I haven't looked at them all yet. I didn't know there was a controversy until today."

"So I did you some good?"

"Absolutely. I am in your debt."

With a playful grin, Sharyne said, "Good. Lunch is on you!"

I loved her spontaneity. "It will be my pleasure. Which way to Mickey D's?"

"Oh no, you don't, Mister Writer Guy! You're taking us to the classiest joint in town."

A few minutes later we had crossed both the Chetco River and Highway 101, and were seated at a table on a wooden deck overlooking the Marina. From Sharyne's description, I was expecting something a little more ritzy, but then I remembered we were in the coastal hinterlands of Oregon and figured I could give up a little ritz for good food.

On Sharyne's recommendation, I ordered a cup of "Award Winning Made From Scratch Clam Chowder (Boston style)" and seafood fajitas, both of which were tasty and expensive. My guest commented on the prices.

"I was kidding about you buying lunch, Travis. These prices are much too high for you to be stuck with the whole lunch tab, so let's go Dutch. I come here because I figure if I'm eating out it's better to pay a little more and get food properly prepared and made from fresh ingredients."

I said, "I agree with that philosophy, but a deal is a deal. I said I'd buy lunch and that's the way it's going to be."

"I see. I also notice you've been opening doors for me all morning. Don't tell me you're one of those chauvinist guys."

Feeling as if I'd just been transported back the 1970s, I said, "Sharyne, opening a door for someone—man or woman—is a gesture of respect, and in my book, respect is earned. If you hadn't earned my respect, you could open your own damned doors."

Sharyne studied my face for several moments, and then said, "I guess I have a tendency to pigeonhole people, and since you travel in lofty circles, I put you in the box labeled 'slick.' My insecurities are showing. I'm sorry."

"What you're saying is, because I'm from Hollywood, I must be a phony, right?"

She shook her head vehemently. "No. I . . . I didn't mean . . . . Look, I said I'm sorry. Okay?"

"You know, Sharyne, I'm sad you feel that way because I'm really starting to like you and liking you makes me want to know you better." After a pause during which she looked at her plate and made no response, I said, "Okay, are we done with the crime scenes tour?"

After a hesitation that was long enough to make me think she was trying to make a decision, Sharyne said, "No. There's one more spot. It's not official and you won't find it in any reports, but I want to take you to a spot that may tie into all this. I'll explain on the way; that is, if you want to see it."

Taking the check from the table, I said, "Sure, I want to see everything even remotely connected with Grover."

At the vehicle, Sharyne offered me the keys as if she thought I no longer trusted her with the Scout, but I said, "You know where we're going, you drive."

Sharyne nodded without comment and off we went. Our destination turned out to be a state park back at the north end of Brookings. We made the short trip in silence.

I wasn't kidding when I told Sharyne I was sad she thought I was "slick." She was quite a woman—one who fascinated and attracted me in ways that were new to me. It wasn't just that she was physically attractive. It was also about the way she thought, her mannerisms, her sense of humor, and a dozen other things. I had the feeling I lost something important over shrimp fajitas at the marina, and that was a shame.

When I saw a sign at the Harris Beach Marine Garden State Park entrance that announced a five dollar daily parking fee, I reached for my wallet, but Sharyne rolled her window down and spoke to the ranger at the gate. "Hi, Ben. We'll just be here a minute."

Ben said, "Okay, Sharyne. Come back when you can stay for a

cup of coffee, okay?"

"Will do, Ben. See you later."

It was obvious from Ben's enthusiasm he liked Sharyne. I could easily imagine that being a common opinion among the young men of Brookings.

HARRIS BEACH PARKING

At the end of the entrance road, we came to a fairly large parking circle. It was surprisingly full for a cool overcast weekday. Sharyne guided my Scout into a parking space facing the beach and turned off the engine.

"I want to tell you about two things I think might be related to Grover, but they could also be nothing."

I said, "Tell me."

"The first thing happened the day after the shootout and fire at the house on the river. A pickup truck was stolen from Sporthaven Marina where we just had lunch. Back then that sort of thing didn't happen often in Brookings, so it made the newspaper."

"The next day, the missing truck showed up right here in this parking lot. It was abandoned with the keys still in it. I know that's what happened because I was out here dropping off some Visitors Association brochures for the park's information booth and I stopped long enough to have a cup of coffee with Ben, the ranger at the entrance gate."

With a smile on my face and in my voice, I said, "I bet that made his day."

Sharyne turned quickly and looked at me, probably wondering if I was being sarcastic. I wasn't, but I'm not entirely sure she knew that.

Continuing her story, she said, "Anyway, I saw a county tow truck hook up the pickup and Ben explained it was left here overnight, which is strictly against the rules in the day-use part of the park.

"I don't suppose anyone went over the truck for fingerprints."

Again Sharyne looked at me. After a moment, she said, "I wondered the same thing, so I asked a deputy sheriff I know. He just shrugged and said, "The truck had been recovered and wasn't damaged, so there wasn't any reason to make a big deal out of it. They just told the owner not to leave the keys in his truck anymore."

"Too bad."

Nodding, Sharyne said, "I assume you're wondering the same thing as me. Did Eric Grover escape the burning house and steal that truck from the marina down river?"

"Yup. The big question is, if he did, why would he leave it here? Also, how did he get across the river without being seen?"

She swung the door open on her side and said, "He could have waited until dark, and then crossed the river on the highway bridge."

"You could be right. It's a safe bet he didn't swim across that river. What is the second thing you want to tell me about?"

"We have to take a short walk for me to tell you about that."

I was following Sharyne to the beach, but stopped to look at a large signboard with all the park rules on it. There were a bunch of them.

Sharyne noticed and said, "Don't worry too much about the rules, it's the squirrels you have to worry about. These little critters will run right up your leg to see if you've got any food. Tourists feed them and that has resulted so many squirrels you can hardly move without stepping on them. They've gotten to be such pests there's talk of rounding them all up and moving them to another location."

As she said that, a gray shape with a bushy tail flashed past me just a few inches from my foot. "I see what you mean."

We walked a short distance south on the beach, and then climbed a low hill that gave us a view of the southern-most stretch of Harris Beach. Sharyne stopped and pointed at a large rock outcropping sticking out into the surf.

"See that big rock out there? It's called Arch Rock."

"I see it."

"Do you also see the people on the beach right next to it?"

I looked more closely. "You have good eyes, Ms Brennan. I didn't see them at first because they blend into the color of the rock behind them. It wasn't until you told me they were there and one of them moved that I actually saw them."

"The reason I brought you to this spot is to put what I'm about to tell you into perspective. I mean, I do have good eyesight and I know how to spot distant objects that are hard to see, but this is still a long shot."

I couldn't help smiling at her. "All right, Sharyne, what did you see out there that might or might not have been what or who you think it was?"

ARCH ROCK

Shar looked back at me for several seconds, as if deciding whether or not I would laugh at her for thinking she saw whatever she thought she saw. Finally, she just said, "Eric Grover."

Still smiling, I said, "I kind of thought that's what you were going to say."

"I ran to my truck for my field glasses, but by the time I got back here, whoever had been out there was gone. Now, I'll admit I have Grover on the brain because he scares the hell out of me, so it's possible I'm forcing pieces of a puzzle into places they don't go, but with the pickup from the marina and all . . . ."

"What you have in your brain is called a hunch, and I like it. I like it a lot."

Sharyne looked surprised. "You do?"

"I do. What time does this beach open?"

She tilted her head in curiosity. "About eight. Why?"

"Tomorrow is Saturday. If you're free, what would you say to finding a good spot out here and doing a little surveillance?"

Now she looked dubious. "Really?"

"Sure. I mean I could come out here and do it by myself, but your eyes are better than mine, which would improve our chances of seeing something down there or in the trees inland from the point."

"You think Grover might still be around here after all this time?"

"I think two things. First, I think there's a strong possibility he escaped that fire or was never in it. Second, I still think there is a reason he made a beeline for Brookings as soon as he escaped. I don't know what that reason was, but it's possible he already knew the area and thought it was a good place to disappear. So, I'm not prepared to walk away from this without at least looking into the possibility he's here or has been here since he was supposedly killed."

"You're also putting a lot of faith in my hunch."

"Sharyne, you're smart, you have skills, and know how to use those skills. Besides, like I told you earlier, you've earned my respect. In my book those things make your hunch at least a possibility. Also, you've been straight about what you've told me, so if I'm betting on the wrong horse, it's my mistake, not yours."

She shook her head, and then just stared at me for several seconds. I said, "Something wrong?"

"Travis, no one has ever treated me the way you do. That respect you talk about is new to me. I'm just not sure how to deal with it."

"Well, I wouldn't worry about it. Pick you up around seven for breakfast?"

I got the idea from her expression that she was making up her mind about something again. After several seconds, she said, "Well, yes, but if you don't have anything else to do, I have tickets to the Brookings Honors Banquet tonight. It's not a big deal, but I'm supposed to receive an award and . . . well . . . ."

While she was searching for words to fit circumstances she didn't encounter often, I gave her a warm smile and helped her off the hook. "Sharyne, if you are inviting me to the banquet, I would enjoy going to the event with you."

She smiled a nervous smile. "It's kind of dressy, so you'd have to wear a suit and tie, but if you don't have one or you'd just rather not, I'll understand. I'm asking because I haven't treated you with nearly the respect you've shown me and I'd like a chance make up for that."

I was watching a grown-up tomboy pouring her heart out. Even if I didn't want to go to her banquet, I owed it to her. Besides, I did want to go. "Well, Ms Brennan, it so happens I have a suit with me and even a tie, so I would be honored to escort you to the ball."

She looked relieved, happy, and still a little nervous all at once. "Oh, good. Thank you . . . I mean . . . ."

"Are you sure you don't mind arriving at the ball in a pickup truck that's more than twice as old as you are?"

Sharyne laughed. "I don't think anyone will be shocked. Besides, it beats the heck out of a pumpkin pulled by mice."

When I thought about it later, her comment about a pumpkin pulled by mice told me some interesting things about how my Cinderella saw our proposed evening. "Then we have a date. What time do I pick you up and where?"

"My apartment is at 600 Pacific Avenue. That's at the corner of Pacific and Fern. There are four two-story apartments in the building, they face the street, and they all have bright red doors. Mine is the door on the far right. The banquet starts at seven and it's at the Chetco Grange Community Center, so if you could pick me up about six-thirty, that will get us there with a little time to spare."

600 PACIFIC AVE.

"Okay, got it. Fourth red door on the right . . . 600 Pacific . . . six-thirty . . . suit and tie. I'll be there."

I drove her back to the Western Oregon Visitors Association office. As I pulled up to the curb, Sharyne took a quick look toward the building, and then leaned over and kissed my cheek. "That's for putting up with my idiot-synchrasies. See you this evening! Oh, and here's my business card. I wrote my home number on the back in case you come to your senses."

Sharyne closed the passenger door and rushed off toward the building's entrance without a backward glance. I think she had just done something totally foreign to her nature, and despite my positive response, her emotions were in an uproar. At least that's the way I read the situation.

I arrived at the last red door on the right in my dark gray suit and electric blue tie at precisely six-thirty and pushed the doorbell button. Sharyne must have been watching for me, because the door opened almost before I got my finger off the button.

To be honest, I was not expecting the vision that appeared in that doorway. She was wearing a sleeveless version of the traditional little black dress with two long strands of beads—one pearl gray and one black—and she literally took my breath away.

All I could think to say was, "Wow!"

She smiled widely and cocked her head to one side. "Forgive me, but I'm kind of new at this. Does 'wow' mean you approve?"

"Sort of. More precisely, it means you look absolutely fantastic!"

It was getting dark outside so I couldn't say for sure, but I think Sharyne might have blushed. "Thank you, Sir. I just wanted to show you I can be a lady when the situation requires it."

"Of that I had absolutely no doubt. Here's a little gilding for the Lilly."

I stopped at a florist on Highway 101 earlier and picked up a white orchid corsage. I handed the clear plastic box to her.

Sharyne took the box and stared at it for what seemed like a long time. During that time her eyes took on a sheen that seemed to forecast tears. I said, "I'm sorry, if flowers are inappropriate, I won't be offended if you don't wear them."

She looked up at me. "Flowers are very appropriate, Travis, and these are beautiful. It's just that . . . well, . . . no one ever gave me flowers of any kind before. I don't even know how to wear these."

"I can help you with that, but the guys in Brookings must be either blind or dumber than dirt."

I pinned the white orchids on her dress, remembering to put them on her right so they wouldn't be crushed if there was any dancing to be done. The flowers added just a light touch of extra style to a woman whose style was a hundred percent natural and original. Then we were off to the ball.

The award Sharyne received actually was kind of a big deal. She was honored as the Brookings Booster of the Year, meaning she had done a lot to attract visitors and promote tourism. That was important because tourism was about all Brookings had going for it.

It was a good thing I remembered which side to put the flowers on because after the awards were handed out and the speechifying was over, there was a lot of dancing to be done to a live band. For a small town event, the organizers showed a lot of class. Another surprise was Sharyne's terpsichorean skills. She was an excellent dance partner. We even did a couple of spins, which Sharyne pulled off with the grace of Ginger Rogers. Sadly, I'm no Fred Astaire, but we had fun.

As the evening grew late, the band slowed their pace and the mood shifted to romantic. Holding Sharyne in my arms was a special delight, and best of all, she seemed to think so, too.

Around midnight I pulled up in front of the last red door on the right and held it open for Sharyne. Inside, she wisely unpinned the orchids, and we stood there for a long moment just looking into each other's eyes. It was one of those moments when we both knew what was going to happen, and the anticipation was part of the magic. Considering the rocky start we got off to that morning, what was going to happen was especially magic.

When our lips met it was a gentle moment that lasted a long sweet time. Then I held her as Sharyne leaned against me. Neither of us said a word. The silence was also part of the magic.

Next came that awkward moment when she was anticipating me wanting to spend the night and her not knowing whether to follow her heart or her head. I suspect Sharyne's head was saying the same thing mine was: Take it slow and treasure the tease of desire.

She looked up at me and her lips parted as if she wanted to say something, but no words came out. This was another of those situations for which life had not yet prepared her.

I kissed her very gently on the forehead and said, "Shar, I want nothing more right now than to hold you in my arms until the sun comes up, but the part of me that thinks about the future is saying, "Wait."

She took a deep breath and sighed. "I know. Part of me is saying the same thing. I can't help thinking you've been to this brink before, maybe more than once, but it's new to me.

"Oh, Ben and I made out a lot when we dated back in high school, but I was afraid to go further. Part of it was I didn't know how to safely go further, and part of it was that silly thing inside all young virgins that says, "Save that special moment for Mister Right."

Her bright blue eyes were fixed on my face and she added, "I know we've only met a few hours ago, but you seem to be the best candidate for Mister Right who's ever come into my life. My grandmother—she raised me from a child—told me something about that once and I've never forgotten it."

"What did she tell you?"

"She said, 'The Great Spirit makes a perfect mate for each of us. When you meet your perfect mate, the Great Spirit will tell you.'

"It might be wishful thinking, but I think He is telling me to pay particular attention to you because you are so different and special in the ways you treat me. I don't want to scare you away, but I hope with all my heart the Great Spirit means us for each other."

Then Sharyne shook her head. "I apologize. I'm babbling now. You don't want to hear that nonsense."

"Shar, what you're saying is not nonsense, it's good sense. If your grandmother is still around, I would like very much to meet her."

Shaking her head, Sharyne said, "Sadly Grandmother is gone, but her spirit still lives in my heart and she speaks to me often. This is one of those times, and I must listen to her."

"Darling, please listen to her for both of us. She was a wise woman, and I could use more wisdom in my life."

Looking at me in a way that made me feel adored, Sharyne said, "I will darling, I promise."

"Thank you. Now, as the old song goes, 'Give me a kiss to build a dream on,' and go tuck yourself in bed. We have an early date for breakfast tomorrow."

I would not have guessed it possible, but our second kiss was even more intense than the first, but in a very different way. The first kiss was between two people who barely knew each other. The second one seemed meant for two people who belonged to each other.

## Saturday, November 17, 2018—Brookings, Oregon

Saturday morning I knocked on the last red door to the right and was greeted with a smile, a quick kiss, and the words, "Du-laa-ha," which she pronounced, "Duh-lah-hah."

"Well, the same to you!"

She gave me an even larger smile and said, "That means, 'Hello, it is good to see you, Darling," in Tolowa lingo." After a short pause, Sharyne added, "Well, I added the 'darling' part. I don't know if there is a Tolowa word for darling because I've never needed one before.'

We piled into the Scout and got moving. It was chilly and overcast, making us appreciate the Scout's efficient heater. This trip I was doing the driving and Sharyne was cuddled up right next to me. That felt even better than the Scout's heater.

My guide directed me to The Blue Pacific Café and Lounge, located in a shopping center just off Highway 101 less than half a mile south of the Chetco River. Sharyne said it wasn't the best breakfast place in town, but it had the advantage of being open early.

The hostess who greeted us turned out to be an old high school acquaintance of Sharyne's. She announced this by saying, "Hey, Sharyne! I haven't seen you practically since we graduated. Come by sometime and we'll catch up."

"Sure, Carole, I'll do that."

Carole was the cheerleader type, an attractive and stacked blonde who was already beginning to show signs of wear around the edges. I also noticed she seemed to be looking at me more than Shar during their brief conversation.

When we were seated, Shar said, "Forgive me for not introducing you, but despite her old-school-chum act, Carole and I were never close. She was one of the rich kids and, of course, I was not. Back then she wouldn't give me the time of day. Now, however, it seems my stock has gone up." She laughed and added, "I think you might have something to do with that, along with getting that award last night. Did you notice the way she was looking at you?"

"Yeah, I also noticed her pasty complexion and elastic stretched to its breaking point. I suspect she's spending more time than is healthy at the local watering holes."

"Say, you're pretty good at this observation stuff. You're absolutely right. Carole married her high school sweetheart and within a few years she caught him in bed with another man. That has to be the ultimate humiliation for any woman. They split up and she's been going downhill ever since."

"She needs a Spirit Grandmother in her heart."

Shar looked at me for several seconds without saying anything, which was becoming a regular thing with her. I didn't mind. I took it as a signal she was contemplating the significance of an event or a comment.

Finally, still looking into my eyes, she said, "You remembered that. I don't think most people would. It is something very personal and important to me, and that you remember what I said tells me so much about you."

"Of course, I remember. Most of what you say makes an impression on me."

"And you don't think I'm silly for saying such things?"

"Silliness never crossed my mind."

She cocked her head to one side and said, "Gosh I'm glad you are part of my life."

I smiled at her. "The feeling is intensely mutual."

After a reasonably decent breakfast, I pointed us back up to Harris Beach. Ben was at the entrance and his expression definitely soured when he recognized the Scout from the day before, saw me in the driver seat, and Sharyne sitting as close to me as she could without being in my lap. I got the idea she was sending him a not so subtle message. That was fine with me.

Ben was very formal and official. "Good morning, Sir. Are you planning to be here for just the day or a longer stay?"

"Just for the day. Maybe only a few hours."

"The daily parking fee is five dollars."

I handed him a five. He took it and gave me a ticket with the date on it. "Please leave this in your windshield while you're here. Have a nice visit."

He was trying so hard to be all business I couldn't help smiling. "Thank you, Ben."

In the rearview mirror I watched Ben standing next to the entrance shack watching us drive away. "I think you just broke that boy's heart."

"We're just friends. We haven't dated for several years."

"I have the distinct feeling he was hoping to change that situation."

From the corner of my eye I saw Sharyne shake her head. "That wasn't going to happen. The only thing Ben and I ever had in common were cases of raging teenage hormones. I never considered Ben a soulmate candidate. I told him so, but I guess he was hoping I would change my mind."

The day use parking area was empty when I pulled into the same parking place we used the day before. We sat there for a few minutes studying our surroundings through windows that were collecting a fine mist, and then I reached under the driver seat and unsnapped the latch on metal box bolted to the floorboards.

From the box I removed a Smith & Wesson Police Model 60 revolver. The box also contained a shoulder holster for the revolver, an Oregon non-resident concealed carry permit, a box of ammo, and a flip-open badge case. I left the shoulder holster in the box.

Shar stared at the revolver with a frown wrinkling her forehead. "Travis, why do you have a pistol in your car?"

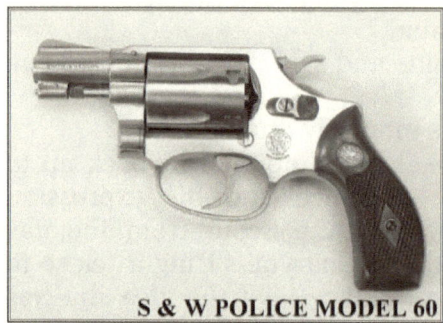

S & W POLICE MODEL 60

"Shar, the world I live in is not as easy going and crime-free as Brookings. The revolver is legit and I am well trained in its use. I have both California and Oregon nonresident concealed carry permits. I am also a Los Angeles County Sheriff's Auxiliary Deputy, which makes me a law enforcement officer of sorts."

She gave me another of her long looks. "Do you really think we might need that thing?"

I flipped the revolver open and checked the cylinders. "No, I don't. I'm hoping we aren't even going to get close enough to Grover that we need a weapon of any kind, but what I hope and what life has in store aren't always the same. Besides, that all assumes Grover is actually still here."

"Or he ever was here."

"If you think you saw him, he was here."

Sharyne smiled. "There you go believing in my hunches again. I warned you about that."

"Yes, you did. There are field glasses in the glove compartment. Let's take 'em along and get into position."

We found a couple of rocks near the spot we visited the day before. They were just up from the edge of the beach and concealed in a dense tangle of underbrush. We sat on one of the rocks and began visually scanning the area around Arch Rock for signs of life.

Next, we scanned the hill behind Arch Rock. When that effort gained us nothing, Shar and I split the area into two parts. She watched the vegetation above Arch Rock and I took the beach between us and the rock.

There was a steady mist falling, and even though we were dressed for the weather, we were still getting damp. That was when the notion we were on a fool's mission began nagging at me. I glanced at my watch. We'd only been there about 45 minutes. Even so, I began thinking about how much longer we should stay.

That was when I heard Shar whispering. We were quite a ways from the surf noise, so I could clearly hear her say, "Trav, there's someone behind us. I think they're about a hundred feet away and trying to move very quietly through the brush."

Since an innocent visitor to the beach wasn't likely to be sneaking up on us, that meant trouble. I said quietly, "On the count of three let's slide forward to the ground and put these rocks between us and whoever is back there. You count."

Without hesitation, Shar quietly counted off, "One . . . two . . . three."

At the precise moment she said "three," the crack of a high powered rifle shattered the air around us. Then we were on the ground and I was turning around as I pulled the Smith & Wesson out of my coat pocket. I raised it and peeked over the rock. Eric Grover now had a full beard, but the same mean eyes as in his mug shot left no doubt it was him.

Grover was almost directly in line with my pistol's single barrel sight. I shifted my aim no more than a quarter of an inch and fired twice.

At the moment I fired Grover was raising his rifle, the Marlin .357 magnum carbine he took from Loring's Sporting Goods. He stopped raising it and stared at me peeking over the top of our rock. He looked confused. I was tightening my trigger finger to fire again when Grover dropped to the ground like a sack of soggy laundry.

I saw the rifle fall with him and decided priority number one was making sure he couldn't use that rifle again. I vaulted over the rock, covering the underbrush between us in seconds.

Kicking the rifle out of Grover's reach, I aimed the Smith & Wesson at his chest. From the way he fell, I was pretty sure Eric Grover had already met his maker, but I wasn't taking any chances. Seeing no signs of life, I cautiously touched his neck and felt for a pulse. If there was one, it was so weak I couldn't find it.

I stood up and over the sound of my pounding heart I heard a racket I hadn't noticed until that moment. It was a siren. Looking up toward the parking access road, I saw a green pickup truck with the shield of the Oregon Parks and Recreation Department on its door. As Ben jumped out, another realization of vital importance struck me: Sharyne had not moved since we slid to the ground on the count of three.

I ran back to our rock and looked at Shar. There was a neat hole in the back of her down jacket just below the collar. I anxiously felt for a pulse and was very relieved to find one. It was weak, but definitely there.

I stood up and saw Ben looking down at Grover's body. With surprise, he said, "Hey, this is that Grover guy!"

I said, "Yeah, but that doesn't matter right now. He shot Sharyne. Do you have a radio in that truck?"

Ben may not have been Shar's soulmate, but he knew how to deal with a crisis. "Yes. I'll call for an ambulance."

He ran to his truck and I watched him talking into the microphone. From that point on things are pretty much a blur.

What I do recall distinctly is the ambulance arrived very quickly, followed by two white Curry County Sheriff's Dodge Chargers and a silver Chevy Tahoe with a State Trooper aboard. The ambulance paramedics immediately loaded Sharyne on a litter and took her to their truck. They wasted no time on Grover. It was obvious to them he belonged to the coroner now.

With the ambulance on its way, more sheriff cars arrived and the mood at the scene of the murder was downright celebratory. I showed the senior deputy my ID, permit, and tried to give him my Smith & Wesson for evidence. He didn't want it.

"That's okay, Mister Radcliff. You keep it. If we need it for forensics or something, we'll let you know. All I need from you is a statement as to what happened and how you nailed Grover there."

It was more like he was a movie fan meeting a celebrity than a police officer taking a witness statement. He pulled a small digital recorder out of his pocket. "I'm gonna tape this if you don't mind. That way I can type up a more complete report and . . . ."

Deciding to see how much slack they would cut me, I interrupted the deputy. "Would it be possible for you to take my statement at the hospital where that ambulance is headed?"

He looked confused. "Are you injured?"

"No, but the woman in the back of that ambulance is very important to me."

"Sharyne? Sure, I didn't realize . . . come on I'll take you there in my cruiser."

"Would you mind if I drove my pickup. I don't feel comfortable leaving it here."

He looked at the Scout and said, "I understand. That's a beauty. Come on, I'll escort you."

I got into the Scout and secured my Smith & Wesson while the senior deputy spoke with his cohort. Then he pulled up next to me in his cruiser and we were off code three. I had to give the Scout's little six-cylinder engine just about all the throttle it had to keep up. The deputy clearly understood the urgency I felt.

The Curry County Medical Center wasn't far. It's just north of the Brookings Police Department, which is just north of Highway 101 where it passes the Fred Meyer store.

The deputy met me at the door, offering his hand. "By the way, I'm Sergeant Bobby Collier. Follow me, I'll get us past the red tape."

Two minutes later Deputy Collier and I were at a nursing station listening to a nurse whose nametag said "Ruth" report on Shar's condition. She said, "The wound is quite serious, but the ER doctor thinks Sharyne has a reasonable chance of recovery."

The nurse glanced at her watch. "They're just prepping her for surgery now. The surgeon is on route from his home, which is close by. As soon as he gets here they'll go right to work fixing her up."

"Is she conscious?"

Shaking her head, Nurse Ruth said, "No, she's still out, but part of that is due to drugs they administered to keep her quiet and stable." Looking curious, Ruth asked, "For the record, are you family?"

"Only if you folks manage to save her. If you do, I plan on becoming her husband."

Ruth grinned a big grin. "You and Sharyne? That's wonderful! Don't worry, we'll save your bride. She means a lot to all of us, too."

Deputy Collier and I sat in an empty surgery waiting room and I said, "Deputy, I really want to thank you for your courtesy. In Los Angeles County I'd have been stuck in an office for hours answering questions and filling out forms."

"You're very welcome, Mister Radcliff. Like Ruth said, Sharyne is a good friend who means a lot to all of us. Now, is it alright with you if we get the facts together for a report on how you bagged Public Enemy Number One?"

He pressed a switch on his little digital recorder and I said, "I think the first thing you need to know is Sharyne is the one who provided the details that gave me an inkling Grover might be near Harris Beach.

"She noticed that a white pickup truck stolen from the marina just down river from the house in which Grover was supposed to have been killed showed up at Harris Beach two days after the shootout. More recently she was taking a walk at Harris Beach and thought she saw Grover out by Arch Rock."

Collier was surprised. "No kidding?"

"No kidding. So putting all the pieces together Shar and I decided to sort of stake out the south end of Harris Beach for a while and see what we could see."

The deputy said, "You know if it was anyone else saying they saw Grover out there to anyone other than you, I'm afraid her observation would have been ignored. You must have a lot of faith in that girl."

"I do, Deputy. I know she is well liked, but I don't think most folks appreciate how bright she really is."

"Well, after what you've told me, I certainly have a new respect for her."

"You know, it would do wonders for her ego if you ever have a chance to tell her that. Anyway, we'd been sitting out there in the mist on a large rock in the underbrush for about 45 minutes when Sharyne whispered she heard someone moving through the brush behind us.

"We counted to three and dropped behind the rock, but on the word 'three,' Grover fired that big three-fifty-seven magnum carbine. He hit Sharyne high in the back, just below the collar."

"Damn!"

"Fortunately, I didn't know that right away or it surely would have distracted me from taking Grover out, which I did while he was lining up to shoot me. I believe I put two rounds into his chest, but you can verify that with the coroner. The weapon I used is a point-three-eight caliber Smith & Wesson Police Model 60 revolver."

We spent the rest of an hour going over details of the morning's events, including the information about how I happened to have the Smith & Wesson and my status as a LA County Volunteer Sheriff's Deputy.

As a screenwriter I've observed many law enforcement officers, and Deputy Collier was damned good at his job. He got the facts and subtleties needed for a thorough and comprehensive incident report without a lot of officious posturing.

When he clicked off his little digital recorder, Collier said, "Do you know where you are likely to be for the next month or so?"

"As long as Sharyne is in Brookings, that's most likely where I'll be. If that changes I will let you know."

"Thank you, Mister Radcliff. I don't know if you'll need to testify at the coroner's inquest or not. Your signed statement may be all they need. I . . . ."

"Hi, Bobby, is this the famous Mister Radcliff?"

Deputy Collier jumped up. "Yes, Sir, Doctor Baxter, it certainly is."

We'd been interrupted by a tall slender fellow who wore green scrubs, a thin mustache, and made me think of Vincent Price. Deputy Collier introduced us. "Mister Radcliff, meet Doctor Baxter. Doc, meet Mister Radcliff."

I stood and shook the hand he offered and Baxter said, "I understand you have a special interest in Miss Brennan, or Sharyne as we all know her."

"I do, Doctor. Even if we were not close otherwise, one tends to have a soft spot in their heart for someone who saves their life."

He looked surprised. "Really? Well, you'll be happy to know we successfully removed the bullet from her back and found very little additional damage. We sewed her up and barring some really unexpected complication, Sharyne should be on her feet in just a few days."

I shook his hand again. "Thank you, Doctor Baxter. Thank you very much. When will I be able to see her?"

The doctor looked at his watch and said, "She'll be in recovery for at least another hour and then . . . I think we can probably let you in for a short visit around one."

After Doctor Baxter left, Deputy Collier and I did a celebratory high five. I said, "Deputy, if you're up for lunch, I'm buyin'."

Bobby Collier asked for a rain check. He needed to go back and check on the crime scene, and then get his reports typed up. I told him he could collect on that rain check any time. That left me on my own for lunch, so I followed the signs to the Medical Center's cafeteria.

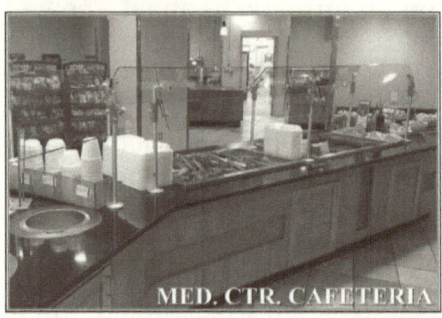

MED. CTR. CAFETERIA

I wasn't terribly hungry, partly because I ate a larger than usual breakfast and partly because killing a man is hard on the appetite. The only things that appealed were a banana and a cup of coffee.

I no sooner seated myself at one of the cafeteria's small tables to eat my banana and calm my nerves when Nurse Ruth showed up with a salad on her tray and asked if she could join me. I couldn't think of a good reason why she shouldn't, so I stood and pulled the chair out for her.

"Thank you, Mister Radcliff. Among other things, I noticed you were a real gentleman at the Banquet last night. That particular trait is one that stands out in a place liking Brookings."

Not particularly wanting to venture further into the realm of my gentlemanliness, I said, "The Brookings Honors folks put on a nice party. I enjoyed myself."

"Yes they did. Of course, whether you knew it or not, you were a center of attention. Everybody was talking about how Sharyne had done very well to catch herself a movie writer from Hollywood."

I looked at her for several seconds, a trick I learned from a certain young woman of my acquaintance. "Nurse Ruth, I'm afraid they have that backwards. It was I who worked very hard at catching myself a wonderful woman. Folks around here may take Shar for granted, but where I come from a woman like her is worth at least ten blonde starlets."

It was her turn to stare for a few seconds. "Well, I'll be. I think you might be worthy of Sharyne after all. A lot of folks were wondering why she was interested in a show business fellow, but I'm beginning to see the reason. I never should have doubted Sharyne's judgment."

"If that was intended as a compliment, I accept it with gratitude."

"Mister Radcliff, it was more than a compliment. It was also an apology. I've behaved frightfully. I hope you will forgive me. My only excuse is that Sharyne is one of our treasures and we protect people like her. We will miss her if she goes away with you."

"Ruth, if I may be so informal, I'm pretty sure Shar would live in Hollywood if I asked her. I also know she would hate it. Come to think of it, I hate it. She belongs in a wide open world with blue skies, tall green trees, and waves crashing on rocks—a place like Brookings. I'm beginning to think I do too.

She clapped her hands a couple of times. "Bravo! I think you belong here, too."

"Now, if you'll forgive me, it's almost one and Doctor Baxter thought Shar might be moved to a room where I could see her about now."

"Oh, I could use the in-house phone to find out for you."

I smiled what I hoped was a kindly smile. "Thank you, Ruth, but I need to move around a little anyway. I'll see you later. Thank you for the conversation."

As I walked away, I reminded myself living in a small town has its drawbacks, too. One is that everybody knows your business and folks aren't hesitant about sticking their noses into it.

At the surgery nursing station, an older woman with a kind smile checked and informed me that Doctor Baxter left instructions that I could see Shar for a short time. No one else, however, would be allowed to see her for a day or two.

Following the directions I was given, I located room S102 and peeked in. Shar was in bed on her side and facing the door. Her eyes were half closed, but a big smile appeared the minute she recognized me.

Her voice was still a little raspy from a breathing tube or something they used during the surgery, but I could understand her just fine. "Travis! Gosh, I'm so glad to see you!"

Standing next to her bed, I took her hand, and then leaned over and kissed her on the forehead. "I'm pretty darn glad to see you, too. For a while there back at the beach, I was afraid I'd lost the most special woman in the whole world."

"When I woke up, I thought the same about you. I mean I thought I'd lost the most special man in the world. The strange thing is, as I drifted in and out of consciousness, I thought about my grandmother and a calmness settled over me as if she was telling me not to worry everything was okay.

"A little later Doctor Baxter came in and talked to me. Of course, my first question was about you. He told me he'd just spoken with you and you were fine . . . and a hero besides. Tell me what I missed out there."

"How about I give you the condensed version now because I have something else to tell you and they're gonna run me out of here pretty soon so you can rest. The bottom line is your good hearing saved both our lives because the person you heard sneaking up on us was Eric Grover."

Sharyne went pale. "No!"

"Yes, I'm afraid so. He must have spotted us out there and thought we saw him. I can't think of any other reason he would want to kill us. Anyway, he shot you just as we ducked and, as I peeked over the top of our rock, he lined up to shoot me, but I was a little quicker. Eric Grover is confirmed dead."

"Thank God! That will be a huge relief to the town when they hear it. Very few people I knew believed he was dead."

"I think most of the town already knows about what happened at Harris Beach this morning. News travels fast around here."

I got a beautiful smile as she said, "That makes you the town hero!"

"Shar, I'm no hero. I just did what was necessary to keep us alive. Now, I want you to pay close attention for just a moment, because I'm about to say what could be the most important thing I ever say and I want to know you are clear about it."

Her smile turned into a frown of concern. "I'm listening."

I took a deep breath and said, "Shar, I love you. There is no doubt in my mind about that. I'm telling you now so you can prepare to be swept off your feet until you agree to marry me."

The beautiful smile returned. "Oh, Trav, I love you, too. I know it just like you know you love me, and just in case you expect me to say yes to your proposal, Harbrook Jewelers in the Harbor Shopping Center is the best jeweler in town, but I think they're closed on Sunday and Monday, so you have time to come to your senses."

I shook my head. "The funny thing is, for one of the first times in my life I feel like I have come to my senses."

"That's wonderful, Darling. We have so much to plan, like

where we want to live and how many kids and . . . just everything!"

On that note a nurse I didn't know walked in. She studied the vital signs monitor screen next to the bed and made a note on her clipboard. "Hmm. Heart rate is a little elevated."

Shar said, "I'm not surprised, Jan. Your pulse might go up a little, too, if the love of your life just asked you to marry him."

Jan looked at Shar, and then looked at me. "Is that so? Well, Mister Radcliff, hero or not, you must stop exciting my patient. Now scoot on out of here. You can come back around dinner time, six o'clock. If you promise to behave yourself I'll even order you a dinner tray."

I said, "Thank you, Jan," and leaned over the bed to give Shar a kiss.

The kiss lasted a little longer than Nurse Jan thought appropriate. "Mister Radcliff! I said you have to behave yourself. Now get out before I call security."

I winked at Shar. "I'm going, I'm going. Dang they've got crotchety nurses in this place."

As I went out the door, Nurse Jan said, "If you don't stop exciting my patient, I'll show you real crotchety!"

## Thursday, November 22, 2018
## Curry County Medical Center, Brookings, Oregon

I divided the next few days of my life between sitting with Shar and developing the film treatment I was in Brookings to write. It took me a while to get a handle on it. In the end, I decided on an approach that saw the events of Eric Grover's escape and time in Brookings through the eyes of a young Native American woman. In writing, the obvious isn't always obvious.

I took a few liberties with details here and there, but I was writing a theatrical film, not a documentary. When it was done, rereading the treatment convinced me I made the right choice. I substituted a sheriff's deputy based on Deputy Bobby Collier for myself throughout the story, but the Sharyne character was clearly the heroine of the story. Shar made an excellent film heroine.

Besides writing and spending time with Shar, I ran errands, did some shopping, and collected Sharyne's mail for her. I was a busy guy.

As Shar improved, she became more and more frustrated, She felt pretty good and wanted to get out of the medical center and back into the real world, but Doctor Baxter insisted she stay put until Thursday morning. I was glad her hospital room windows did not open. If they had, I think Shar would have tied her bed sheets together and shinnied down three floors.

The Curry County Medical Center's food was about the only saving grace from Shar's point of view. She found it both tasty and appropriate to her healthy eating habits. I even found the healthy parts edible on those occasions when I joined her for a meal.

It also turned out that hanging around Shar's hospital room was a great way to meet a large part of Brookings' population. On average she had five or six visitors a day, and after a few days there were so many flowers in her room the bed was lost among the foliage. Shar asked the nursing staff to spread the floral cheer by taking about half of the arrangements to brighten the rooms of other patients.

Tuesday was a red letter day. Doctor Baxter ordered Sharyne out of bed with instructions to walk around the medical center and get some exercise. I walked with her on some of those outings and I was darn near running to keep up with her, and she was pushing a wobbly IV stand.

Despite a spell of cool weather, her favorite haunt was the outdoor cafeteria seating area. Nurse Jan provided a small blanket Shar put over her shoulders for such arctic adventures.

Wednesday night Susie and I were dispatched to Shar's apartment with specific instructions on what clothes to bring back for her medical center departure the next day. She was not going to celebrate her departure in dirty clothes, especially a top and a jacket with bullet holes in them. To solve that dilemma, we also stopped at Fred Meyer's gigantic store and Susie picked out a colorful warm knit sweater to replace Shar's jacket for the occasion.

Thursday morning Sharyne took a shower with Nurse Jan's help to keep the dressing dry. Next step was donning the outfit I brought from her apartment. After that it was breakfast time.

Finally Doctor Baxter showed up and cut Shar loose. Her smile on hearing that news was almost as big as the one I got when I first saw her at the med center.

In her new sweater and with her arm tucked through mine, Sharyne had to say goodbye to nearly everyone in the hospital as we headed for my Scout in the parking lot. I opened the passenger door, prepared to help her climb into the seat, but she scampered up before I could offer her a hand.

"I SURE LOVE YOU..."

From the seat, Shar looked down and smiled. "I sure love you this morning, Mister Radcliff."

"Oh, I bet you say that to all the boys you're engaged to."

Putting on an insulted expression, Shar said, "I do not! Besides, we are not officially engaged. I believe something was said about a ring, which I have yet to see."

I snapped my fingers as if suddenly remembering about the ring. "That's right. I must get around to doing something about that.

By that time in our relationship, Sharyne could tell when I was kidding her. She glowered at me. "Darn right you'd better do something about that. I bet Ben wouldn't take that long to find a ring."

I made a face and closed the door. Climbing into the driver seat I started the Scout and headed for Shar's apartment. We had detailed plans for this day and I was following them to the letter.

At her apartment Shar checked the mail I'd carefully stacked on her kitchen counter. After that, I got a suitcase down from her closet shelf and she proceeded to pack a few days' clothes. When she was nearly done, I noticed her black dress was still in the closet.

I called her attention to it, saying, "Don't you think you should pack that, too?"

Shar looked at the dress, and then back at me. With suspicion in her voice, she said, "I should? I thought I was going to your hotel to recuperate, not to party."

I shrugged. "It's up to you. I'm just a firm believer in being prepared for every eventuality."

Carefully folding the dress to fit in the suitcase, she gave me a sly look. "Regular little Boy Scout aren't you?"

Finally, she put a very sexy black silk negligee' into the bag. Before closing the suitcase, she turned to see if I noticed the lacy black garment she just packed. She could tell I had and simply said, "It goes well with engagement rings."

I carried her bag out to the Scout while she locked the fourth red door on the right. Our next stop was the Beachfront Inn in the harbor area south of the Chetco River. For propriety's sake and

Sharyne's comfort, I had moved out of my old room and into a two-room suite.

By this time the desk clerk and I were old pals. He greeted us warmly and we headed for the elevator. Since he didn't greet Sharyne like a long-lost cousin, I thought I might have found the only person in Brookings who wasn't on a first name basis with her.

Exiting the elevator on the third floor, I directed Shar to the left and we walked to Room 312 at the end of the hall. I opened the door and we entered our private sanctuary.

Shar took a look around and said, "This is very nice. I've been to functions here, but this is the first time I've actually been in one of their rooms. Certainly nobody could ever ask for a better view."

Pointing to the connecting door, I said, "That's where you bed down, unless you'd rather have this room, in which case I will sleep in there."

Shar looked through the connecting door. "This looks fine," and then she walked over to me and gently put her arms around me. She still had tenderness in her upper back and shoulders.

"Travis, I want you to know how much I appreciate the way you've taken care of me since I was . . . hurt. Like this room. I suspect a lot of men in this situation would have just gotten one room and expected me to go along with the sleeping arrangements. Now, I might actually like to try sleeping together, but this way the choice is mine. That's respect on the most personal level and I love you for it."

"This just seemed like the right thing to do so you would have privacy, but I could still be close by if you needed anything."

We kissed. It was a gentle sweet kiss that said "I love you" more than "I want you."

With my arms still around her waist, I said, "What's next on the agenda?"

"I think I could use some rest. In my hurry to get out of the medical center, I may have overestimated my stamina a little. Would that be okay?"

"That would be fine."

Concern wrinkled her forehead. "Will you be here?"

"Absolutely. There is no place I need to be but here with you."

"Then would it be okay if I stretched out on one of those loungers on our balcony? I would like to enjoy the fresh air and still know you're nearby."

Suddenly I realized something that hadn't occurred to me before. "Shar, have you been experiencing nightmares about what happened?"

She looked down like a kid caught with her hand in the cookie jar. "Yes, Travis. How did you know?"

"It's a perfectly natural reaction to what we experienced. Besides, if I'm having them, it's likely you are, too. When you have another one, yell out. One of my jobs here is nightmare exterminator."

Sharyne looked up into my eyes and said, "Add another item to the list of reasons I love you more and more every day."

I laughed. "Will do. Now go get comfy on the balcony. By the way, When you get thirsty, there are bottles of water and fruit juice in the fridge."

Ten minutes later I looked up from my laptop to see Shar already sleeping soundly on our balcony. It was a beautiful day out there with the sun making sparkles on the water and soft breezes blowing ozone in our direction. After a while, I succumbed to the temptation, and reclined on the chaise lounge next to hers.

When I woke up Sharyne was still next to me, but her hand was holding mine. That felt good, but a heavy cloud cover was moving in from the northwest and blocking the warming rays of the sun. It was getting downright chilly.

I sat up and kissed Shar on the forehead. Her eyes opened slowly. "Mmm . . . what a wonderful way to wake up."

"I hated to wake you , but there's a storm moving in, or at least some heavy clouds."

She shivered. "I can tell. The temperature has dropped a bunch."

Pushing the sliding door to our balcony closed behind her I asked, "Do you think you could use some lunch? It's nearly one."

Nodding, she said, "Yes, I think I could. Does the hotel have a restaurant?"

"No, but they use a seafood place across the street for room service. I've had a couple of meals sent up and they were pretty good."

"Oh, The Grotto. Yes, their food is good. Do you have one of their menus?"

"Sure do. Look over there on that little table under the TV screen."

Shar asked for a small shrimp Louie and I ordered a bowl of Boston chowder. From there, the afternoon just sort of drifted by with me at my laptop and Shar looking over my shoulder to see what a writer actually does. We also watched giant drops of water make little craters in the beach and Sharyne took another nap on the couch. After all that excitement, we watched an American Plains Indian documentary on the Discovery channel.

Around nine-thirty I gave Sharyne a hug and a goodnight kiss at the door to her room. I closed the door after her, but a minute later the door reopened and Shar asked, "Will it bother you if I leave this door open?"

"Not at all. I just thought you might appreciate a little privacy."

Tilting her head to one side, Shar looked at me. "Travis, do you really intend to marry me?"

Wondering why she chose that moment to ask such a question, I said, "Absolutely."

"Then you need to forget about privacy, Darling, and I know we aren't married yet, but we might as well get used to what living together is like."

## Friday, November 23, 2018—Brookings, Oregon

As it turned out, leaving the door open was a good idea. Around two in the morning a moan from Shar's room woke me. I jumped out of bed, but by the time I got through the connecting door, the moan turned into a scream.

I ran to Shar's bed and gently shook her. When her eyes first popped open, she cringed away from me for a second, but then reached for me with both hands. "Oh, Travis. It was terrible! Grover kept shooting you and I couldn't make him stop!"

Sitting on the edge of her bed, I said, "You can relax now, Darling. You know that was a nightmare and it's over now. Nothing is going to hurt us."

Sometimes nightmares are worse than real life, and this one left her sobbing. I stretched out next to her and held Shar in my arms until she began to relax and her sobs quieted.

When I woke up again sunlight was streaming through a gap in the window curtains and Shar was laying half on top of me with her head on my chest. She wore a sleep shirt to bed and it was hiked up far enough to offer a display of two long, shapely legs from hip to toe.

I gently kissed her forehead. Shar's eyes opened slowly and it seemed to take several seconds for her to comprehend that we were not only in bed together, but we were entangled in an embrace that was tempting the hell out of me. It was clear she was feeling the same temptation.

Shar skootched up a little and kissed me on the lips. It didn't take long before that kiss and her position were having a physical effect of me. She pressed herself closer to me and I said, "Shar, not yet, Darling. There's still that matter of a ring."

"WHOSE FAULT IS THAT?"

She propped herself up on one elbow. "Whose fault is that?"

Before I could say it was my fault, she pressed the inside of her right thigh harder against me, and when she felt what was happening there, Shar put on a big grin and asked, "Does that mean I turn you on?"

When I didn't answer right away, she giggled gleefully. "It does! It does! Gosh, I'm glad I turn you on. It would be awful if I didn't!"

I slid my leg out from under hers and started to get up, which made the male physical reaction on which she was focused even more obvious under the shorts I sleep in. Shar giggled. "Oh, my! I did that? And I did it without even trying." Then adding an erotic tone to her voice, she said, "It makes me wonder what would happen if I put some effort into it."

I made a face at her. "Trust me, you don't need to put any more effort into it."

She smiled. "But I want to be the best for you."

"You're already that and then some.

Shar grinned. "Are you sure you don't want to come back to bed?"

"You're only saying that because you know I won't."

Her smile got even bigger. "Try me!"

After a light breakfast at The Grotto we took a walk on the beach among the large pieces of driftwood the waves swept on the beach during the storm. Now, the driftwood was all that was left of the storm and the sun was warming the air nicely.

"Travis?"

"Yes?"

"I'm sorry for what I put you through this morning. I was in a playful mood, but I was being more than playful. I know we have sort of an agreement about sex, but waking up in your arms and . . . well, like that, is more temptation than I can handle in my weakened condition."

I smiled at the last part. "Shar, you have no weakened condition. You're pure vixen through and through, and you came very close to getting something else through and through."

She stopped and look up into my eyes. "I know. And you know what else I know?"

"Tell me."

"If you had come back to bed I'd have given myself to you without hesitation. I feel I know you so well now, and I feel so good about who you are that even the idea of losing my . . . you know . . . to you doesn't concern me in the slightest.

"Maybe me giving myself to you in that way wouldn't seem like much to some men, but I think you understand what it means to me, and I know without any doubt I can count on you to do what's best for both of us, and if it comes to a choice between what's best for you and what's best for me, you've already proven . . . well, that I come first. A woman could ask for nothing more in a husband."

I may have blushed a little, but I managed to say, "That is my idea of what loving someone means. It's probably old fashioned these days, but if you can't trust me, why on earth would you want to be my wife."

A momentary frown crossed Shar's face. "But do you feel you can trust me, darling?"

"Hell, I knew that the minute I met you that day in your office. Even then I knew I could trust anything you said to me. Do you remember when you handed me that cardboard box to put up on the shelf?"

Shar nodded and I said, "I think that was the moment I knew you were a very special person. It was the first time I saw your face and heard your voice. That's all it took."

She looked surprised. "Really? That particular moment?"

"I think so."

All she said was a soft "Wow."

The rest of Friday passed in kind of a lazy haze, but I watched Shar closely for signs of fatigue. I'd put some big plans in motion, and I hoped she would be up to the excitement. By five that afternoon, I decided the show would go on.

She was stretched out on the couch reading one of the screenplays I'd given her so she could better understand what I do. I walked over and sat on the arm of the couch.

"Shar?"

"Yes, Darling?"

"Do you remember what you were saying this morning about trusting me?"

"Of course."

"Then, if I asked you to do a couple of things without any explanation, would you do what I asked?"

Now I had a hundred percent of her attention. A smile was tugging at the edges of her lips as she said, "I would."

"Good. Please go and get yourself all gussied up in that sexy black dress."

One of the things about Sharyne I'd learned is that when something makes her curious or puzzles her, she tilts her head to one side. She tilted and said, "Sexy black dress, huh?"

Handing me the script she'd been reading, Shar said, "Okay, Mister, one gussied up Indian girl in a sexy black dress, coming up. It'll take a little time, though."

I smiled. "No hurry."

"And you know that bandage on my back is going to show, don't you?"

I nodded. "I do, but anyone we encounter in these parts will know how it got there and will think of it as a badge of courage."

While she took a shower and changed, I used the other bathroom to do the same, putting on my dark gray suit. While at Fred Meyer buying her sweater, I also picked out a bright red tie. I put it on instead of the blue one.

I'd just looked at my watch, noting that the time was going on six, when Shar made a grand entrance through the connecting door. Just as the first time I saw her in that black dress, she took my breath away.

She grinned widely. "May I assume from your expression you still approve?"

Shaking my head in amazement, I said, "I don't know what I did to deserve the most beautiful woman in the world, but I got her."

"You sure do. I doubt 'the most beautiful woman part,' but you have me, that's for sure."

"In that case, there is something I need to do." Taking her hand, I said, "Come over here please."

I led her to the couch closest to the glass doors overlooking the beach. "Please sit here."

Shar sat on the end of the couch and I opened the glass door a few inches. The tide was in and the waves were breaking closer to the hotel so we could even hear the hiss of the water as it slid back from the beach. "That's for ambiance."

Next I went to the DVD/CD player attached to the big screen TV and pushed the play button. A second later Herb Alpert's voice from another of my Fred Meyer purchases came softly from the TV speakers:

You see this guy?
This guy's in love with you.
Yes, I'm in love.
Who looks at you the way I do?
When you smile I can tell
We know each other very well . . .

I think most love songs are written from a woman's perspective, but the one Herb was singing is a love song from a guy's point of view, which makes it different from all those songs by Gershwin and Cole Porter. Shar's big bright eyes were following my every move.

"Sharyne, in a very short time you have captured my heart and completely changed my life. Your grandmother told you the Great Spirit makes a perfect mate for each of us, and when we meet our mate, the Great Spirit will tell us.

"Well, I have come to believe in your Great Spirit and He has made it clear to me that you are the woman He intends for me. So, with that and a heart overflowing with love, I ask if you will please make my life complete by becoming my wife?"

The tears rolling down both of Shar's cheeks did not surprise me. They simply meant she understood my words.

"Travis, the words you just said to me are the most beautiful I will ever hear. Yes, Darling, I want to be your wife more than almost anything on earth!"

I'm pretty sure there were a few tears in my eyes, too, when I said, "Thank you, Sharyne. Thank you with all my heart."

She leaned forward and we kissed gently. Then I remembered

the little box in my hand.

"Oh, I almost forgot." Opening the box, I said, "This is a small reminder of the love I feel for you."

Shar took the box and stared at the ring. "Travis, this the most beautiful ring I have ever seen! The two shades of gold blending together are perfect. They are you and they are me. They are us together!"

"Let's see how it looks on your finger."

Carefully removing the ring from its box, she said, "I hope it fits."

"You know, that's an interesting part of all this. When I told the man at Harbrook's who the ring was for he just happened to have your ring sizes on file."

Sliding the ring smoothly on to her finger, Shar said, "Yes, isn't that an amazing coincidence? But don't get the wrong idea. I took my mother's engagement ring in a while ago and had it resized so I could wear it, and Harbrook's keep files on ring sizes for all their customers. Oh, Travis, I love it!"

Not only did the ring fit perfectly, it fit Sharyne's style perfectly. The ring cost me just about three grand, but, as engagement rings go, that's not outrageous. Seeing the smile of Shar's face as she held her hand up to the light made the ring worth a hundred times what it cost.

"I love it, too, Shar. More important, I love you and all you mean to me."

"Travis, even though I knew you had something like this up your sleeve, I had no idea your words and the ring and . . . well everything would be so perfect. It all hit me squarely in the heart. Bulls eye!"

"I'm glad. I want it all to be as perfect as I could make it. Now, let's get your coat. We're steppin' out."

Grinning again, Shar said, "There's more? I suppose our destination is a secret, too?"

"It is. Rest assured, however, you are dressed appropriately."

While Shar went to get her coat, I snuck out on the balcony and placed a quick cell phone call to my co-conspirator and said we were on our way. Then, having carefully studied a road map earlier, I followed the back streets route to the Grange Community

Center where the next phase of the night's excitement was already in full swing.

I doubt if my twisting, turning route fooled Sharyne, but at one point she did ask if I was sure I knew where I was going. When we were within site of the Grange hall, she said, "Looks like there's some kind of event on at the Grange tonight."

"So it does. Maybe we should drop in and see what's going on."

As I pulled into the parking lot, I sensed her looking at me. "Travis, what have you done?"

"Me? I ain't done nothin'."

Even though the building was all lit up, it was quiet as a church outside the hall. When Shar stepped through the door I held open for her, however, all hell broke loose. A small dance band played a fanfare and roughly fifty people stood and applauded. Then we were surrounded by Sharyne's closest friends, all congratulating us on our engagement and wishing us a wonderful life together. A giant white banner with large red letters over the bandstand spelled out CONGRATULATIONS, SHARYNE AND TRAVIS!

When things calmed down, I got Shar seated not far from the bandstand and walked over to the band's microphone. The musicians faded themselves to silence, and using their microphone, I said, "Good evening everyone!

"As you all know by now, I have asked Sharyne for her hand in wedded bliss and she has agreed." I paused to look at her. "Since it wouldn't be much of a party if she said no, the first person I want to thank for giving us something to celebrate is Shar. Thanks, Darlin'."

That comment was met with another burst of applause. When it was quiet again, I continued my speech. "My next thank you goes to Susie Carter. She's the one who made about a zillion telephone calls to put this party together at the last minute. Send me your cell phone bill, Susie. This month is on me."

I watched Shar shake her finger at Susie as if scolding her, and there was more applause before I could go on. "Now, more very important 'thank yous' go out to Doctor Baxter and Nurse Ruth and all the other folks at the Curry County Medical Center who pulled our girl through a rough surgery and recovery. You guys are gold!"

I went on with a few more specific thank yous before thanking everyone for turning out on such short notice. Then I said, "Now we can get back to the festivities and I'm going to kick things off by asking my future bride to dance with me. The tune is one we'll both remember all our lives."

I nodded to the band leader who counted off a tempo for THIS GUY'S IN LOVE WITH YOU while I took Shar's hand and led her onto the dance floor. Right on cue all of the lights except those directly over the dance floor dimmed and we danced.

Shar whispered in my ear, "Travis, you are even more amazing than I thought. I have no idea how you and Susie pulled this off and kept it a secret, but thank you, thank you, thank you. Practically everyone I know is here, even the mayor for crying out loud!"

"That's a tribute to you. You are an important member of this community and they almost lost you. They're here to show you how important you are to them. According to Susie a lot of plans were cancelled at the last minute so everyone she asked—and I mean everyone—could be here. I even saw Ben a few minutes ago."

"Don't you think the fact that I am now engaged to the most wonderful guy on the planet might have something to do with it?"

"Nope. There are only two reasons I mean anything to these people."

"What reasons, Darling?"

"First, they want to know I'm going to make you happy. Failure to do that in this town is a Class A Felony."

"I see, and the second reason?"

"Second, they all want to know for certain I'm not going to take you away to the big city."

Shar leaned back to look at my face. Her expression was one of surprise, but she was smiling. "You aren't?"

"No, ma'am. Unless you vote otherwise, we are staying right here."

"But you work in Hollywood. What about all that?"

"I'm established now, I don't have to be in Hollywood to write. Besides I have a more important job here."

With a twinkle in her eyes, she asked, "Oh, what job is that?"

"Making my new wife the happiest woman on the planet."

Shar pressed her face against my chest. "Oh, Travis."

After our dance, I escorted Shar to the buffet table, which was sagging with the spread arranged by Susie and laid on by an outfit called The Tuxedo Bistro. The food was excellent and there was plenty of it.

After we ate, Shar made a circuit of the room thanking everyone for coming. By the time she'd made it around the entire room, she was drooping a little. I flagged Susie down and said, "I think Shar is getting a little tired. She's only a week out of major surgery. Will you please make our apologies to everyone after we sneak out?"

Susie nodded. "I noticed she looked tired. I'd be happy to do that, but first I want to thank you. I've known Shar nearly all my life, and despite her physical weakness right now, I've never seen her so . . . so radiant and happy. Thank you for making that happen."

I nodded. "Susie, with Shar and me it's kind of a mutual thing. For every one of her smiles, I smile twice."

Susie is a fairly short woman, but she stood on tiptoes to kiss my cheek. Of course Shar caught us.

She gave me a playful whack on the arm. "Darn, I turn my back for a second and you two are over here making out at MY engagement party."

Susie grinned at her. "Then don't turn your back. You should have already figured every woman in town is gonna try to steal this guy."

"Well, they can't have him. I found him and he's mine!"

I agreed with her and escorted my bride-to-be out of the hall. Back at the Beachfront Inn, Shar collapsed on the couch. I said, "Tired?"

She looked up at me. Her face was drawn and a little pale. "A little."

"I hope we didn't overdo it tonight."

Shar shook her head vehemently. "No, Darling. Yes, I'm a little tired, but even so this has been the most wonderful, exciting night of my life. I'll remember it all my life. Thank you, thank you!"

"You're welcome. Now get in there and put your jammies on little girl. I'll come in and kiss you goodnight in a minute."

She stood up. "The hell you will." Holding up her left hand, Shar flashed her new ring at me. "After all I went through to get this, I'm not going to miss any of the benefits. Get ready for bed, darling husband. I'll be back in a few minutes."

When Shar came back, I was propped up in bed and all the lights were off but one on the nightstand. I wouldn't have thought she could, especially as tired as she was, but Sharyne took my breath away yet again.

She was wearing the black silk negligee, but that wasn't what left me speechless. What did that was a soft glow—an aura—about her that gave her an amazing grace and radiance.

Trying to give her every out, however, I said, "You look

absolutely lovely, but if you're thinking what I think you're thinking, are you sure you don't want to wait until we're actually married?"

She sat next to me on the bed and kissed me. It was a kiss that grew steadily in intensity until we were both panting a little.

"No, Darling, I don't want to wait for anything. I think weddings are like funerals. They are a technicality. Having a funeral doesn't make a person any deader than they were. As far as I'm concerned, we pledged love tonight when you asked me to be your wife and I said yes. A wedding will be fun to share with our friends, but it won't make us love or care about each other one bit more than we do right now."

Her logic was clear, but what I saw even more clearly was the love in her eyes. Shar saved the most special moment in her life for me and this was that moment. She was offering me a precious gift she could only give once in her lifetime.

I gently accepted that precious gift with appreciation for the spirit in which it was offered. When we collapsed an hour or so later, Sharyne rested her head on my bare chest. I will remember the last words she said before falling asleep until the day I die.

"Thank you, Dearest Travis. Sometimes I'm not as wise as you are, so please help me, Darling. Help me be the woman the Great Spirit intended me to be . . . your woman."

## THE END

# Meet H. P. Oliver

H. P. Oliver began his career with a degree in journalism from San Jose State University and spent the next twenty-some years writing award-winning entertainment and educational media. Now he applies his creativity and imagination to writing historical mysteries.

About mystery writing, Oliver says, "To be truly engrossing, a mystery needs a little meat on its bones—something more than just figuring out who did the evil deed. Taking a story back in time or even basing it on actual historical events is a great way to endow a good yarn with even more color and depth. Historical periods and locations give the writer an opportunity to take most readers where they've never been before."

H. P. Oliver lives in northern California and spends much of his time working on projects throughout the west. In addition to his love of history, Oliver's interests range from vintage film to restoring classic cars.

For information about H. P. Oliver's books, including synopses, previews, video trailers, and purchase links, visit his fan site at www.HPOliver.com, where you will also find illustrated history articles, a free library of original short stories and other fascinating features. Plan to stay a while.

# Books By H. P. Oliver

## NEW THRILLER
### FATE'S FAULT
(E-Book & Paperback)

## CLASSIC MYSTERIES IN HISTORY

| | |
|---|---|
| THE TRUTH BE TOLD | E-book |
| AND THE ANGELS SING | E-book |
| SILENTS! | E-book/Paper |
| WINGING IT | E-book/Paper |
| ESTELLE | E-book/Paper |
| GOODNIGHT, SAN FRANCISO | E-book/Paper |
| SO LONG, LA | E-book/Paper |
| H. P. OLIVER OMIBUS | E-book/Paper |

## JOHNNY SPICER CAPERS

| | |
|---|---|
| THE FIRST CAPERS | E-book |
| PACIFICA | E-book/Paper |
| REVOLVER | E-book/Paper |
| TEMBO | E-book/Paper |
| S.N.A.F.U. | E-book/Paper |
| PAYBACK | E-book/Paper |
| JAKE | E-book/Paper |
| LOS ANGELES NOIR | E-book/Paper |

H. P. Oliver's books are available at Amazon.

www.ingramcontent.com/pod-product-compliance
Lightning Source LLC
Chambersburg PA
CBHW021707180626
46816CB00011B/2194